A QUIET PROMISE

OTHER BOOKS AND AUDIO BOOKS
BY ANITA STANSFIELD:

First Love and Forever

First Love, Second Chances

Now and Forever

By Love and Grace

A Promise of Forever

When Forever Comes

For Love Alone

The Three Gifts of Christmas

Towers of Brierley

Where the Heart Leads

When Hearts Meet

Someone to Hold

Reflections: A Collection of Personal Essays

Gables of Legacy, Vol. 1: The Guardian

Gables of Legacy, Vol. 2: A Guiding Star

Gables of Legacy, Vol. 3: The Silver Linings

Gables of Legacy, Vol. 4: An Eternal Bond

Gables of Legacy, Vol. 5: The Miracle

Gables of Legacy, Vol. 6: Full Circle

Timeless Waltz

A Time to Dance

Dancing in the Light

A Dance to Remember

Barrington Family Saga Vol. 1: In Search of Heaven

Barrington Family Saga

VOLUME TWO

A QUIET PROMISE

ANITA STANSFIELD

Covenant Communications, Inc.

Cover image *Her Favorite Place* © Daniel F. Gerhartz.

Cover design by Jessica A. Warner, copyrighted 2007 by Covenant Communications, Inc.

Published by Covenant Communications, Inc.
American Fork, Utah

Printed in Canada
First Printing: August 2007

11 10 09 08 07   10 9 8 7 6 5 4 3 2 1

ISBN-13: 978-1-59811-373-0
ISBN-10: 1-59811-373-9

For Benjamin K. Hall and Isaac Morley,

neighbors in Nauvoo in 1840,

and great-great-grandfathers to dear friends and

partners in struggle in the twenty-first century.

Prologue

James Barrington stepped out of his Iowa home and walked through the woods toward the river that ambled through his property. His son, David, held one of his hands, and his daughter, Iris, held the other. The small group of people walking with them included most of the people in this world that mattered to him. Frederick and Lizzie were more like family than employees; the same applied to Amanda Leichty and her son, Ralph, who came in six days a week to help wherever it was needed. In the time since James had brought his family to America, they had all grown close and comfortable. But he sensed that the rest of them felt a level of enthusiasm for this event that he was lacking. He couldn't find any logical reason to protest his wife's decision to do this, but he wanted to anyway.

At the edge of the river, James watched with the others while his dear wife, Eleanore, stepped into the water, holding to the arm of Brother Yeats in order to remain steady in the gentle current. They'd met the missionary the previous week while taking a little vacation, and James couldn't deny that their coming together had certainly been no coincidence. Eleanore had been praying for two years to find a connection to this religion that she'd known in her heart was true ever since she'd read a discarded Book of Mormon that she'd happened upon. Once Eleanore had met Brother Yeats—as he insisted on being called—and had known for certain that he shared her beliefs, what could James do but invite him to their home so that he could share his vast knowledge of the gospel with Eleanore? James had listened in on many of their conversations, and he couldn't deny feeling intrigued with what he heard. But for reasons he couldn't fully explain or understand, he felt hesitant to become too involved. He respected his wife's beliefs and supported them. As long as what she believed was Christian, they were of one mind and one heart. And that was all he cared about.

James watched as Eleanore was lowered fully into the water and then lifted up again. It was a beautiful ceremony, and she clearly glowed with happiness. He could find no credible basis for the sudden uneasiness he was feeling, but he found himself looking over his shoulder, as if he expected to find someone standing behind him, watching them with malicious intent. He shrugged the sensation away and told himself the very notion was ridiculous for more reasons than he could count. Eleanore stepped out of the water, and he helped her up the bank, wrapping her in a blanket, and then in his arms.

"Are you happy, my dear?" he whispered.

She tightened her arms around him and let out a little laugh, an expression of perfect joy. "I never dreamed I could be so happy."

"Then I'm happy too," he said and let go of her to offer a hand to Brother Yeats to help him step out of the water. Lizzie quickly provided him with a blanket as well. The river was far from warm with summer still weeks away.

"Thank you," he said to James, adding a nod toward Lizzie to repeat the sentiment. He then smiled at James, saying lightly, "It's still not too late, Brother Barrington."

"That river is far too cold for me," James countered glibly. "Eleanore's much braver than I am." He put his arm around his wife and started back toward the house if only to halt the conversation. Brother Yeats and the rest of the household followed close behind.

Back at the house, once they'd changed into dry clothes, Brother Yeats put his hands on Eleanore's head and gave her a special blessing, officially pronouncing her a member of The Church of Jesus Christ of Latter-day Saints. James contemplated the tears on Eleanore's face while he listened to the words of the blessing and considered their meaning. Again an uneasiness tugged at him, but he couldn't put a finger on it.

That evening they all shared a feast akin to Christmas dinner to celebrate this important step in Eleanore's life. James had never seen her so happy. And considering the loss she'd endured not so long ago, that couldn't be anything but good. She should have been significantly pregnant now, but the baby had been born dead weeks earlier. Eleanore did well at bearing her grief with courage, and she was not the kind of woman to allow one challenge to outweigh all else that was good in life. Her positive outlook had always been a great example to him, and he did his best to heed it. Still, neither of them could deny the heartache, even if they spoke of it rarely. But now there was a new light in her eyes.

That night as James slipped into bed, Eleanore eased into his arms and rested her head on his shoulder.

"Thank you," she murmured.

"For what?"

"For supporting me in this. I'm certain many husbands would be opposed to their wives joining some new religion."

"I just want you to be happy."

"Oh, and I am!"

"Good," he said and kissed her good night. She fell asleep in his arms while he pondered what the future might entail as a result of Eleanore becoming a Mormon. As far as they knew, she was the only one in the area. Brother Yeats had told them that members of their religion were gathering together and establishing communities. James had almost feared that Eleanore would want to move and join them, but she'd not even mentioned it. And he was relieved. This was their home now. God had guided them here, and his heart told him they needed to stay.

Brother Yeats left the following day to return to his home, and James knew that Eleanore was sad to see him go. They'd talked many long hours, and she had absorbed this man's knowledge with eagerness and enthusiasm. Prior to their meeting, she'd had nothing but the book she'd found, and she'd read it over and over. Conversations with the missionary had satisfied something in her, and she'd thrived on them. But Brother Yeats had a wife and children somewhere in Illinois, and he'd done what he declared the Lord had sent him into their lives to do. He had been the answer to Eleanore's prayers.

James couldn't deny that there was an extra radiance about his wife. Surely nothing but good could come out of the choices she'd made in regard to her religious beliefs. Each day, he struggled to convince himself of that, while a formless nagging sensation hovered around him like a cobweb that refused to be brushed away. But he kept it to himself, certain it would never make sense even if he tried to explain it. And surely it would pass with time.

Chapter One

WHAT THEY DO
IN MISSOURI

Iowa City—1840

James dismounted his chestnut stallion and tethered it to the rail outside the general store. He went inside to purchase just a few more seeds and some odds and ends, which he tucked into his saddlebags before throwing them over his shoulder. His thoughts were preoccupied with visions of the garden he would start planting today. He'd arrived in Iowa with his family late the previous summer, following a long journey from their home in England. The land he'd purchased was mostly uncultivated around the home that had already been there, but he preferred it that way. He wasn't a farmer, and he didn't need the means to make a living since he'd inherited more than enough to comfortably care for his family for two lifetimes. But he'd become obsessed with bringing the garden to life. The previous owners of the home he'd purchased had apparently moved out in the middle of summer, leaving their huge garden with neat rows of vegetables to rot in the sun. But it had all been plowed under now. The soil was black and rich, waiting to join with seeds and sun and water. And James couldn't wait to get his hands dirty and make it happen.

He stepped back outside and inhaled the fresh warmth in the air while he turned his face briefly toward the spring sun. His thoughts gravitated naturally to Eleanore. He thought of buying her a gift, even though she always told him that he didn't need to, that she had everything she could ever want. Still, he loved to indulge her. And perhaps he hoped to compensate for the loss that was still close to her heart. The baby would have been due next week. But thankfully her recent baptism had buffered the loss for Eleanore, and James felt certain anything he might buy her would pale in comparison.

James walked down the street a little way and bought some candy for the children, then he went into the tavern for a drink. It was more the socializing than the liquor that drew him here. Having recently immigrated to America, he enjoyed immersing himself with the locals and observing their behavior. He liked the people in this community for the most part, and he delighted in being a part of them. He'd become acquainted with the owners and some local merchants who frequented the place, even though he only came here once or twice a week himself. He was disappointed when he entered not to see any familiar faces other than the man serving drinks. But James ordered the usual, and the two of them chatted for a few minutes before he needed to clear some tables.

While James took a careful sip of his drink, he rubbed a hand over his face, unaccustomed to its smoothness. He'd worn a beard throughout the winter but had shaved it off just this morning. He fondly recalled Eleanore's surprise when she'd seen him, how she'd touched his face and kissed him, telling him she'd missed the smell of his shaving lotion. He smiled, missing her now. And he'd only been gone an hour. His mind wandered again to visions of his garden until two men at a nearby table became too boisterous to ignore. They'd clearly had too much to drink, but it was the word *Mormon* that caught his ear. He listened discreetly, uneasy even before he heard one of them say, "Yeah, they're gone and good riddance. Whole family up and left in the middle of the night."

The other man laughed. "I guess a little harassment goes a long way in keeping the filthy scum from getting too comfortable around here. I hear the Weller boys roughed up his wife pretty good."

"Whatever it takes." He laughed as well while James felt physically ill. Surely this couldn't be what it sounded like! Then the man added, "It's too bad we can't do what they do in Missouri. Smart man, Governor Boggs, making it legal to kill Mormons."

James fought to keep his countenance steady while his feelings exploded inside of him. He struggled to appear disinterested and nonchalant while his every nerve tightened until he wanted to scream. This was America, for the love of heaven—the land of religious freedom. How could such atrocities truly occur? *And his wife was a Mormon!* He couldn't help recalling how Missouri had been one of the places where they'd considered settling. How grateful he was that they hadn't! But did that matter?

"Yeah," the other man chuckled, "if we could just shoot 'em with the blessing of the law it would be a whole lot easier."

James took a careful swallow of his drink and told himself to get up and leave, but he couldn't find the strength. Instead he put his head in his hands, hoping he appeared to be brooding over his drink and oblivious to his surroundings. His alarm deepened as he heard the conversation continue with horrific details of an entire community of Mormons being driven like cattle from their homes in the middle of winter with nothing but the clothes on their backs, of men being whipped and beaten, women and children tormented—all with the apparent approval of the law. James felt certain the men were exaggerating. Surely such repulsive acts could not really be happening. He glanced discreetly at the men making light of such atrocities, and wondered what kind of person would take pleasure in the suffering of others.

As anger began to smother his shock, James knew he had to get out of there before he did something he would surely regret. He coolly pushed aside the drink he'd barely touched and left the tavern with practiced indifference, not wanting to draw any attention to himself. He quickened his pace as he walked to where he'd left the horse. By the time he'd mounted, he felt so consumed with fear he could hardly breathe. *What had they done?* Eleanore had wanted to join this church and he had encouraged her to do what she wanted. And now what? How could he douse the light he'd seen in her eyes with news such as this? But he had no choice if he was going to keep her safe.

James cursed and drove the stallion hard and fast, almost fearing his wife would be discovered and killed before he could get to her. He guided the horse off the main road and onto the lane that led to his home. The horse answered his will as it picked up speed through the trees, over the bridge, and down the gentle hill that sloped toward his home. The two-story, white-painted house sat against a background of woods and next to a large red barn where he dismounted but left the horse free, hoping it wouldn't go too far.

"Eleanore!" he shouted before he got to the house. And just inside the door, he called loudly, "Eleanore! Where are you?"

He peeked into the kitchen and saw Amanda, busy as usual. He didn't even acknowledge her before he moved up the hall toward the front of the house.

"Eleanore!" he shouted and threw open the door to the library, her favorite room. She wasn't there. He cursed under his breath and took the stairs three at a time. He reached the top to see her coming out of their bedroom at the other end of the hall.

"I'm here," she said, alarmed. "What's wrong?"

James heaved a sigh of relief just to see her. She was tying a black hair ribbon around the bottom of the thick, dark auburn braid that hung over her shoulder. He took her arm and guided her back into the bedroom, throwing the door closed. Before he could even consider how to tell her, he wrapped her in his arms, holding her desperately close as if some hideous predator might slither into their lives and snatch her away from him.

Eleanore felt desperation and panic in his embrace that crept into her even though she had no idea what was wrong. She eased back and looked up at him. "What is it?" she asked. "What's happened?"

"Oh, Eleanore," he murmured, holding her face in his hands. "Have you told anyone outside our household that you're a Mormon? Anyone at all?"

She shook her head, more confused. "No, not yet. I—"

"Not *ever!*" he said with such vehemence that it frightened her. She wanted to ask how she could possibly keep from sharing with others the joy she'd received from embracing the gospel. But she was too stunned to utter a sound. "Never, Eleanore. You must never let it pass your lips. You must never let what you believe go beyond the walls of this house. Do you understand?"

His silence made her realize he was expecting an answer. "No, I *don't* understand, James. What could possibly be so—"

"I heard two men talking," he said. "In the tavern. They were pleased because a Mormon family left in the middle of the night; they said the harassment had paid off, that the wife had been roughed up." She gasped and stepped back, as if doing so might help her discredit what he was saying. "They called the Mormons filthy scum, said they didn't want them getting too comfortable around here."

"I can't believe it," she said, her heart pounding.

"Oh, it's worse," he said.

"How could it be *worse?*"

"They said that in Missouri it's *legal* to kill Mormons."

"No." Eleanore could hardly breathe.

"They talked of them being driven out of their homes, beaten and tormented."

"No!" she repeated, even more breathless. "Surely there must be some mistake," she insisted. "Something so . . . drastic . . . so horrible; it just *can't* be true."

"I don't care if it's true or not. If there are people out there who feel that way about Mormons, then *no one* will *ever* know that one is living in *this house.* Do you understand?"

Eleanore felt a piece of her heart breaking. She'd experienced such joy in finally being a part of these beliefs that she knew beyond any doubt were true. She longed to share those beliefs with others, to spread this joy and see it flourish. And now she was being told that she could only hold it in her heart and never speak of it, that she might even have to lie if the need arose. Tears burned into her eyes, and her throat turned hot. She looked up at her husband, wanting desperately to explain, to convince him to change his mind. She only managed to get one word out of her mouth. "But . . ."

"You must trust me, Eleanore," he said before she could go on. "I am your *husband.* It is my privilege and my obligation to protect you, and I will do whatever it takes. I honor your beliefs, but I will *not* have you put at risk. There will be no compromise on this matter. Do I make myself clear?"

Eleanore then heard words in her mind that she'd heard once before. She'd just received a letter from Palmyra, New York, in response to her request for more information about the Mormons. She'd addressed it to the postmaster, and months later he'd responded. Before she could open the envelope the words had come to her plainly. *Trust your husband. He will protect you. Trust in Me. I will guide you when the time is right.* She gasped as the words took on new meaning—for this moment, *and* for when she'd first heard them. She'd handed the letter to him, had asked him to read it. James had told her it said the Mormons had left the area years ago, and their whereabouts were unknown. He'd asked her if she wanted to read it. She'd declined, and he'd tossed it into the fire.

James watched his wife's eyes become distant and puzzled. He allowed her a minute to absorb what she'd just heard, then he took her shoulders and repeated more gently, "Do I make myself clear?"

She seemed to emerge out of a daze, then tears fell down her face. He wondered if she would try to argue or protest, if he would have to become some kind of tyrant over the matter in order to see it stand. But she said with a broken voice, "Yes. Quite clear. I'll say nothing." James sighed deeply and hung his head, surprised when she added, "What did the letter say?"

"What?" He looked up.

"The letter . . . from New York. You were protecting me when you read it, weren't you." It wasn't a question. "What else did it say?"

He didn't know how she knew, but he'd long ago learned her instincts and perception were sharp. "I don't . . . remember exactly," he said, glad to be able to say that truthfully.

"But the tone of the letter was . . . what?"

He sighed and stepped back, putting his hands on his hips. "The same as what I heard today. It said the Mormons were gone; good riddance. Something like . . . with any luck you'd never find them."

She turned her back and wiped her hands over her cheeks to dry them. "And yet you stood by me in this decision."

"It's what you wanted, Ellie. Your convictions over this matter are no small thing. How could I stand in the way of that? But now . . . we must be careful. So careful."

"Of course," she said and moved unsteadily to the edge of the bed.

"Did Brother Yeats say anything—anything at all—about such happenings?"

Eleanore fought the shock in her brain to recall what he'd said. "He told me that . . . there had been some trouble, that . . . the people had . . ." She took a deep breath. "How did he put it? That they'd not been well received in some communities."

"That would seem a gross understatement," James snarled, then watched new tears roll down his wife's cheeks and realized she was trembling. He sat beside her and took her in his arms. "I'm so sorry," he murmured.

"I just don't understand," she said. "How could something like this happen?"

James took her shoulders into his hands and looked at her firmly. "Eleanor, is there anything . . . anything at all in what you know of these beliefs that could be considered . . . extreme . . . or a threat to others?"

"No." She shook her head and sniffled. "As far as I can see it's . . . Christianity. But James," a familiar conviction rose in her eyes, "I know that it's true! How can people be so against something that's true and right and good?"

James thought about that for a second. "Perhaps for the same reason the disciples in the New Testament were all eventually done away with. It's good versus evil, my dear. But we will fight the battle quietly and privately." She nodded and sniffled again. He handed her his handkerchief and said, "I expected more protest. Why are you so agreeable?"

"Am I generally *dis*agreeable?" she countered.

"No, of course not. I just know how much your religion means to you. Perhaps I expected you to be willing to face any risk in order to live it in the way you wish."

She looked down. "I think God prepared me for this moment. That day . . . when the letter came. I heard the words in my head, so clearly, that I should trust you, that you would protect me." She looked at him and touched his face. "I heard them again, exactly the same . . . just now. I was also told that He would guide me . . . when the time was right. He's guided every step of my life. How can I doubt that He'll keep doing so?"

"Then surely all will be well," he said and kissed her brow. "Do you think Lizzie or the others have said anything . . . to anyone?"

"I wouldn't think so, but we should make sure." She sighed and added, "I should be hugely pregnant, you know."

"I know," he said. "But we must look to the future. There will be more babies." He held her chin and kissed her lips. "I want a daughter who looks like you." He kissed her again. "Make that three daughters." And again. "No, four."

"And sons?"

"Sons too." He kissed her still again. "We could try right now." Their kiss became long and sweet.

"It's tempting, Mr. Barrington," she murmured and urged her lips to his once more. "But the children will be wondering where we are, and I've got work to do." He made a noise of exaggerated disappointment that made her laugh, but he was glad to see that she could find laughter in the face of today's difficult news. "Besides, I thought you were going to plant that garden today, or at least get a good start."

"One more day won't hurt," he said and kissed her again before he leaned on one elbow just to look at her.

Eleanore reached up a hand to touch her husband's face. She'd become accustomed to his beard over the last several months, but now he looked more like the man she had married. She pushed her fingers into his thick, dark hair, pressing some abandoned locks back off his forehead where they had strayed from how he'd combed it. They'd only been married a year, and yet it felt as if they'd lived a lifetime together. It was difficult now for her to imagine that they'd once resided in an enormous manor house in England. He had been lord of the manor, and she had been the governess for his children following the death of his first wife. At the age of forty, he was twenty-two years her senior, but she'd never felt the difference in their age beyond certain moments in their early relationship when his life's experience had starkly contrasted with her own naiveté. From the day he'd proposed, he'd always treated her as his equal in spite of disdain and criticism from those who had disapproved of him marrying into a lower social class. But they'd not been married very many weeks when they'd set out for America, where no one ever saw them as less than equals. And she liked it that way. To see him now, no one would ever guess his former aristocratic status, except perhaps by his natural dignity and refinement. But he dressed as commonly as the farmers who lived around them, and he mixed well with the people in the community. The life they were living suited him, and it showed in his countenance.

While she was pondering how much she loved him, he murmured with conviction, "I love you, Eleanore." The words still felt miraculous each time she heard them. It hadn't been so many weeks since he'd been holding to a firm declaration that he had no love to give her. His proposal of marriage had been completely unexpected and a matter of practical compatibility and convenience. She'd agreed to be a mother to his children. He'd promised to be a good husband and to provide for her every need. But he'd made it clear that love would not be part of the deal. His first wife had betrayed him, and the hurt was deep; he'd had no qualms about admitting that his heart was broken and off limits. And then he had contradictorily proceeded to show love for her every hour of every day while she had gradually come to love him more than she'd ever believed possible. He had finally come to accept and admit to the truth of his feelings only after they'd lost the baby. She believed that the trauma had brought him to a deeper awareness of the importance of all they had come to share. In that regard, she couldn't entirely begrudge the loss, because she had gained her husband's heart. Still, thoughts of her baby inevitably came with some measure of grief and an emptiness that would only be filled when she was able to have a child of her own.

"What would we have named him?" she asked, putting a hand against his chest. The baby had been far enough along that there was no question about it being a boy.

"It doesn't matter," James said, certain that avoiding sentimentality on the matter would be best. "All of our children will be given fine names and . . ." The knock at the door was clearly that of a child. "Speaking of our children," he said, and they both sat up. "Come in," he called, and David opened the door, peering timidly into the room.

"I took care of your horse," the child said.

"Oh, thank you." James held out a hand, and David took it. "I was in a hurry to talk to your mother and I forgot all about it." He hugged the boy. "You're awfully good help. Are you sure you're only eight? Maybe you're really eighteen and you're just pretending to be eight."

David laughed. "No, silly. Mama's eighteen."

"Truly?" James looked at his wife, pretending to be shocked. He spoke in a ridiculously loud whisper, "Well, don't tell anybody or they won't believe she's your real mother. Most people would never understand the magic that made her your real mother."

They shared a knowing smile, and James was glad to see peace in his son's eyes. Both of his children had struggled with the fact that their natural mother could only claim the title due to actually having given birth to them. Beyond that, she'd wanted little to do with them, and her attitude had caused a great deal of damage. David especially had contended with anger and confusion over his mother's death, and Eleanore had been highly instrumental in guiding him to the peace he'd found. Now, he behaved more like a normal child than he ever had. In fact, it had been his idea that he wanted some kind of magic to happen in their family so that Eleanore could be his real mother. That's when James had told both him and his sister, Iris, that something magic *had* happened. It was easy for them to understand that the love she gave them made her more of a mother than the woman who had given birth to them.

Iris appeared in the doorway, never far behind wherever her brother went. Like David, she was fair in coloring, similar to the woman who had given birth to them, but Eleanore swore they both bore a strong resemblance to their father, even if he couldn't see it. Iris climbed onto Eleanore's lap and said to her father, "Mama said when you got back we would pwant the garden."

James laughed and touched her little blonde head. Iris was nearly six but still struggled with an adorable speech impediment. He felt sure she would grow out of it. For now, he loved the way she called herself "Iwis."

"Well then," he said, "we should go plant the garden. I have just a couple of things to take care of, and then we'll meet you there. I have candy in my saddlebags." They both grinned. "You may each have one piece and put the rest in the jar in the kitchen. And give a piece to Ralph." Amanda's son had to be close by.

They ran from the room, cheering with excitement as if candy were like unto Christmas morning. Eleanore turned to her husband and said, "I love you too, James." She kissed him. "Thank you . . . for making me their real mother."

"I made you Mrs. Barrington," he said. "You did the magic." He stood up. "I should talk with the others. We can't take any chances."

"Of course," she said, and he saw her eyes turn cloudy again as she was reminded of today's bad news.

"I'm sorry," he said, "that this is so difficult."

"I can't help thinking that you were guided to hear that conversation. What if you hadn't? Better this than finding out the hard way that some people are not fond of Mormons. At least we can be prepared."

James sighed deeply and touched her face. "Always finding the positive in everything. How do you do it?"

She smiled up at him as if nothing in the world were wrong. "It's not so difficult when I'm married to a man who has given me an absolutely perfect life."

He bent to kiss her, then cleared his throat and moved toward the door. "We'd best hurry, my dear. We must 'pwant' the garden."

"Indeed," she said and laughed.

James found Amanda still in the kitchen. "May I talk to you, Amanda?" he asked. In the past he had clung to a certain formality in addressing her, but with his more recent convictions on their household being American, he'd found he preferred using given names. In fact, he'd become quite adamant about it. In spite of his being their employer, he considered those who worked for him to be equals.

"Of course," she said, giving him her attention.

"Have you mentioned anything at all to anyone about Eleanore's new religious convictions?"

"No, sir," she said, looking concerned. "I've had no cause to. Is there a problem?"

"Apparently it's not very popular with some people around here, to the point of foul play."

"Good heavens!"

He repeated what he had heard, wanting her to understand the profound need for absolute secrecy over the matter. She heartily agreed, and he asked that she talk with her son Ralph about it so that he would also understand and be careful.

James found Frederick on a stepladder in the parlor, dusting cobwebs from the ceiling, while his wife, Lizzie, supervised. They had both served in his household in England. For many years Frederick Higgins had been as much a friend as a right-hand man to James. When he'd made the decision to sell his estate and move to America, he knew he could never survive without Frederick. In addition to the numerous ways in which James had come to rely on him, Frederick also had knowledge crucial for starting a new life in a new land. James had been raised as a gentleman, but Frederick had grown up on a farm and had served in many occupations that gave him practical experience in matters foreign to James. Lizzie had been a dear friend of Eleanore's mother, and the two had been close ever since her death. James had told Eleanore to choose one of the servants to come along, and the choice had been obvious. The arrangement became even more tidy when Frederick and Lizzie had been married on the ship while crossing to America. The journey from there had become even more challenging, and they had all worked together to do what needed to be done. Along with that, becoming Americans had naturally closed gaps in any social distinction, so even though Frederick and Lizzie were technically employees, they all lived together in the house like family. This summer, however, they would build a separate home for them on the property, but only a stone's throw away. They all *preferred* living like family. Lizzie was expecting a baby, which had come as a surprise since she'd believed she was too old. She and Frederick were naturally thrilled at the prospect of becoming parents when neither of them had believed they would ever marry or have a family of their own. But the pending arrival had become bittersweet for James and Eleanore with the loss of their own baby. Still, they were happy for their dear friends. And perhaps by the time the baby came in the fall, Eleanore would be pregnant again.

"Good, you're both here," James said, entering the parlor. "I need to talk with you."

"Is something wrong?" Lizzie asked, concerned. She was average in build with a roundish, freckled face and carrot-colored hair full of tight curls.

"In a way, yes," James said and closed the door. Frederick came down from the ladder. He was more then ten years older than James, tall and thin with graying blond hair. "Have you mentioned anything at all to anyone about Eleanore becoming a Mormon?"

"No," they both said at the same time, and James took a deep breath of relief. The secret was safe. "Why?" Frederick added.

"Sit down," James said, and they did. He repeated what he'd heard, speaking more openly with them than he had spoken to Amanda about his feelings on the matter. As always, they offered perfect compassion and support. He finished by saying, "We need to respect her beliefs, but we must be very careful."

"Certainly," Frederick said.

"We're not going to live in fear," James added. "We just need to remain cautious." He stood up and lightened his tone. "Now, the children are impatiently waiting to plant this grand garden, and since I have absolutely no idea what I'm doing, the dusting will have to wait."

"Fresh air is better than dusting any day," Lizzie said and led the way.

Everyone spent the better part of the day in the garden, except for Amanda, who was in charge of keeping the rest of them fed. While they were working, James carefully instructed his children on the secret that needed to be kept. He told them that normally he would not condone being dishonest, and perhaps they would never have to be. But in this case it could mean their safety, or even their lives. He didn't want to alarm them, but he did want them to know this was serious. They seemed to understand without being afraid, and he prayed that they would all remain safe and that no problems would arise in the future.

After supper, Eleanore found her husband standing at the edge of the garden. The striped shirt he wore was dirty, and the sleeves were rolled up haphazardly to just below his elbows. His suspenders crossed in the center of his back where she put her hand as she came up beside him.

"Do you think it will grow any faster if you stand here and watch it?" she asked, and he chuckled.

"Maybe," he said and put his arm around her. "Are you trying to tell me I've become eccentric?"

"I like your obsession with growing things," she said. "It suits you."

"Does it?" he asked, as if she'd told him he had royal blood.

"So I'm absolutely certain you would love to see what I found today."

He looked intrigued. "Show me."

She took his hand and walked to the side of the house where a long, railed porch wrapped around from the front of the house and went the full length of it. And all along the edge little green shoots were coming up. "There're weeds, obviously," she said. "But see the consistency of these." She pointed at a thick, somewhat random row that all looked the same. "Lizzie says it looks like iris."

"Iris?" he echoed.

"The flower you named your daughter after," she said.

"Our daughter."

"She wasn't mine when you named her, but she is now."

"Well, I named her after my grandmother. I didn't know it was a flower."

"Truly?" She laughed.

"Does that make me a fool?"

"No, James." She kissed him. "It makes you adorable." He chuckled, and she surveyed the lengthy flowerbed. "When they bloom it will be beautiful."

"I can't wait," he said, and she moved away from the house, keeping his hand in hers.

"Walk with me," she said and headed toward the woods.

"Where are we going?" he asked.

"Exploring," she said, and they moved into the trees, walking slowly.

After several minutes of silence, he asked, "What are you thinking?"

"I was thinking about Sally Jensen."

"The woman who used to live here."

"That's right." Eleanore only knew her name because the neighbors had known the family. The Jensens had been long gone before they had arrived to purchase the home. According to people in the area who had known them, no one knew their reasons for moving, but Eleanore had often wondered. It was such a beautiful home, surrounded by acres of rich land. "I was thinking about her planting iris bulbs next to the porch, and then leaving them behind. Now we will reap the benefits."

"So we will," he said, and they walked on in silence, coming to the edge of the narrow river that ran through their property—narrow only in comparison to the Mississippi. It was certainly significant enough. "You're thinking again," he said. "You have that faraway look in your eyes."

"I'm still thinking about Sally Jensen."

"Why?"

"I don't know. I just do now and then. I find myself wondering about her. What was her life like in this home? Was she as happy here as I am?"

"*Are* you happy?" he asked.

Eleanore felt astonished by the question. "Of course I am."

"Even though you have to live your religion secretly and alone?"

She looked away and sighed, unable to deny her own heartache in that regard. Still, she readily admitted, "I have much to be grateful for."

"Yes, you're very skilled at counting your blessings. But it's still hard."

Eleanore looked at her husband and found compassion in his eyes. "Yes," she said, "it's still hard. But beyond that, my life is perfect."

"Now you're lying," he said, and again she felt astonished. "What you really mean is that your life will be perfect when you have a baby."

Eleanore turned her back to him as if that might ward off the truth. "I was trying not to think about that."

"An hour doesn't pass when you don't think of that," he said. "I can see it in your eyes. Don't get me wrong, Eleanore. I admire your courage, your faith, and your positive outlook. You are an inspiration to me. I just want you to know that when your heart is hurting, you don't have to hide it from me. You don't have to be brave with me. It was my son, too." Eleanore couldn't hold back tears, as if they'd only needed his permission to appear. "We had a death in the family, Ellie. If we need to grieve over that, so be it." He put his hands on her shoulders and said behind her ear, "I love you, Eleanore Barrington. And we're going to get through this . . . together."

He turned her to face him, and she crumbled in his arms, sobbing against his chest while the empty ache of losing her baby swirled into the heartbreak of having fear and secrecy shatter the perfect happiness she'd found in embracing the gospel. He just held her and let her cry, proving to her the truth of what she'd told him. She had much to be grateful for.

Chapter Two

T H E   L E T T E R

Eleanore sat on the bank of the river next to her husband for nearly an hour with his arm around her, while they spoke of the loss of their baby and cried together. It wasn't the first time they'd talked about it and shared their grief. But each time the weight seemed to ease a little. When there was nothing more to say, they sat in silence for long minutes while the sound of rushing water hovered peacefully around them.

"They'll be wondering where we are," James said.

"I told Lizzie we might go for a walk."

He made no effort to move, as if he were as content and relaxed as she.

"Why don't you write her a letter?" he asked.

She lifted her head from his shoulder. "Lizzie?"

"No," he chuckled, "Sally Jensen."

Eleanore let that sink in and wondered why she hadn't thought of it. "The Plummers might know where to send it," she said, liking the idea very much. Their neighbors had been asked by the Jensens to sell the property in their absence.

"Actually, they don't," he said with confidence. "But the attorney who handled the transaction for us sent them the money for the sale of the house. And the Jensens mailed me a receipt; I wanted proof that they'd received what was owed them. It's in my desk."

Eleanore jumped to her feet, inexplicably thrilled at the thought of actually communicating with this woman she'd thought about so much. "Come along," she said, hurrying back toward the house.

He followed after her, saying, "You can't mail it until tomorrow."

"It's nearly dark anyway," she said and hurried on. "The children will be expecting their bedtime story."

They went through the back door and straight into the office where James kept track of their finances. Eleanore paced and fidgeted while he opened a drawer and flipped through an organized stack of papers. He closed that drawer and opened another one.

While he was searching, he said, "When you write, ask her why that couch is so ugly." He nodded toward it. He'd often commented on it, but they'd never made the effort to replace it. He smiled and added, "Perhaps that's why they left it behind."

"All of the other furnishings they left behind were perfectly lovely. Since it's in the office, I'm guessing her husband picked it out, and he had very poor taste."

"Perhaps." He smiled again.

"What do men know about choosing furniture?"

"I know that's an ugly couch. Here it is," he said, and her heart quickened. "Unless they've moved in the last six months, I would assume this is where you'll find them." He handed her the envelope, pointing out the return address as he said, "Mark Jensen. Nauvoo, Illinois."

"Nauvoo?" she echoed. "Surely not!"

James was startled by the way she snatched the envelope out of his hand to see for herself. "Is that not what it says?" he asked.

"I can't believe it." She touched the written words as if that might *help* her believe it.

"What?" he demanded, completely baffled.

"Surely you remember."

"I have no idea what you're talking about."

"Brother Yeats said he'd come from Nauvoo." Her eyes

widened with wonder. "This is where the Saints are gathering, James. Nauvoo. I believe it's solely a Mormon community."

He *hadn't* remembered. He must have missed that conversation. But something eery smoldered inside him just before he saw Eleanore teeter slightly and put a hand to her brow.

"What is it?" he asked, reaching out to steady her. "Are you ill?" A dizzy spell due to being pregnant sounded like a pleasing explanation. With his arms around her he became aware of her labored breathing, and the envelope fell from her hand to the floor.

"That's why they left," she said, leaning heavily against him. "Heaven help us, that's why they left." The eeriness in him took hold firmly as she recounted the same information going through his mind. "They left their furniture, their dishes, even the china. They took only their books and personal belongings. They left a flourishing garden and a shovel sticking in the ground." She took hold of his upper arms and looked up at him as if he might save her from inevitable destruction. "That's why they left, James . . . to join the Saints . . . and they probably left in a hurry because . . ."

"Because they were in danger," he said, angry and scared. Or perhaps one emotion was attempting to squelch the other. "Well, we're staying safe *right here*. And we are *not* going to join the Saints, wherever they may be."

Her voice was defensive. "I would not have suggested that we might."

"Good. Because this is our home. God guided us here, and we're staying."

She moved unsteadily to the ugly couch and sat down. "Yes," she said, getting that faraway look in her eyes, "God guided us here. I was praying to find people who shared my beliefs, and God guided us to *this* home. It can't be coincidence, James."

How could he possibly try to say that it was? There had been so much uncanny *coincidence* over this that he almost felt more afraid. He would have preferred to keep any evidence of God's hand out of the matter, which would have made it much easier to distance her from every possible connection to this new religion. But the evidence of God's involvement in his wife's quest continued to mount. There was something chillingly right about this Church. He wouldn't embrace it, but he couldn't dispute it. He kissed her brow and told her she was surely right, then he went upstairs to put the children to bed.

Eleanore sat at her husband's desk and wrote a lengthy letter to Mrs. Jensen. She said nothing about her own beliefs or suspicions. Instead she simply wrote of how she loved the home and how her thoughts had been drawn to the previous owners. She wrote of planting the garden and of the flowers peeking up by the porch. *I assume it's iris,* she wrote, *but I'll have to wait and see, unless you write back and tell me before they bloom.* Eleanore gave a brief description of her own life, how they had ended up in Iowa, and the people who shared this home with her. Hoping to coax some information out of Mrs. Jensen, she wrote that she couldn't help being curious over their reasons for leaving, and she asked questions about Nauvoo. What were they doing there? What was it like? *Were they safe and well?* She resisted writing that last question but kept it in her heart, praying for the Jensen family even as she wrote.

James found his wife at the desk and leaned his shoulder against the door frame, holding the lamp that had guided him through the darkened house. "Come to bed," he insisted gently. "It's late. You can finish it in the morning."

"It's finished," she said and stood up, extinguishing the lamp on the desk.

As they walked up the stairs together, James tried to think of something positive to say that might help her mood. Knowing their secret was safe and she wouldn't try to coerce him into joining the Saints in Nauvoo, he felt more confident in expressing what seemed obvious. "This is not something to feel glum over, my dear. God sent you a friend, even before you knew you needed one."

Eleanore stopped in the middle of the stairs and turned to look at her husband, stunned into silence as a warmth in her heart beckoned her to believe it was true.

"I would say," he added, "that the timing is evidence that God is with you. It's as if He's given you a gift to compensate for what we learned earlier today."

Not for the first time that day, Eleanore pressed her face to her husband's chest and wept. He guided the lamp from his hand into hers and lifted her into his arms. He carried her to their bed and laid her there, then took the lamp and set it on the bedside table. He stretched out beside her and took her fully into his arms. She held to him and cried herself into a familiar silence. Funny how easy it had become for her to find such perfect solace in the love he gave her. It had been just a year since he'd completely shocked her with his proposal of marriage. Prior to then, she'd seen nothing in him but her employer, the father of the children in her care. And now he was the center of her life. When he'd very practically promised to always see that her needs were met, she never could have imagined how thoroughly he would keep his promise. She tried to imagine where her life might be if she had declined marrying him. The thought made her shudder.

"Are you cold?" he whispered.

"No," she murmured and eased closer, tightening her arms around him.

"You should get some sleep. It's been a difficult day."

"More good than bad," she said, touching his face. "But it would have a perfect ending if you'd kiss me, Mr. Barrington."

He smiled and pressed his lips to hers with a kiss that was warm and familiar. Eleanore eagerly succumbed to the greatest joy of being his wife, then slept contentedly exhausted in his arms.

* * *

Eleanore mailed her letter with a prayer, then put her focus fully on the present. She kept busy with her household duties and spent time each day teaching the children their school lessons. And she pretended not to notice the time passing when her baby should have been born.

Iris was delighted to learn she'd been named after a flower, especially when she saw how beautiful they were. The irises along the edge of the porch had sprung up tall and bloomed in varying shades of purple. Their fragrance often lured Eleanore to the side porch where she would sit with the children and read or play games, and sometimes her husband would join them. Pregnancy continued to elude Eleanore, but she reminded herself hourly of the great joy she found in being a mother to David and Iris. She loved them as deeply as a mother could. But even if they were her own, she would still be longing for another child.

Eleanore continued to find peace each day from reading in the Book of Mormon. It was undoubtedly her most precious possession; it had been since the day she'd found it more than two years ago. And while she found great fulfillment in knowing that she had officially become a baptized member of this great Church, she felt as alone in her beliefs as she always had. James was endlessly supportive, but he had shown no specific interest in her beliefs, and she'd not felt compelled to share them beyond a minimal point here and there. So, she read and pondered and shared with her journal the things she felt, daily praying for the safety of the Saints, as well as her own household.

While most of their property, a combination of woods and prairie, remained in its natural state, the ground surrounding the house, barn, and corrals gradually became well-groomed and beautiful. Eleanore loved working in the yard with her husband, and she loved the way he kept the children involved, teaching them to work while at the same time enjoying just being together. She loved the way he'd become so passionate about making things grow and nurturing them with fastidious care. She could hardly comprehend the man who had once been lord of the manor.

Every Sunday the entire household attended church together. There were many denominations of religion available in the area, and they had attended at least one meeting of each until they'd decided to remain somewhat passively involved with one particular sect. Eleanore felt that each meeting they'd attended lacked something, and James agreed on that point. But they also both agreed that God would want them to attend a church meeting on the Sabbath, and it was an important example to set for the children. Their biggest reason for choosing this particular sect had more to do with having friends who attended, as opposed to the teachings having any great impact. Most particularly, they'd become rather close to the Plummer family that lived only a five-minute ride from their own home. Andy and Miriam Plummer were some of the kindest people Eleanore had ever known. Almost from the day they'd moved in, the Plummers had been gracious and warm, and they'd been spending time in each other's homes. They quickly established a habit of having the Plummers over for Sunday dinner once a month, and in turn they would have dinner at the Plummer home once a month. While the Plummer children were much older than David and Iris, they still got along well and always had a marvelous time together. James occasionally went to visit with Andy, or they went into town together. And Eleanore did the same with Miriam. Together they attended a ladies club meeting in town once a week, and occasionally they would just spend an afternoon together and visit or help each other with a project. There were other families in the area that they'd grown acquainted with and liked, but the Plummers were truly friends.

While warm weather was abundant, James hired a builder to erect a small home on the property for Frederick and Lizzie.

Back in England they had all lived in the same house, but it had been an enormous manor house with servants' quarters and many wings. Here in Iowa, Frederick and Lizzie had been using a bedroom in the house, and since they all worked and ate together, it was a comfortable and practical arrangement. But Frederick and Lizzie were going to have a baby, and James and Eleanore hoped eventually to fill the bedrooms in their home with more children. The house being built was only a stone's throw from the big house and much smaller. They would still eat with the family, so there wouldn't be full kitchen facilities. But it would be nice and more than adequate.

Meanwhile, green sprouts had started showing in the garden, and James was almost as excited as the children. He taught them how to distinguish between the weeds and the vegetables, and every day they all worked together to keep the garden immaculate and thriving. The air grew increasingly warm as summer crept closer, and the garden became a lovely variety of green brilliance growing out of the black soil of Iowa.

On a beautiful June day, Eleanore sat at the kitchen table shelling peas that the children had picked. Amanda was busy chopping carrots and potatoes from the cellar; she would soon take these vegetables out to the summer kitchen to add to the broth she had simmering for lunch. David, Iris, and Ralph were all sitting at the table around her, taking turns reading aloud from a children's story that was one of Eleanore's favorites from her own youth. While Ralph was nearly five years older than David, the boys got along well most of the time and had proven equitable playmates. Ralph was a good boy, as polite and hard-working as his mother. Like David and Iris, Ralph had chores assigned to him each day when he came to work with his mother. But time was also taken daily for studing and reading, and Ralph had naturally joined the children, since he was always around. His reading skills had improved a great deal in the months he'd been in the household, and his mother had many times expressed pleasure over this positive influence on her son, which she regularly declared was one more blessing added upon Mr. Barrington for giving her employment following her husband's death. She'd also mentioned a number of times her pleasure at Ralph spending time in a home with a father figure present whom he could look up to and learn from in the absence of his own father.

"That was excellent," Eleanore said to Ralph when he'd finished his turn. The boy smiled at her, then tried to steal some of the peas she'd just shelled. She playfully slapped his hand, and he laughed. It was a common game between them. "Now it's your turn, Iris," Eleanore said, and the boys each heaved a sigh. Iris was younger and not so proficient at her reading, and she also had difficulty pronouncing certain letters, which often left the boys impatient—especially on such a pleasant day when they were longing to finish reading and go out to play. Eleanore wasn't so much concerned with them having to endure Iris's reading as she was with Iris's self-consciousness over their attitude.

"Iris is doing very well," Eleanore said. "When you boys were her age, I wonder if you were doing so well." The boys offered no response, but Iris gave a faint smile as she began to read.

A few minutes later James returned from errands in town and tossed a letter on the table in front of her. She glanced at James, who was smiling, then back at the letter, hardly believing her eyes. At first she thought it might be from Brother Yeats. She'd written two letters to him but had never heard back. But it was addressed to Mrs. Eleanore Barrington, from Mrs. Sally Jensen, Nauvoo, Illinois.

"I can't believe it," she said, picking it up, her heart quickening.

"You should really have more faith," James said facetiously.

Eleanore nearly opened the letter right then and there, but she felt unmistakably emotional, and there were too many eyes in the room watching her. She said to Amanda, "Have Iris finish the page she's on, and then the children can play."

"Glad to," she said, and Eleanore hurried out of the kitchen. She walked up the long hall to the front of the house and into the library, where she closed the door and sat in the center of the couch. For more than a minute she just held the letter and looked at it, convincing herself it was real, savoring the anticipation of what it might say. Would it gladden her heart, or would she feel sorrow or dismay?

Eleanore finally took a deep breath and carefully opened the envelope, pulling out three pages folded together. A quick glance showed that they were filled front and back with lovely delicate handwriting. She felt some excitement at the letter being lengthy. There would be more of it to savor. Before she even began reading, she felt an impression of deep affinity with this woman whose home she now lived in.

Dear Mrs. Barrington, I cannot begin to express my joy at having received your letter. It arrived at a time when joy was fragile, and your effort in writing was very much appreciated. I confess to shedding some tears over your mention of all that I left behind. The irises are so lovely in the spring. I loved to sit on the porch and enjoy their aroma. It gives me great pleasure to think of you doing the same, and to know that the home we built is housing a family. You asked about our reasons for leaving Iowa. The answer to that is the greatest source of joy and sorrow in my life.

Eleanore took a sharp breath and put a hand over her quickened heart. While she strongly suspected the reasons, she was struck with how perfectly this woman had described her own feelings regarding the gospel. She eagerly read on as Sally briefly described how she and her husband had been led to the gospel, had wholeheartedly taken it into their lives, and then had suffered for it when there were people who had been zealously opposed to having Mormons in their community. Those against the Mormons were a minority, but frighteningly volatile. She said that they had tried to be discreet, and even most of the neighbors hadn't known of their beliefs. The open candor of the letter left Eleanore wondering if Sally felt an instinctive affinity between them that prompted her to speak so freely. She didn't say what specifically had happened, but the tone of her wording implied that it had been horrid.

Looking back, I wonder if we should have been more careful about keeping it a secret, but I know we needed to make the move, and perhaps the struggles were necessary to prompt us to that decision.

She went on to briefly say that it had been difficult for the family in Nauvoo, but she didn't say why. She expressed appreciation for the timely purchase of their property that had given them money when they'd needed it very much. Apparently things were better now, but a subtle tone of ongoing struggle seeped through her written words. When she said they were building a home that was nearly completed, Eleanore wondered where they'd been living in the meantime. Sally concluded the letter with a firm and tender testimony of her knowledge that the religion for which they'd suffered was true. She realized then that this woman was purposely sharing her beliefs as Eleanore wanted so desperately to do.

Sally's final written words were, *Thank you again for your letter and for keeping my once-beloved home. I would love to hear from you again and to know more about you and your family. May God bless you and your loved ones. Kindest regards, Mrs. Sally Jensen.*

Eleanore read the letter through again and wept tears that were a combination of joy and sorrow. How perfectly her new friend had phrased the contradictions of life. Words like suffering, struggles, and grief hovered in her mind, and she wanted to know and understand the depth of meaning beneath such words. Her own sorrow on behalf of her new friend was deep, but deeper still was the joy she found in knowing that God had guided her to this woman's home, that they were of one heart across the distance.

Eleanore looked up to see her husband leaning against the door. She'd not heard him open or close it. She wiped at her tears and forced a laugh. "Where did you acquire the skill of entering rooms so quietly? You used to do that to me all the time, you know."

"Do what?" he asked, his concern evident.

"When I was taking care of your children, I'd look up and find you watching us, and I'd have no idea how long you'd been there. I was never sure if you were just trying to observe the children while they were unaware, or if you wanted to catch me doing something wrong."

"That would be impossible," he said. "You never did anything wrong." He stepped slowly toward her. "I *was* observing the children, but I was also falling in love with you. I just didn't realize it at the time. I wanted to be in the same room with you." He sat down beside her. "I still do."

Eleanore wanted to tell him all she was feeling, but didn't know where to begin. Consequently she remained silent beyond her sniffling as she attempted to get her tears under control. He handed her his handkerchief and asked, "Why did her letter upset you?"

"It's wonderful, really. And tragic, too." She handed it to him, certain that talking about it would be easier if he knew what it said. "Before you read it, I just want to say . . . how grateful I am . . . that you were led to know that we need to be careful, and for your insistence on the matter. I only wonder why . . ." She became too emotional to speak, and he put his arm around her shoulders.

"Why what?" he pressed gently.

"Why God would spare us and not others."

James focused on the letter in his hand and started to read while Eleanore's question hung uneasily in the air. He took his arm from around her to turn the page over while the meaning behind what she'd said sank in more deeply. Eleanore stood and idly paced the room while he finished the letter then tossed it onto the table. He leaned back and put an elbow on the arm of the couch.

"I wonder what happened to them," she said, looking out the window.

"Whatever it was, it wasn't good. I shudder to think." He thought of the men he'd overheard and didn't even want to consider what men like that might be capable of.

Nothing more was said, but Eleanore appreciated her husband's offer to watch the children while she answered the letter. She felt anxious to do so right away and went to the office where she sat behind the desk and pondered exactly what to say. While she was thinking, she noticed the plaster impressions of the children's hands hanging on the wall. She smiled as she recalled helping them make the gift for their father back when she was their governess. James had declared more than once that it was one of his most prized possessions. She thought of how much the children had grown, since she was very familiar with the present size of their hands.

Turning her attention back to writing a letter, Eleanore realized that her own experience in searching out the gospel and being led to this home seemed the obvious place to begin, and she wrote the story in detail. She expressed boldly her belief that God had not only guided her family into this home, but had prompted her to write to Sally, and she made no hesitation in admitting how she felt that she now had a dear friend who understood her, which eased the loneliness she felt in living the gospel solely and in secret. Eleanore then asked questions about Nauvoo. What was it like? And what manner of struggles had they endured? A part of her didn't want to know, but something deeper needed to understand the sacrifices and hardships of those who shared her beliefs. Eleanore mailed her letter the following day, sending with it a prayer on behalf of Sally and her family, and with gratitude for being given this connection to life in Nauvoo.

* * *

Summer brought with it a sticky heat that was especially challenging for a houseful of people who had spent their lives in England. The sunshine was a pleasant contrast to what they'd known in their homeland, but the accompanying intensity of the heat was less appealing. The huge shade trees surrounding the house were a great blessing, and by keeping all the doors and windows of the house open, being inside could almost be tolerable. Eleanore gained deeper appreciation for the summer kitchen a short distance from the house that kept the heat of cooking from making the problem worse. And they found ways to cool off, like regularly playing together in the river, or getting purposely wet while they worked to keep the garden watered.

With the heat came memories of the previous summer when they had been making the wearisome journey by wagon to Iowa. The experience had been miserable even before Eleanore had started getting pregnancy symptoms that had made her horribly ill. She was *so* glad to have that behind her, but longed every day for evidence that she was pregnant again. She was willing to endure any amount of illness, if only to have a baby. The progression of Lizzie's pregnancy couldn't help but make her aware of the passing of time, but she could never begrudge Frederick and Lizzie having a child, and she was truly happy for them. And even happy for herself. Having their baby in the home would be greatly exciting and would surely bring with it more joy.

In struggling to understand her own inability to conceive, Eleanore searched out stories in the Bible that might give her some insight and peace. She loved the story of Abraham and Sarah. And also that of Elizabeth, the mother of John the Baptist. Both stories were miraculous evidence of women having children when no one had believed they would. But Eleanore was drawn most of all to the story of Leah. She had first been led to Leah prior to her marriage when she had been contending with the fact that the man she had promised herself to had boldly claimed he would never love her. In the Bible she'd found the words, *And Leah conceived, and bare a son . . . for she said, Surely the Lord hath looked upon my affliction; now therefore my husband will love me.* Leah had been deceptively arranged into a marriage with a man who did not love her. And in the story as recorded in the Bible, Leah gave him many sons, and yet she still had reason to doubt Jacob's love for her. Eleanore was grateful beyond words to have her husband's unquestionable love, and she knew that if she never gave him children he would love her no less. Still, there was something about Leah's heartache that connected to her own. She had evidence that she was capable of conceiving, but it wasn't happening. And she wondered why God would deny her the opportunity to have a baby. She knew that she couldn't question God, and she needed to trust Him. Still, it was hard.

As the summer heat increased, the children often went into the woods to play where it was cooler. They were all repeatedly reminded about the rules for remaining safe, which included never going far enough that they couldn't hear their father's shrill whistle or one of their mothers calling from the house when they needed to come in. They were also not supposed to get close to the river without having an adult present. Eleanore could see the woods from the kitchen window, and she or Amanda often shouted and waited for an answer from the trees just to be certain the children were safe.

Amanda Leichty was a kind, gentle woman, older than Eleanore but younger than James. She was average in build with light brown, unruly hair. And her countenance was rarely without a smile. Eleanore enjoyed Amanda's company as they worked together in the kitchen. While all of the cooking was done in the summer kitchen, they used the kitchen in the house for much of the food preparation. Mixing and kneading bread, cutting vegetables, and mixing batters all took place in the house while they chatted. Eleanore was often in and out of the kitchen, where Amanda oversaw the responsibilities, and it was nice to always find her there and to partake of the gentle constancy this sweet woman had brought into their home.

On a typically hot morning, Amanda informed Eleanore that she would be looking out for the children so that Eleanore and her husband could enjoy the picnic she had prepared for them.

"Why?" Eleanore asked.

"I don't think the two of you hardly ever get time alone in daylight," she said. "You're always busy with one thing or another, and the children are never far. It's good for a married couple to have some time together; you should do it more often."

"You talked me into it," Eleanore said. "Thank you. As always, you are too kind."

Amanda offered a humble smile. "You've made my life rich," she said. "Working here and being a part of your family is a blessing I'd never imagined possible when I lost my husband. Now, hurry up and change. Daylight's wasting."

Eleanore was just buttoning a dress that didn't look as if she'd been cleaning house in it when her husband came into the room. He smiled and said, "I've been informed that I'm going on a picnic."

"Can you imagine the audacity of that woman?" Eleanore asked facetiously.

"Indeed," he said and put an arm around her from behind, pressing a kiss to her neck. "I'm ashamed for not thinking of it myself."

"If you thought of everything, you'd be close to perfect."

He made a disagreeable noise, and she laughed.

A short while later they were headed into town in the buggy to see to a few errands before finding a spot to share their picnic lunch. They both went into the general store to get a few things. James went into the bank while Eleanore sat in the buggy and read, then they stopped to pick up the mail. Again she read while he went inside. When he returned and sat beside her, he handed her an envelope without speaking. Eleanore set her book aside and took it from him, turned it over to look at the front, and gasped.

"Now that she knows you're a Mormon," he said, snapping the reins, "you'll never stop hearing from her."

He smiled when he said it, and Eleanore replied, "I would hope so."

"Aren't you going to open it?" he asked after she'd just stared at it for a minute.

Eleanore did so but almost felt afraid to read it, and at the same time, her excitement made her want to put it off a little and savor the experience. "She must consider us good friends now," she said. "The salutation says 'Dear Eleanore.' Last time it was 'Mrs. Barrington.'" She let out a quiet laugh and added lightly, "It's a good thing you've finally started calling me Eleanore; otherwise, I would think that Sally cared more for me than you do. We were married for months before you ever called me Eleanore, you know."

"There's no need to remind me," he said with mock chagrin, driving out of the city and down the lane that led back toward their home. "I'm well aware of my past hypocrisy." He smiled at her. "I'm just glad I had the good sense to figure out how in love with you I am. I can assure you that *no one* cares for you more than I do."

She smiled in return. "How delightful! You must know, however, that I don't mind your calling me Mrs. Barrington now and then. It reminds me that I'm yours, that we share the same name."

James looked at her and felt overcome with one of those moments when the love he felt for her consumed him. He wondered if his years of living a lie—married to his first wife in the midst of betrayal, surviving her horrific treatment of him and the children—had made him more appreciative of what he had now. Whatever it was, he pulled on the reins to stop the horses and leaned over to kiss his wife as if that might let her know how dear she was to him. When a simple kiss didn't feel adequate, he said, "Here, hold these." He put the reins into one of her hands while she held her letter in the other. Before she could question him he put both his hands into her hair and pressed his lips to hers, kissing her the way a husband should kiss his wife.

"James," she muttered breathlessly, opening dreamy eyes to look at him. "We're in the middle of the road."

"We are completely alone," he said and kissed her again. "Are you complaining?"

"No, but . . . it is a bit . . . awkward."

He noted her holding the reins and admitted, "So it is." He took them from her and drove the buggy off the road and parked it where the horses could graze. She stuck the letter and her book into her satchel that she always carried. He helped her down, then took out the picnic hamper and blanket. They walked for a few minutes until they found a pleasant shady spot with a stream close enough that they could hear the faint gurgle of running water. James set down the hamper, spread out the blanket, took Eleanore's satchel from her, and set it aside as well before he took her face into his hands. "Now, where were we?"

Between bouts of passionate kissing they shared the delicious lunch that Amanda had prepared. James declared that they didn't do nearly enough kissing these days, and getting away on a picnic was a very good idea. "We're practically newlyweds, after all," he said, lying on his back to gaze up at the trees that blocked the view of the sky.

Eleanore sat beside him to eat a second piece of cake, since Amanda had made her favorite. "So we are," she said and fed him a bite. "It's hard to believe. I can't even remember what it was like not to be married. Imagine how we'll feel in ten or twenty years."

He chuckled. "I will be very old, and you'll still be very young."

"Which means you'd best stay *very* healthy and live a *very* long time."

"I'll do my best," he said, and she finished her cake.

Eleanore leaned back on her hands and soaked in the serenity of their surroundings while James closed his eyes and became completely relaxed. Then she remembered the letter in her satchel, and she hurried to take it out. She opened it quietly and felt jittery inside as she began to read.

Dear Eleanore, How can this be anything but a miracle? Though we have never met I feel as if we are sisters in spirit. To think of someone such as you living in the home that was once mine, and to know how you were led there, warms my heart beyond any words I could find to describe. I've reread your letter a dozen times, and I can only say how grateful I am to you for writing to share your experiences, and to a merciful Father in Heaven who would guide us together this way. I hope that one day we will meet, but for now it seems best if you stay where you are, as you said in your letter. We have found many blessings living in Nauvoo, but many hardships as well. Brother Joseph . . .

Eleanore stopped and pondered the name. Could she possibly mean Joseph Smith? She knew he was the translator of the Book of Mormon, and it was through him that the gospel had been restored. Brother Yeats had told her the story in much detail. Joseph Smith surely had to be one of the most amazing men who had ever walked the earth. Could Sally truly be referring to him? She read on.

Brother Joseph purchased the property as a place for us to gather and be free from persecution. No one can doubt the inspiration of a prophet . . .

She *did* mean Joseph Smith! Oh, to hear any news of him was such a joy.

. . . And surely this is where God wants His people to be at this time, although we can never guess by what means God will test and

try us. If Moses and his people wandered in the wilderness for forty years, and Nephi's people wandered for eight, we can only trust in our Maker and strive to endure well, and learn the obedience and patience that they learned.

Eleanore took a deep breath and put a hand over her quickened heart. Such faith! Such perspective on eternal matters! She loved this woman already, and admired her deeply. And she'd barely begun to read Sally's lengthy letter.

Chapter Three

ELEANORE'S WISH

Sally went on to write vaguely about the persecutions that had preceded their coming to Nauvoo, and more specifically of the fever that had befallen every member of their family and countless others of the Saints while most of them were living in tents, or wagons, or even with no shelter at all. They had suffered greatly, and many had died. The Jensen family considered themselves greatly blessed that they'd all survived the illness. She tenderly wrote of how it had seemed the effects of the disease would afflict them eternally, and death began to seem preferable. And then the Prophet Joseph had gotten himself off his own sick bed, going from tent to tent where the people were living, to offer holy priesthood blessings. Sally bore emotional witness of how she had felt the sickness flow out of her body as the Prophet's hands had come upon her head and his words had surrounded her with a nearly tangible sensation of the Holy Spirit. And while she read, Eleanore wept quietly. Sally wrote of her absolute knowledge that Joseph Smith was indeed a prophet of God, repeating some things about him that Eleanore had heard from Brother Yeats, and other things she'd never heard before that both saddened and amazed her. And Eleanore continued to cry.

"What's wrong?" James asked quietly without opening his eyes.

"I thought you were asleep."

"I'm not." He looked at her and took her hand. "Tell me."

"She's just . . . talking about Joseph Smith and how he—"

"Who?" he asked.

Eleanore felt astonished. "Surely you remember. Brother Yeats told us all about Joseph Smith. He's the one who translated the record that became the Book of Mormon and he—"

"I wasn't privy to your every conversation."

"I'd forgotten," she said, wondering how she could ever convey her feelings about this great man. "Have you never heard me mention his name before?"

"Not that I recall," he said, and Eleanore wondered why, when they were as open as they were with each other, she had never discussed things that were so important to her. "Who is he?"

Throwing caution to the wind, Eleanore said, "He's the founder of the Church; the prophet, and he—"

"Wait a minute." James leaned up on one elbow. "A prophet? As in . . . a man who communicates with God?"

In spite of his skepticism she said firmly, "That's right."

James considered such a statement in light of knowing that Mormons were persecuted and driven. If they had no qualms about declaring that their leader was a man who spoke with God, he could perhaps understand why some people were put off. Still, given that they lived in America, people should be entitled to believe whatever they wanted, and worship how they chose. If people wanted to believe a man was a prophet, so be it. His concern was that his *wife* believed it. He noted the conviction in her eyes, but it was mingled with concern. He reminded himself that no matter *what* she believed, he couldn't let it create discord between them. He simply asked, "Are you saying then that this Joseph Smith speaks with God the same way that Moses or Abraham would have?"

"Of course," she said, as if it took no stretch of faith or imagination to grasp such a concept. "And why wouldn't there be prophets today as there were in centuries past? Are the people of Old Testament times the only ones privy to living prophets?"

"But what about all the time between then and now?"

He didn't expect her to have an answer, but she did. And she spoke it firmly. "After Jesus died and the original Apostles were gradually done away with, the true gospel faded from the earth along with the proper authority. Since that time the world has lived in some manner of darkness. Joseph Smith is the man God has used as an instrument in His hands to restore the full gospel to the earth."

James fought to keep the skepticism out of his voice as he asked tonelessly, "And how does Mr. Smith know *he* is that man?"

"Because God told him."

"Face-to-face?"

"Yes."

"And where did you learn all of this, my dear?"

"Brother Yeats told me."

"And you believe him? You believe it's true?"

"I *know* it's true."

"How, Eleanore? How can you *know* it's true?"

Again he expected her to become uneasy, or unable to answer the question. But the resolve in her eyes only deepened as she said, "The scriptures tell us that by the Holy Ghost we may know the truth of all things. Brother Yeats told me I didn't have to take his word for it, that it was up to me to pray and receive my own witness as to the truth of these things. I already knew beyond any doubt the Book of Mormon is true; it is what it claims to be. Joseph Smith was guided by God to the ancient record and given the power to translate it. If the book is true, then the means by which it was brought about are also true. I know, James; I know he is a prophet."

Eleanore saw doubt in his eyes, even though he was trying to be supportive. She took advantage of the silence between them to complete her testimony. "I know it sounds strange, James, but truly . . . I know my heart, and I know it's true. Joseph Smith saw God the Father and Jesus Christ as two separate beings. They spoke to him, and through him all of the keys and authority that were lost centuries ago were restored. You said yourself that the difficult things happening to the Saints were likely for the same reason the original Apostles were all done away with. I believe that the evil conspiring against the Church only adds evidence of its validity. Surely Satan would not want this work to go forth."

James considered everything she was saying and the emotional strength behind her words. He'd always admired her instincts and the way she lived by them. He'd always trusted her intuition. Could he doubt it now simply because it sounded strange? In his mind he tried to connect what he knew of organized religion with what she was telling him. As if she'd read his thoughts she said, "You believe the Bible is true; I know you do."

"Yes, I do."

"If you read with an open mind," Eleanore said, hoping she wasn't babbling too much, "you will find much evidence in the Bible that supports and coincides with the Book of Mormon, and with what Joseph Smith teaches. But I believe that in such matters, it is what we feel, not what we can logically assess that matters. Still, if you believe that Moses truly spoke to God and parted the Red Sea, why is it so difficult to believe that a man of our day would do the equivalent?" She was grateful for the concept she'd just read in Sally's letter that gave strength to her explanations. "In spite of the miracles Moses performed through God's hand, he wandered with his people in the wilderness for forty years. Are the followers of God in this day likely to be tried any less?"

James thought about that for a minute, combined with all he knew of his wife's character. He simply couldn't fathom her being taken in by something harebrained or irrational. But truthfully, if it were *not* for the longtime evidence he had of her character, he might be seriously concerned. As it was, there could only be one thing to say. "I will always respect your beliefs, Eleanore, whatever they may be."

Eleanore looked down, hoping to hide the threat of tears. He didn't believe her. She told herself that she couldn't expect him to, not with so little to go on. Still, with the closeness they shared in every aspect of life, it was difficult to feel divided on this one point. In spite of that, he was telling her he would respect her beliefs. She counted that as a blessing when she felt certain that another man might have told her it was ludicrous and prohibit her from having anything to do with it.

He moved his head to her lap and put his arms around her. "So long as it doesn't come between us, Eleanore, I will stand behind you."

Eleanore wanted to say thank you, but she feared that speaking at all would reveal her raw emotion over the matter. In fact, until this moment she'd not realized how tender her feelings were in regard to her desire to share the gospel with this man she loved so dearly.

She felt James relax and became aware of his even breathing, which indicated he was asleep. She finished reading the letter from Sally, soaking in details and information about this church she belonged to and other people who shared her faith. She read the letter again, silently thanking God as she did for sending her this priceless connection. She was grateful for the wealth of information Sally shared, as well as the warm association that eased her loneliness over the matter. With that blessing uppermost in her mind, she pushed away any discontentment she felt over her husband's lack of interest, praying that with time his heart would be softened and his mind opened. She felt certain he was more likely to appreciate and respect her beliefs if she wasn't aggressive about them.

After pondering Sally's words, Eleanore considered taking a nap as well, but didn't feel sleepy. Instead she picked up the book she had with her and silently reread some of her favorite passages; it was truly one of her most cherished novels. James kept his head in her lap and remained relaxed there even though she knew he was now awake. Eleanore's mind began to wander, and she said to her husband, "What do you suppose it might have been like if we'd met differently? If you had courted me in a way that was more typical?"

He opened his eyes to give her a curious glance, then he lifted the book that was open on her lap to see what she was reading. "Jane Austen again? Your romantic notions are insatiable, my dear."

"I wouldn't say that. I would say that my romantic notions are met rather well right within my own marriage." He lifted one eyebrow, and she laughed quietly before she added, "You are a man who carries a hair ribbon in his pocket sprayed with my perfume. You speak tender sentiments to your wife each and every day, and you clearly adore her simply by the way you look at her. You're a sentimental fool, James Barrington, yet you tease me for having romantic notions."

James made a comically disagreeable noise and sat up, taking the book from her, keeping his fingers on the page where she'd had it open. He looked at it skeptically, as if it might be the root of some horrid discord between them. *"Pride and Prejudice?"* he said in a mocking disapproval that was so exaggerated it made her giggle. He then opened the book to where she'd been reading and read in a histrionic voice, "'In vain have I struggled. It will not do. My feelings will not be repressed. You must allow me to tell you how ardently I admire and love you.'" Eleanore giggled again, and he read on. "'Elizabeth's astonishment was beyond expression. She stared, coloured, doubted, and was silent. This he considered sufficient encouragement, and the avowal of all that he felt and had long felt for her immediately followed.'" He set the book face-down, keeping it open on the specified page and growled with humor, "Good heavens, woman, what lures you to read such nonsense?"

She shrugged. "Romantic notions."

"Yes, and look where they've gotten you." He leaned over and kissed her in a tender way that completely contradicted his teasing.

"Yes," she said, putting a hand to his face, "for all my romantic notions, I married a man who declared he would never give me his heart."

More seriously he said, "And why did you do such a ridiculous thing?"

"I knew it was right," she said, equally somber. "But I never imagined I could be so happy."

"Nor did I," he said and kissed her again. "You are everything I only dreamed a woman could be."

"There you go again," she said lightly. "Spouting off romantic diatribe as if it might win my heart, or something."

"It is *not* diatribe!" he insisted with a smile. "It comes from the heart."

"There you go again," she repeated. "But you know what? It's working." She kissed him and eased her fingers into his hair. "Your love for me sustains and keeps me, James. I would be utterly lost without you." She kissed him again.

"I could say the same," he said and kissed her still again, this time with more passion.

A short while later James drifted off to sleep again with his wife close beside him. He couldn't figure out why he was so sleepy unless it was simply the fact of being away from all of the usual responsibilities. He woke to find Eleanore reading, leaning back on one hand, holding a book with the other. He eased his head into her lap and murmured with a sleepy voice, "Indulging in more silly nonsense, are you?"

"I would have to argue that point," she said severely. "I won't dispute that reading Jane Austen is purely for recreation, but what I'm reading now I will defend vehemently. So be careful what you say."

James lifted his head to see that her face was hidden behind the Book of Mormon. He resumed his comfortable position and pondered her words. He'd passively respected her beliefs, but had never made any effort to understand them. In spite of his skepticism on some points, he wondered how he might feel if she disregarded something that was of value to him. Did she believe that he placed the worth of this book at the same level as the romantic novels she read? There were many books they'd read that they discussed at length, likely with the exception being that he preferred not to talk about the romantic tales she read, and she didn't appreciate his studies on politics. But this was religion. He considered himself a religious man, or perhaps more accurately a very spiritual one. So, why did he steer himself away from any interest in what meant most to his wife beyond the life and love they shared together? Besides feeling somewhat dubious over modern-day prophets and visions, he could admit to some fear on her behalf, and perhaps he hoped that by keeping himself distanced from her religion he might be more able to keep her protected from those who opposed it. But that was certainly no reason to avoid even discussing it with her. If only to express his respect for her as his wife, he felt sure it would be appropriate to show some polite interest in what she was reading. Perhaps their earlier conversation had sparked his interest. Perhaps he hoped that learning more about her beliefs might aid him in helping her keep a prudent perspective. And perhaps he'd simply been awakened to the fact that he had a blind spot in regard to his wife.

"Tell me about what you're reading," he said.

She peered around the book with dubious eyes. "Why?" she asked.

"I'm curious."

"I've been reading practically every day from this book for as long as I've known you. Why are you asking about it now?"

"Perhaps my interest is overdue."

Somewhat facetiously she said, "But it was translated by a modern-day prophet and—"

"Just . . . tell me what you're reading about," he said. "We can analyze it some other time."

Eleanore couldn't hold back a smile. Prayers that she'd barely uttered already seemed to be heard. If he showed any interest at all, even if it was only a little here and there, perhaps he would eventually come to know what she knew. She silently thanked God, then told James the story of Samuel the Lamanite prophesying of Christ's birth, and how he was protected from the people who were trying to kill him. Then she told him of Christ's appearance following His resurrection, and the miracles that took place. James didn't comment, but he listened attentively. And when she concluded that she'd told him enough for one day, he admitted that it *was* an amazing book. She left it at that, grateful for the conversation, and praying that more would come eventually.

That evening Eleanore wrote Sally another lengthy letter, this time pouring her heart into it with no restraint. She truly had found a friend.

The following day Eleanore pulled weeds from around the tender squash plants in the garden, a wide-brimmed straw bonnet shielding her face from the sun. The children had each done their allotted weed pulling and had gone off to play in the woods where it was cooler, but she could hear them nearby. James was at the opposite side of the garden, examining the budding stalks of corn. Eleanore heard some laughter and excitement from the children, with David's voice rising above that of Iris and Ralph. Then David came running out of the trees, calling with enthusiasm, "Mama, Mama! Look what we found!"

Eleanore rose from her knees and noticed James step over the rows of corn to see what the excitement was about. Following after David and coming before the other children was a dog. Eleanore had rarely seen David so excited about anything, and she felt relieved to note that the dog was friendly and pleasant. She'd rarely had any encounter with dogs herself, but James immediately squatted beside the animal and started looking it over.

"I think he's hungry, Papa," David said. "May we feed him?"

"Well, we can't let him go hungry," James said and rubbed its pointed ears. The animal was grayish brown with dirty, matted hair that was more long than short. He had a significant tail and was about medium sized as far as dogs went.

"He needs a bath," James added. "A good scrubbing. And then we need to find out who he belongs to."

The last declaration immediately changed the bright expressions of the children into prominent frowns. "Can't we keep him?" Iris asked, her eyes going wide, her lips pouty. David and Ralph silently echoed the question.

"He's obviously lost," James said. "Someone has given him a lot of love or he wouldn't be so friendly."

"I told you it was a boy," Ralph said, and James chuckled.

"Yes, it's definitely a boy. Let's get him something to eat and get him cleaned up—along with the rest of you—and then we'll take care of him while we ask around and find out who he belongs to."

"We know he can't be from any of the homes in the area," Eleanore said. "We know all of those people—and their pets. We've never seen this dog before."

"Still, the neighbors might know where he's run away from." James stood up and brushed his hands. As if to test the animal he said, "Sit." And the dog did so immediately. "Lay," he added, and the command was honored. The children were beaming with pride at the intelligence and obedience of their discovery.

Eleanore couldn't help but be drawn to the animal—but only with the prospect of that scrubbing James had insisted on. She said to her husband, "Apparently you know something about dogs. I don't recall a dog ever being in your home in England."

"We had dogs when I was a child—three, in fact. My father was very fond of them. They each died eventually, and so did my father. I had plans to travel abroad and never bothered to get another. But I admit it . . . I like dogs."

"Well, don't get too attached," she said. "I'm sure you're right; it must belong to someone around here."

Even though the dog was treated as a temporary visitor, the children insisted on finding a suitable name, not wanting to just call him "the dog." While "the dog" was eating, a number of possible names were suggested. During the course of a lengthy, very thorough, and comical scrubbing of the dog in a tub that had been moved to the yard, they unanimously and firmly decided to call the animal Jack. Once clean, Jack took a nap on the porch while the children sat close by, apparently fascinated by him even while he was motionless. When naptime was done, he seemed eager to accept the children's attention and wanted to play. Eleanore saw a different side of her husband as he initiated some type of wrestling with the dog that Jack clearly enjoyed, and it made the children giggle. Then it became evident that Jack's previous owner had taught him to play fetch rather efficiently. The children each took turns throwing a stick, and Jack repeatedly brought it back and dropped it at their feet. It was debated whether or not Jack should be tied up when it came time for supper and no one was watching him, but it was determined that if he needed to go find his owner, he would. They found him lounging on the side porch, however, where he was fed again. And in the morning he was still there.

Over the next several days, inquiries were made among neighbors and in town regarding the dog, but no one knew anything about him. And they asked virtually everyone they could think of, every person they knew and many they didn't. After two weeks it seemed evident that Jack was staying. They'd decided that perhaps he'd run off from a passing wagon train or the like and his owners were long gone. "Or maybe," Eleanore speculated, "God sent him to us because He knew Jack needed someone to care for him, and we needed a new friend." The children liked that theory, and Jack quickly became a member of the family. At first Eleanore was reluctant to let him in the house. But it was quickly proven he would bark at the door if he needed to go out, and not once did he do anything in the house that required anyone to clean up after him. While the children quickly grew to love the dog, and the adults enjoyed having him around, it was James who spoiled him, sneaking food to him under the dinner table and letting him sleep on the couch. Eleanore told her husband, "That's fine, as long as *you* clean the hair off the furniture." He gladly agreed.

A few times Jack disappeared into the woods and didn't come back for many hours. But he *did* come back. At first they thought the dog had a mind to go seeking its original owner, a thought that caused everyone, the children especially, much grief. But inevitably Jack returned. Since David occasionally wandered off without thinking, occasionally giving his parents a scare, they declared that he and Jack were much alike. James and Eleanore both gently scolded David for wandering away and worrying them. He would always apologize and feel bad, but it seemed a habit of his to simply allow his mind to drift and his feet seemed to follow without any thought given to what he was doing. As a result, his parents kept close track when David went out walking, and they called out frequently to be certain he was close enough to answer. Eleanore recalled times in England when he'd run off to be alone, and once he'd become lost in a storm, and a horrible illness had resulted. She had no intention of allowing that to happen again.

Summer slipped toward autumn, with the garden being the focal point of all family activity. The harvesting and using of all they had grown became mutually fulfilling, and Eleanore loved the way her husband thrived on the life they were living. She found some of her greatest pleasure in just watching him with the children while they worked and played together.

The new little house for Frederick and Lizzie was completed before the heat of summer began to relent. Furniture and other necessities had been ordered to Lizzie's specifications, and James had humbly and quietly paid for everything. He made it clear that having a place to live was part of their employment agreement; they'd been loyal and hardworking, and he wanted them to be comfortable and happy. Eleanore couldn't recall Lizzie *ever* being so happy. But then, they all seemed to be doing well with their new way of life. Only Eleanore's desire for a baby caused her any real grief. Other challenges were minimal, and she felt certain time would work them out. She tried to feel the same way about her longing to be pregnant, but on that point she felt less prone to being positive. Instead she simply avoided talking about it, and tried not to think about it.

The weeks of harvest were busy but gratifying as the produce was picked and preserved. The cellar became filled with food for the coming year, and it would be enjoyed by all who had contributed to the process. The harvest season merged summer to fall. The cooler temperatures and changing colors of the leaves were pleasant and breathtaking. Eleanore marveled that they had now lived in Iowa for more than a year, but she found joy in recognizing that, in spite of certain struggles, it had been the best year of her life.

With autumn came the birth of Lizzie's baby. She was a beautiful redheaded girl, who came into the world healthy and strong but caused enough problems for her mother that an emergency surgery was performed right after the birth. Lizzie would never be able to have more children, but she was likely too old to do so anyway. Lizzie and Frederick were grateful to have a child at all, when neither had ever imagined that they would. They named the baby Mary Jane, after both of their mothers. Lizzie recovered quickly while Eleanore and Amanda worked together to care for her and help with Mary Jane. Eleanore loved holding the baby and being involved with her care, and she spoke only with James about her bittersweet emotions. She was happy for Lizzie and Frederick and grateful to have a baby around, but her own heart ached while her womb remained empty.

Eleanore also found a bittersweet delight in the regular exchange of letters with Sally Jensen. Gradually Eleanore had learned through the written words of her new friend that the city of Nauvoo was being transformed from the swampy land they had first encountered on their arrival. While many miracles had taken place, the effects of the ongoing fever had continued, but were now easing up for most people. Still, Sally boldly declared that she preferred the security of Nauvoo over what had befallen them before going there. She only hinted at what had specifically happened to them in Iowa preceding their move to Illinois, but Eleanore could sense in her letters the personal trauma to the Jensen family, and how grateful they were now to be among the Saints and feel safe in spite of struggles they'd faced there. Eleanore longed to be with the Saints as well, but in her heart she knew this was her home—at least for now—and this was where she needed to stay.

Sally wrote of the happenings in Nauvoo, and often made mention of seeing Brother Joseph here or there. Eleanore wondered how it would be to actually meet and interact with Joseph Smith, a man who had seen visions, personally translated the ancient record that had become the Book of Mormon, and who was now the leader of this great Church and a true prophet of God, not unlike Moses or Jacob of the Old Testament. In her heart she knew he truly was a prophet; she didn't even have to question it. She'd long ago felt the truth of his own words written at the beginning of the Book of Mormon, prior to the beginning of the translated text.

Through Sally's letters, Eleanore learned that at one time Joseph had been illegally imprisoned for a period of months, and during that time a large number of Saints had been driven

from their homes in Missouri amidst great horrors. Sally veri-
fied things that James had heard, that it truly had been made
legal by the governor of Missouri to do whatever it took to get
rid of the Mormons. While Sally had not lived in Missouri, she
had come to personally know many people who had been
deeply affected by this chain of events. The stories were heart-
wrenching, but were also further evidence of Satan's battle to
destroy the going forth of Christ's work, and of the faith and
perseverance of the righteous who were striving to do God's
will in spite of horrific obstacles. Eleanore often wondered why
she would be preserved from such horrors, grateful for the
safety and security of her Iowa home, knowing she had God's
blessing to remain here, hidden from those who would do harm
to Mormons. A part of her longed to be with the people who
shared her faith, and consequently to be free of the loneliness
she felt in her solitary worship. But her mother had always
taught her to count her blessings and to find the good in any
situation. Eleanore's life was good; she could not dispute that.
So she allowed herself to enjoy it and appreciated the long-
distance friendship she'd gained through letters with Sally that
didn't leave her feeling quite so cut off from the rest of the
Saints.

Eleanore wrote and told Sally that she would be happy to
send anything that had been left in the house that Sally might
want. She knew they'd left in a hurry, likely with little wagon
space. And even though the purchase of the house legally
included all of its contents, Eleanore was more than willing to
part with anything that had value for Sally or her family, or that
they might need. And she said so firmly. But Sally wrote back
and said they had everything they needed and Eleanore should
enjoy the contents of the house, especially the china, since it had
belonged to Sally's mother. Eleanore had never used the china
and wasn't sure she ever could. Realizing it had sentimental
value, she felt even more certain Sally should have it, but she

didn't know how she could ever send it without risk of it breaking. So she just left it in the cupboard and admired it on occasion.

Eleanore also received a couple of letters from Brother Yeats, the man who had baptized her. He was kind to write, and it was good to hear from him and to know he was keeping track of her, but his letters were brief, and she was grateful for Sally's lengthy epistles, filled with detail and emotion.

Eleanore stopped meticulously counting the days of her monthly cycles, when doing so only gave her more dread than hope. Whenever thoughts of it entered her mind, she immediately forced them away, allowing herself only a few tears each month when she found that she was not pregnant. She appreciated the coming of Christmas and the opportunity to have something extra to keep her busy and her mind occupied. The delights of the holiday season were even more gratifying than the previous year as new traditions settled in more deeply. The men cut an evergreen tree and put it up in the parlor, where everyone helped decorate it, and they gathered around it to read from the Bible and exchange gifts. Laughter and warmth filled the kitchen as the women baked extra treats and prepared an unparalleled Christmas feast. The heavy snow kept Amanda and Ralph from returning to their own home throughout the holiday, but they all agreed that they preferred it that way. They all felt like family. Even Jack had become an inseparable part of their home. He loved to lay close to the fire almost as much as he loved getting attention from anyone who would give it to him. While he clearly loved all of the children, he was most often found close to James, as if he had chosen him as his favorite person.

The new year came with heavy snow and bitter cold. The daylight hours were short, and the long nights lured Eleanore's ache closer to the surface. Still, she forced her thoughts away from the calendar, refusing to watch it and count the days.

During intimate moments with her husband she never allowed her mind to wander to the possibility of conceiving a child. She focused instead on the tenderness they shared and the ever-strengthening bond between them. Her gratitude for his love deepened daily with the ongoing evidence of what a fine man he was. But she knew that he too longed for a baby, and she ached to give him one, to share the experience of bringing a new little life into the world. Still, pregnancy eluded her, and they'd stopped talking about it at all.

On an especially cold night, Eleanore crawled into bed and watched the strange shadows that the fire cast on the ceiling. James came into the room after checking the heat in the children's rooms and slipped into the bed, immediately putting his cold feet close to her warm ones.

"You're a scoundrel," she giggled.

"Yes, I am," he declared with bold sarcasm and a quiet laugh. "The only reason I married you was to keep my feet warm."

"That's what I thought," she said, loving his teasing words.

"But it only works if you go to bed first." He snuggled close to her and kissed her cheek. "Do you know why I *really* married you?"

"As I recall, it was a matter of convenience."

"Convenient only because God had planted you right there in front of me long before I realized how perfect you were."

"No, not perfect."

"Perfect for me . . . in every way."

Eleanore wanted to say that she was a woman incapable of giving him children, but she couldn't allow such a conversation to even begin. She turned toward him and touched his face. "It's the other way around." She kissed him. "You've always taken such good care of me."

"That has *never* been difficult, my dear." He kissed her again. "Do you know when I first started to fall in love with you?"

"*Fall* in love with me?" she asked lightly. "How can that be when you so boldly declared that you were not capable of love? You were far too disciplined and wise to *fall* in love."

"Now you're mocking me," he said with a laugh.

"Well . . . you did prove yourself a hypocrite."

"Yes, I did," he said proudly, as if that were as admirable as being a scoundrel. "I fell in love with you long before I asked you to marry me. I was just too afraid and prideful to see the truth, let alone admit it."

"But you admit it now," she said, touching his face again.

"Eagerly," he said and kissed her hand. "I love you, Eleanore. But you're changing the subject. Do you know the first time I started falling in love with you?"

"No, tell me."

"You were sitting in my office, telling me that you would not divulge the secrets David had shared with you—even though I was his father. And when I tried to talk you into it, you said . . ." He raised his voice to mimic her. "'If *you* had told me something in confidence, Mr. Barrington, I dare say you would not want someone else wheedling it out of me.'"

"You wouldn't, would you?"

"No, of course not. That's just the point. You put me so neatly in my place. You had a way of doing that. But that was the first time I remember looking at you and thinking, 'Where *did* she come from? She's incredible!'"

"And I'd been under your roof for years."

"But you *came* from heaven, my dear . . . like an angel, a gift from God, everything I'd ever wanted or needed." He tightened his embrace and kissed her brow; his voice became earnest. "I still wonder sometimes what I'd ever done to deserve you."

"It's the other way around, James," she repeated and urged her lips to his. *I only wish* . . . she nearly added but kept the wish to herself and kissed him again.

He made love to her with all the care and tenderness that was typical of his nature. She felt perfectly loved and utterly content as she drifted toward sleep in his arms, until he whispered near her ear, "Perhaps this will be the magic moment, hmm?"

Tears tingled in her eyes, but she blinked them away, grateful her back was to him. "It's always magic, James," she said, proud of her own steady voice.

"You know what I mean," he said. She made no comment, and he added, "Not talking about it won't make it any easier, perhaps only harder."

"I *can't* talk about it," she admitted, her voice less firm. "If I don't talk about *that* then I can easily admit that my life is perfect."

"But it's *not* perfect," he said, touching her shoulder to roll her toward him. "Admit it, Eleanore; this is hard, and it hurts, and maybe we *should* talk about it."

"James," she said firmly, "if God were to ask me what I might be willing to give up in return for a baby, I would prefer to remain barren over losing anything that I've been blessed with. I have so much to be grateful for that it's impossible to make a list long enough."

"I admire your faith and your gratitude, my dear; I do. But that doesn't change the fact of this challenge we face."

"So, let's talk about it," she said, sounding sharper than she'd intended. "Will it help either one of us feel better if I admit that there's something wrong with me?"

"How can you be sure it's you?" he countered, equally sharp.

"You fathered two children through your first wife."

"And you have been pregnant before. It doesn't matter *what* the problem is, Eleanore. There is no way of knowing such things and it simply doesn't matter. This is *our* marriage and we are in it together. Whatever life brings, we face it together. But it's begun to feel like we're sharing this battle on separate battlefields because we don't want to talk about it. Sometimes I fear that you're holding it in until you'll explode with the pain. You need to talk to me, Eleanore. Tell me it hurts, that it's hard; curse and cry if you have to. But don't shut me out of your heart . . . I beg you."

Eleanore was startled at how quickly her emotions responded to his invitation. She sobbed and took hold of him, pressing her face to his chest, crying so hard that her head hurt and her throat became dry and raspy. When her tears subsided, she whispered her greatest fear. "What if we are never able to have a child together, James?"

"Then we will be happy living the nearly perfect life that we share. But you mustn't give up hope, my dear. You are still so young. There are many years left for us to have children."

"Forgive my stating the obvious," she said, "but you are not so young." She rose up on one elbow and looked into his face. "I want you to live long enough to see our children raised. I want you to be healthy enough to be an active part of their lives. Chronologically you're old enough to be a grandfather to my children, but I don't want it to feel that way to them."

"Are you questioning your judgment in marrying an older man?" he asked, not entirely serious.

"No, I am not!" she said, wholly serious. "I just *want* to have your baby, and I feel dreadfully impatient."

"The matter is in God's hands, Ellie. Perhaps there is nothing physically wrong at all. Perhaps it's just not the right time for us to have children, for reasons we may never understand. If God wishes to teach us patience, we would do well to learn it and not question *His* judgment. All we can do is exactly what we're doing. We must live our lives one day at a time, finding happiness in all that we share and making the most of all that we have. And we must trust in God."

Eleanore looked into his eyes and touched his face. A smile overtook her, almost against her will. "You tell me you admire my faith, while you seem so oblivious to your own. You are an inspiration to me, my darling. You are my strength; you're what holds me together."

"God is your greatest strength, my dear wife. We both know He comes first in your life, but that's the way it should be."

"He gave me you . . . to take care of me while He is so far away."

"Not *so* far," he said and kissed her. "I love you, Eleanore Barrington. And all will be well."

"As long as you are beside me, reminding me of that, then surely it will be."

Chapter Four

THE SECRET

Eleanore slept in James's arms and woke in the morning to find the fire stoked but her husband absent. Recalling their conversation in the night, she couldn't deny that she felt a little better than she had in a long while. When she saw James before breakfast, he asked her how she was feeling, and teased her about naming their first son Jack, after the dog. She assured him that Jack was a fine name, but already taken in their household.

The next morning James suggested that Eleanore go into town with him, just the two of them. He thought it would be good for her to get out, even though it was so cold. He wanted to take her to lunch at a restaurant in town where they went on occasion. Eleanore was feeling a little under the weather but didn't want to turn down such an opportunity. Midmorning he helped her into the buggy and adjusted a heavy quilt over her lap before he sat beside her and snapped the reins. He moved the reins to one hand and put his arm around her as the horse pulled them toward town. Eleanore laid her head on his shoulder and closed her eyes, feeling unusually tired. She was mentally attempting to assess the reason for her fatigue when the motion of the buggy suddenly made her dizzy and a little queasy. She sat up straight abruptly, which only enhanced both sensations. She noted her husband's question and concern, but before she could explain, her stomach lurched.

"Stop!" she said, putting a hand on his arm. He pulled back on the reins, and she jumped down before the buggy came to a full stop. She rushed into the trees where she lost the contents of her stomach and found James's hand on her shoulder before she was finished retching.

"Oh, I hate it when you do that," she said, taking the hand-kerchief he offered and pressing it over her mouth, attempting to catch her breath.

"Do what?" he asked, baffled.

"You really could keep your distance while I'm throwing up. I can manage on my own, you know. It's terribly degrading."

"I'm concerned for you," he said as if it were nothing. "Besides, I haven't watched you throw up since . . ." He didn't finish.

"Since our journey to Iowa, I know. And then it was every day." The implication hit her, and she looked up at him, feeling startled. His eyes let her know that he'd thought of it before she had. "No!" she said, not willing to get her hopes up. "I am *not* pregnant just because . . . I have a little upset stomach. I'm sure it's nothing; it will pass."

"You sound like I did when I was trying to declare that I didn't love you—when I really did. And I was making a fool of myself."

Eleanore hurried past him and back to the buggy. They were on their way toward town again before he asked, "Is your cycle late?"

"Don't ask me that."

"Why not? I'm your husband."

"And you're trying to give me false hope. There have been too many times when I've been certain I was pregnant because of a little . . . dizzy spell . . . or an upset stomach. And my hopes were always shattered. So don't do this to me."

He was silent for a couple of minutes then repeated, "Is your cycle late?"

Eleanore glared at him. He returned her gaze firmly, with no apology. She looked back to the road. "I don't know. I've stopped counting. I'm certain it's nothing."

"Fine. It's nothing. But I'm still taking you to see Dr. Garner . . . so he can tell me it's nothing." She glared at him again but he ignored her. She almost felt angry when he took her straight to the doctor's office. Then it occurred to her that if she were examined and declared to be not pregnant, she could put this argument to rest and fully set aside her hopes once again. She recalled from being pregnant before that the doctor had told her physical changes occurred in a woman right away that a doctor could detect very clearly. At least this would keep her from wondering, and her husband from speculating.

Inside they were told the doctor was with a patient and he could see her as soon as he was finished. Eleanore was relieved and at the same time wished he was gone making a house call. She wondered then if she preferred to hang on to some degree of hope—even if it were false. But she couldn't admit to that, not even to herself.

When the doctor was ready to see them, James did all the talking. He explained the symptoms, said he was concerned, and mentioned nothing about suspicions of pregnancy. But Dr. Garner immediately said, "I'd like to do a standard examination and see if she's pregnant, first of all."

James waited in the other room, and the doctor said nothing until he was finished. Then James went back to sit beside Eleanore and hold her hand. The doctor sat as well, saying nonchalantly, "There's nothing to be concerned about. You are undoubtedly pregnant, Mrs. Barrington."

Eleanore sucked in her breath and used all her will to keep from sobbing audibly. She squeezed her husband's hand and wondered if it was him or her trembling.

"Check back every few weeks," the doctor said, "and we'll do everything we can to keep you healthy."

"Thank you, Doctor," James said and urged her out of the office.

Just outside the door he took her in his arms and held her tightly while she discreetly wept against his chest, oblivious to any passersby who might find their behavior strange.

"Oh, Eleanore," he murmured, a quaver in his voice, "I don't know what to say."

"Just tell me it's really true." She drew back and wiped at her tears with her gloved hands. "Tell me it's not a dream."

He smiled and helped wipe her tears. "It's true," he said and kissed her brow. "We must take very good care of you." He kissed her brow. "Are you up to our errands, or should I take you home and do them myself later?"

"I'm fine," she said. "And you promised me lunch. We need to celebrate." She put a hand to her stomach. "In fact, I think lunch now would be a good idea. I need to keep food in my stomach. I remember this feeling very well. Even if he hadn't told me, I think I'd be more prone to believe it now than I was an hour ago."

James chuckled and guided her toward the buggy. "Perhaps, but if we'd not gone to the doctor you'd still be arguing with me."

"Perhaps," she admitted and settled onto the seat, attempting to accept the reality. *She was pregnant!* At last! It was a miracle.

* * *

Eleanore's illness made it impossible to keep her pregnancy a secret, even though she felt some trepidation in having everyone know. Having lost the last baby, she recalled too well the grief of everyone in the household as well as her own—especially the children. She didn't want to live through that again, for more reasons than she could count. And she prayed hourly that this baby would go full term and come into this world healthy and strong.

Dr. Garner estimated she was nearly four months along when the illness began to settle and her anticipation of having a baby heightened inside of her. The arrival of spring added to her growing contentment. Her life truly felt perfect in every regard. She received a letter from Sally in response to the news that she was expecting, and her friend expressed sincere excitement and congratulations. Eleanore sat on the side porch, breathing in the scent of the irises while she read Sally's words. She had also written that she had already started making a little quilt for the baby and would send it as soon as it was completed. After reading the letter, Eleanore went upstairs and into the room next to her own that had been designated as the nursery. She refolded all the little clothes and blankets they had collected during her first pregnancy and throughout this one. She'd never felt happier.

The following morning at breakfast, Eleanore felt no prior warning to the sudden cramping low in her belly. Horror tightened her heart at the same moment she met the fear in her husband's eyes as his attention was drawn to the evidence of her discomfort.

"What is it?" he asked softly, taking her hand across the corner of the table.

"I don't know," she muttered and stood. "Perhaps I should lie down."

She only took a few steps before the pain struck again, stopping her progress. She found James right beside her, his hands on her shoulders, silently questioning her. She felt tears on her own cheeks before she even realized she felt like crying. He scooped her into his arms, saying, "Frederick, would you go for the doctor, please. Lizzie, look after the children."

"Certainly," they both said at the same time, Frederick already on his way toward the door.

Eleanore's crying increased as he carried her up the stairs; the pain was undeniable and familiar. Once in the bedroom it only took her a minute to assess that she was bleeding, and she sobbed while James held her. She sensed his barely holding back his own torrent of grief.

"There must be some other explanation," he muttered, his voice trembling and husky, rocking her in his arms as if she were a child. "There has to be something that can be done."

Eleanore just held to him more tightly and continued to cry. In her heart she knew the truth. There *was* something wrong with her. She was incapable of carrying a baby full term, even when she *could* get pregnant. And her heart was breaking.

The doctor arrived and pronounced what she already knew. By the end of the day she was no longer pregnant. The drama was over, the signs washed away. Eleanore felt hollow and empty, no less in shock or consumed with grief than when she'd lost her mother. Maybe more so. She was grateful when the doctor gave her something to ease the pain and help her sleep. She only wanted to drift into oblivion and stay there.

James had the painful duty of informing the children that the baby was gone. They were both genuinely saddened, but their childlike faith inspired James. They both insisted that someday their family would have a new baby. He hoped they were right.

James returned to the bedroom and watched his wife sleeping while he wept silently. He couldn't even fathom facing her with this. He didn't know what to say. He wanted her to be happy. He ached to fix it, to make it right. But there was nothing he could do. The loss felt brutally deep. She hadn't been as far along as last time, but this loss was compounded upon that one, and the time it had taken her just to get pregnant made its untimely end feel harshly cruel. Memories of grieving over the loss of their first baby washed over him. What had felt healed was now torn open and added upon. He'd often pondered his gratitude for having that trial behind them, wondering how they'd ever gotten through it. He hated even thinking about the seemingly countless times they'd talked and cried together, attempting to heal and find peace. And now it was starting all over again. What could he say to her? What might he do? The answer was, of course, nothing. He could only love her as he always had, be there for her hour by hour, day by day, and hold tight to her as they shared this burden.

In the middle of the night James was awakened by a light knock at the door, then it opened and light peered through from a lamp that illuminated David's face as he stepped timidly into the room.

"What's wrong, son?" James asked, sitting up.

"I had a dream," he said and moved to the edge of the bed.

James took the lamp and set it on the bedside table, then he urged David into the bed between him and Eleanore, who opened her eyes and touched the boy's face. "A nightmare?" James asked.

"No," David said. "Just . . . strange. It felt strange. It almost felt like it was really happening."

"Tell us about it," Eleanore said sleepily.

"It was me holding a baby. It was my brother."

James met Eleanore's eyes that were suddenly alert. But it was difficult to tell if David's dream enhanced her pain or gave her comfort.

"What else?" James asked.

"That's all. It was just me and my brother." David rolled onto his side and said, "Can I sleep in your bed?"

"No," James said and stood up, pulling him out of the bed, at the same time tickling him. They laughed together, then he added more seriously, "You're far too big and take up too much room. Besides, your mother doesn't feel well and needs to rest without your wiggling." James picked the boy up with a dramatic groan to indicate how big he was getting and carried him back to his room while David held the lamp.

Once David was tucked back into bed, James returned to find Eleanore either asleep or pretending to be. He left her to rest, hoping that David's dream might give her some hope. For some reason it had made *him* feel better, whether it held any profound meaning or not.

For days, James stayed very close to Eleanore, hardly daring to leave her alone. The grief they shared was deep, but he quickly noted she would put on a braver face with everyone except him. Especially when she was with the children, she would hold them close and wipe their tears and assure them that with time they would have a baby in their home. She reminded them of how wonderful it was to have little Mary Jane, who was now crawling and full of giggles. While James knew that having Eleanore spend time with the children every day was important, he also insisted that she have time without them, if only to encourage her to spill her grief freely. He couldn't fix her broken heart or solve the problem, but he could cry with her and hold her close. He never wanted her to doubt his love for her, especially not now.

Less than a week after the loss of the baby, Eleanore was still hovering close to her bed, even though the doctor had assured them that she was physically fine and should be able to get up and go about her normal activities, provided she didn't overdo. James prayed that she would find her inner strength and move beyond this, and he reminded himself that it hadn't been so long. Surely she was entitled to some days of staring at the wall and wanting to be alone.

James went into town to pick up some things, including the mail. He felt his prayers being heard when there was a letter from Sally. Her letters always cheered Eleanore. Even when Sally wrote of difficult matters, the bond between these two women always gave Eleanore a light in her life.

Back at the house he went straight to the bedroom to find his wife. She was propped up in the bed with pillows, reading a story to David and Iris. He kissed all three of them and handed her a bouquet of flowers he'd purchased from a woman selling them on the street near the general store.

"Oh, they're lovely, James," she said. "Thank you." To David she added, "Would you go to the cupboard in the kitchen and fetch a vase?"

"Should I put water in it?" David asked on his way out the door.

"Yes, please," Eleanore said, then to Iris, "Tell Papa what you can say."

She grinned up at him and said, "Irises are pretty."

He laughed and pretended to be more surprised than he was. He knew she'd been trying very hard to overcome her inability to say the r's in certain words. "What?" he teased. "Not 'iwises are pwitty'?" She giggled, and he added, "You sound very grown up, young lady. But you know what? You've always been prettier than any flower." She laughed again and jumped into his arms. He was tickling her when David returned with a vase, and Amanda was right behind him.

"I just had to see these beautiful flowers," she said and raved about them while she delicately guided David as he arranged them in the vase. James knew her coming upstairs had little to do with seeing the flowers, and more to do with keeping the children from causing Eleanore any anxiety. When that was done, she said to the children, "I could use some help baking a pie for supper."

The children ran out the door, and Amanda winked at Eleanore before she left, closing it behind her to leave James alone with his wife. She offered him a wan smile and said, "The flowers really are lovely, James. Thank you."

"A pleasure," he said, "but I've got something else that I know will put my flowers to shame." He held out the letter, and her face brightened immediately. "See there," he said with a soft laugh.

She held out her hand for him. "You know I would be devastated without every little thing you do for me."

He kissed her brow and ignored the compliment, wishing with all his heart that he could take away her sorrow. "I'll leave you to read your letter. Andy asked that I come out and help him repair something that requires extra hands. Then there's grass to cut and weeds to pull." He kissed her lips. "You take care of yourself, my dear. I'll see you later."

"I'll be fine," she said and looked briefly into his eyes. He wanted to believe her.

Eleanore watched James leave the room before she turned her attention to the letter in her hands. The same as every time she received a letter, she took a minute just to look at it and take in the wonder of this miraculous connection she had to life in Nauvoo. Beyond her family and the gospel, her friendship with Sally was one of her greatest treasures. Through their letters they had shared many joys and sorrows and a level of understanding that she'd found nowhere else beyond her husband. But Sally was a woman, and she was also a Mormon. She had an insight that James could never understand, for all his efforts. She felt certain God understood that need in her; Sally's letters were evidence of that.

Eleanore carefully opened Sally's letter, fully prepared to read of her ongoing excitement over Eleanore's pregnancy, and how she was still working on a quilt for the baby. Eleanore shed some tears, swallowed hard, and read on. But Sally's letter was more brief than normal, with none of the usual details of everyday life and the happenings of the Church that Eleanore craved. Instead she stated that her six-year-old daughter had unexpectedly become ill and passed away. "No!" Eleanore muttered into the empty room, then she set the letter aside for several minutes while she wept without control. Her own grief meshing with the grief of her dear friend momentarily felt unbearable. When her tears subsided into a familiar shock that now felt more intense,

Eleanore took up the letter again, rereading the horrible news if only to be assured that it was true. Eleanore had heard many details of each of Sally's children, their ages and activities, their challenges and interests. She didn't even know what these people looked like but she felt as if they were family. Eleanore read on and found in Sally's words an unexpected turn. She wrote of feeling unquestionable peace, of knowing beyond any doubt that this child's spirit lived on, that they would be reunited one day. Even if she didn't know exactly how that might be possible, in her heart she knew that it was. She wrote, *Of course I miss her, and I always will as long as we are separated, but even in my grief I feel the evidence in my heart of what my Savior did for me, and for each member of my family who is touched by this tragedy.* Sally bore witness of the Atonement of Jesus Christ in easing her pain and comforting her sorrow. And then she briefly wrote of how the cornerstone had been laid for a temple in Nauvoo, and that the prophet had spoken of many great and eternal blessings that would take place there once it was built. Eleanore finished the letter feeling more awe than sadness, without being able to quite define the reasons. It was as if Sally's fervent testimony had seeped into her aching spirit and strengthened it. If Sally could find peace over the death of a child who had lived and breathed and been a part of her family for years, surely Eleanore could find peace over losing this baby. Sally's pain did not diminish her own, but it gave her a shining example to follow, and a perspective that strengthened her gratitude for all that she *did* have.

Eleanore got cleaned up and dressed and immediately sought out David and Iris, just wanting to hold them close for a long moment and be in the same room with them. She found deeper appreciation for them in the simple evidence of their living and breathing, their laughter and even their little tiff over some trivial matter related to the game they were playing in the yard. James still hadn't returned home from helping Andy Plummer, so she went to the office to write Sally a letter.

My dearest Sally, We are sisters in grief at this time. Your letter arrived within days after my pregnancy ended tragically, but your faith has inspired and strengthened me. She wrote in detail of the event of losing her baby, and even more details of the previous loss and her heartache in waiting so long just to become pregnant. She cried as she wrote and found that sharing her burden with another woman brought an added measure of solace. With her letter sealed and ready to be mailed, she went outside and found James weeding in the garden. She quietly stepped over the neatly planted rows and began to pull weeds nearby. He looked up in surprise, watched her for a long moment, then stepped carefully toward her to take her in his arms.

"You're feeling better?" he asked, touching her chin.

"Yes, actually." She looked down. "Sally's letter gave me a fast lesson in perspective."

"What's happened?" he asked with concern.

Tears preceded her saying, "Her daughter died." She held to him and cried for several minutes before she could tell him what else Sally had written. As he held her and listened, he kissed her gently, then together they worked at clearing the weeds away.

Throughout the following weeks Eleanore prayed every day to feel peace over the loss of her babies. And her prayers were answered. Some days were harder than others, but her greatest remedy was gratitude. As she looked around and counted her blessings, her heart would become too full to hold sorrow for long. In fact, she felt her prayers being answered on a deeper level when she found herself watching her loved ones as if through new eyes. Observing Lizzie and Frederick with their sweet little Mary Jane left her thinking of the evidence of miracles. A few years earlier they had both been middle-aged and single, neither having any hope of ever marrying or having children. And now they were a family. The effort they put into their work always went far beyond any requirements of their employment. Their genuine love and concern for the Barrington family was one more blessing. And Eleanore felt similarly grateful for Amanda and her son, Ralph. She recalled the day that James had hired Amanda, how she'd been close to destitution following her husband's death. They were fine people, kind and charitable. Their place in the home felt as right and natural as anyone else there, and Eleanore wondered what she'd ever done without them.

Eleanore's wonder over the children hovered with her for days. She found herself just watching them in ways she never had before, as if their very lives were miraculous. Perhaps it was knowing Sally had lost a child. Perhaps it was the Spirit helping her find a more profound joy in all that she *did* have, which helped her to feel less concerned about what she *didn't* have. Probably both. But suddenly their fascination with the bugs in the yard was as entertaining as their giving Jack a bath. They read stories and played and did their chores with energy and untroubled joy. They didn't have to think about whether or not they were happy. They just were. A skinned knee or a minuscule disagreement would only impede their happiness for a few minutes. And their greatest source of dismay was having to cut playtime short to go to bed.

Eleanore also felt herself seeing her husband through new eyes. Her mind wandered through memories of the early weeks of their relationship. She'd worked in his household, been distantly in awe of him, and then had worked more closely with him in caring for his children. But never in her wildest dreams would she have imagined becoming his wife. She never actually saw him as a man until after he'd proposed marriage, and initially she'd felt nothing for him beyond respect and a deferential admiration. She thought of how terrified she had been when she'd suddenly realized that she would be expected to share a physical relationship with this man. But he'd been sweet and tender, talking to her about things that no one had ever bothered to prepare her for. He'd gently guided her through that aspect of the life they shared, just as he'd cared for her in every other way. What they had come to share in that regard was one of the most blissful aspects of her life, made more so by knowing it was right and good in the sight of God; they were husband and wife, committed and bound together. And she loved him so much!

Eleanore watched her husband at the breakfast table, trying to imagine him as once being an English lord. She watched him chopping wood and carrying it into the summer kitchen, and she thrilled at the thought that she was his alone. She felt as if she were falling in love with him all over again and wanted only to be in the same room with him. At lunch she couldn't stop watching him, and after he caught her doing it more than once she saw intrigue in his eyes, as if he sensed her thoughts and feelings. Had they been together so long that such a thing was possible? They hadn't truly been married so terribly long in the perspective of a lifetime, and yet it felt like forever. And yes, they had quickly grown to be sensitive and perceptive to each other.

After lunch, Eleanore entered the parlor to find him standing at the window with Iris in his arms and David by his side. They were looking out, talking quietly of what a beautiful day it was. They all turned toward her in spite of her efforts to remain quiet. For the briefest moment her husband's eyes connected with hers, and she saw there a sparkle of the secret part of their lives they shared behind closed doors. The subtlest of smiles touched his lips, echoing the tenderness in his eyes, and she knew beyond any doubt that he was thinking her same thoughts, remembering what she remembered.

The moment ended when Iris squirmed down from his arms and ran toward her. Eleanore bent down to hug her, then she greeted David the same, although he approached more slowly. While she talked with them about simple things, she was aware of her husband watching them, his eyes warm with contentment. A minute later Lizzie came in, saying she'd promised the children a walk in the woods since it was such a beautiful day.

"Thank you, Lizzie," James said as they were leaving the room. She smiled and closed the door, leaving Eleanore alone with him. For a long moment they just watched each other while her mind wandered back to days when they'd been newly engaged, and the very fact that they shared any kind of a relationship had left her often feeling as if it were all a dream. He had stepped into her life, changing it quickly and irrevocably. And now she couldn't imagine living any other way. But in that moment the newness they'd once shared came rushing back over her, as if she'd been too numb to fully appreciate at the time how wondrous their blossoming relationship had been. That dreamlike sensation hovered around her while she wondered what it might be like to go back in time and be alone with him, knowing they would share a lifetime of joy and grief. She'd been so young and inexperienced, so naive and simple. If she had known then what she knew now, she would have been so thoroughly in awe she likely would have melted into the floor.

Eleanore saw the silent question in his eyes as he reached out a hand toward her. She stepped forward slowly, slipping her fingers into his, tingling from his touch as she might have the first time he'd touched her, had she not been so terrified of the uncertainty of such drastic changes in her life. He pressed her fingers to his lips, then stepped close enough to press a kiss to her brow. She closed her eyes and inhaled the familiar aroma of him, a combination of shaving lotion and the masculine soap he bathed in. She looked up at him while he gingerly touched her face and hair.

"You are so beautiful," he said and meekly touched his lips to hers, like a first kiss, but so much more wondrous with all that they had shared. He'd kissed her a thousand times at least, but she was still affected and prayed she always would be.

"I love you, James," she whispered and lifted her lips to his again while he wrapped her in his arms with a comforting familiarity. "Thank you."

"For what?" he asked, looking at her so closely that their noses almost touched.

"For asking *me* to marry you, and not some other woman."

"There was no other woman who could hold a candle to you, my dear." He kissed her again. "Thank you for saying yes. Every day I am grateful for the life we share."

Eleanore's heart nearly burst with undeniable joy. He *could* read her thoughts, or at the very least he shared them so fully that they were of one mind, one flesh, one heart. "As I am," she said, a quiver in her voice. He just wrapped her more fully in his arms as if he needed no further explanation.

The following day James initiated a picnic, and Eleanore thoroughly enjoyed having some time away from the house alone with him. And later that night while lying close to him in bed, a thought came to her mind, seemingly out of nowhere. It brought both excitement and fear, and she had to mull it around for a few days before she firmly suppressed the fear in order to go forward. After much prayer and contemplation she absolutely knew that she needed to pursue this idea. But first she needed the approval of her husband. She could never do anything without consulting him first. Thankfully, he was a reasonable man and willing to talk things through with her. And in most cases he allowed her to do whatever she liked. But she had reason to doubt this was one of those cases.

Eleanore found James at his desk, meticulously going over the finances. He smiled and leaned back in his chair as she closed the door behind her.

"Hello, my dear," he said.

"Hello." She crossed the room and kissed him quickly before she sat across the desk from him.

"What can I do for you?" he asked with a subtle crease in his brow, letting her know that he sensed she had purpose in her visit.

"I need to talk to you about something . . . and I ask you to . . ."

"To what?" he asked when she hesitated too long.

"To . . . keep your mind open, and your spirit. There's something I feel I should do, but clearly it needs to be a matter of prayer . . . for both of us. I would never want to do anything to bring harm to . . . any of us." His brow furrowed further but he didn't speak, so she hurried on. "I've been feeling that . . . I need to share the gospel with Miriam Plummer." She saw him lean back, heard him take a deep breath. Still he didn't speak. She quickly passed along her reasoning. "I just . . . can't get the feeling to leave, and . . . well . . . I know I can trust her. I'll speak with her privately, carefully. I'm certain she'll keep my beliefs in confidence. If she's not interested, that's fine. But maybe she will be."

"And then you would have a friend who shares your beliefs."

She looked down. "Yes. Yes, I would."

"Is that why you want to talk to her about it?"

She looked up. "I can't deny that would be nice . . . but . . . that's not my reason. I just . . . feel like it's the right thing to do."

"And what if she doesn't keep your secret?" His question was almost sharp, catching her off guard.

"She's my friend; of course she'll keep my secret."

"What if someone in her family finds out . . . even inadvertently? What if someone just slips and—"

"Why do I feel like I'm on trial here?"

"Just answer the question."

"I can't answer the question, James. I can't predict the outcome."

"Then it would likely be best for you to keep your beliefs to yourself."

Eleanore was stunned. She had expected some discussion over the matter, and for him to need some time to consider it. She'd not expected such harshness. She felt compelled to admit her overriding thought. "Why do I suddenly feel like a child, like you're my father, telling me what I can and can't do?"

"A man has a right to govern his wife's choices." Again she was startled by such an attitude.

"I know that, James. But whatever the law or social expectations might dictate, you've always treated me as an equal, respecting my beliefs and opinions—until now. Why?" He didn't answer, and she said more firmly, "This is not like you, James. Why are you not even willing to consider this?" Still he said nothing. "You're afraid, aren't you?"

"Yes, I am," he admitted without hesitation. "And I've got good cause to be."

"Fair enough, but if the Spirit guides me to do something, I must have the faith to do it, and to believe that I will be protected."

"The way the Saints are protected?" he countered crisply.

"The Saints are in God's hands. We cannot question how He tests and tries his people."

"And will He guide you to share the gospel and open the door for new measures of testing and trying for us?"

"And if He does, we must take it on with faith, James. My heart tells me I must do this."

"Even if I forbid it?"

Eleanore couldn't believe what she was hearing. "You wouldn't! Surely you would at least give it some thought . . . some prayer." She forced herself to remain calm, knowing anger would solve nothing, and their words were getting precariously close to that. "If you pray about it, James, and you can look me in the eye and tell me not to do this with the same confidence you've had over other important decisions we have made in our lives, I will honor your wish. If you can't, then I will do what I feel I must do." She stood up. "I promised to honor you. I only ask that you not impose decisions that affect me without honoring me equally." He only stared at her, and she added, "Am I out of line, Mr. Barrington?"

James studied his wife a long moment while a thousand memories assaulted him at once. Her attitude brought to mind things he'd rather not be reminded of, but she'd also made it clear that *he* was out of line. Their relationship was based in honesty, and he needed to be fully honest with himself before he could be honest with her.

Eleanore saw her husband's countenance soften as his eyes turned down.

"Please don't call me that," he said.

"You call me Mrs. Barrington all the time and—"

"Only in affection, my dear. When you . . . say it in that tone of voice . . ." He hesitated, and she realized he was having a hard time admitting his thoughts. "It reminds me of when . . ." He didn't finish.

"When you called nearly everyone but me by their given names because you were too afraid to let me into your heart?"

He took a sharp breath abruptly, as if he'd been hit in the chest. She saw defensiveness in his eyes for only a moment before it melted into raw humility as he looked away. "Yes, then."

"Talk to me, James," she pleaded, and his eyes met hers. "With all we have been through, there is no reason we can't talk about this sensibly. I understand why you're afraid; I'm afraid too. But we can't deny what God would have us do, simply because you are afraid. Still, if you really don't want me to talk to her, and you can give me a valid reason, with prayer behind it, I will do as you wish. But I'm asking you to at least consider it."

James knew she was right. He also knew there was a part of him that *did* fear the opening of any doors in regard to this religion, and where it might take them—literally or otherwise. He loved the life they were living and didn't want to see it change. But he was a man committed to honoring his wife and obeying God. He could not in good conscience refuse to do as she'd asked.

"Forgive me," he said. "You know me well enough to know that I let fear distort my judgment. I *will* pray about it and give it some thought. I appreciate your consulting me first. Some women wouldn't do that."

"Why wouldn't I?"

"Because you knew I wouldn't be happy about it. You could have talked to her first and then told me about it."

"I promised you," she said firmly. "I promised you I would never tell anyone. I could never go back on that without talking to you first."

James sighed and leaned back in his chair. For the first time in many months, he thought of his first wife. Her deceitfulness and flair for contention were difficult to imagine in contrast to this amazing woman. Long before he'd asked Eleanore to marry him he'd marveled at the depth of her integrity. But he wondered if she could ever know what it meant to him.

Chapter Five
DISCUSSING RELIGION

Eleanore couldn't help but feel pleased and excited when James told her that she most certainly should follow her feelings and share her beliefs with Miriam. He knelt and prayed with her before she set out to visit her friend, but she could easily imagine him pacing and wringing his hands until she returned. Eleanore asked Miriam if they could take a walk together, wanting complete privacy as opposed to being in her home where family members might come and go and possibly overhear. They walked slowly together through the woods while Eleanore wondered where to begin. Miriam was closer to James's age than her own, but they'd always felt completely comfortable with each other from the day they'd met, when Miriam had graciously given Eleanore biscuits in her kitchen to help ease the nausea of her first pregnancy. Miriam had a well-rounded figure and was taller than Eleanore, with blonde hair and a pleasing countenance. She always had the appearance of smiling, even when she wasn't.

The two women chatted typically of trivial matters until Eleanore asked Miriam what she thought of the sermons they'd been hearing on Sundays. They'd been going to church together for many months, but had never actually discussed religion. Eleanore was surprised by the way her friend hesitated and seemed mildly nervous.

"It's all right," Eleanore said. "You can admit anything to me. I'll not repeat a word."

Miriam's eyes showed a glimmer of relief before she said, "Truthfully, Ellie, I'm not always comfortable with what we hear over the pulpit. But how can that be? I pray to understand, but answers don't seem to come. How can I feel like something is missing? Is it not wicked to question what . . ." She stopped speaking when Eleanore stopped walking. Eleanore knew her own astonishment was evident when Miriam asked, "Are you all right?"

While Miriam was apparently waiting for Eleanore to endure a dizzy spell or some other malady, Eleanore felt a warmth settle into her spirit. Her feelings about sharing her beliefs with Miriam were an answer to Miriam's prayers. But Miriam didn't know it yet.

"Oh, my dear friend," Eleanore said, putting a hand on her arm. "We must sit down." They found a shady spot where the grass was cool and sat to face each other. Eleanore prayed silently for guidance in her words, at the same time thanking her Father in Heaven for such a glorious opportunity.

"Miriam," she said, taking her arm, "there's something I need to tell you; I've been feeling like I *need* to tell you. And what you just said makes me realize that . . . well . . . I think that what I have to say may just be the answer to your prayers."

Miriam's eyes showed intrigue. "Tell me," she whispered, as if something magical might spew from Eleanore's lips. She started at the beginning, telling her friend everything from the day she'd found the Book of Mormon in the road, until she'd finally found a missionary in Iowa and had been baptized. She told her of their reasons for concern and secrecy, and she told her the reasons Sally Jensen and her family had left Iowa, and details of the life Sally was now living in Nauvoo. Eleanore talked about Joseph Smith. And she shared her firm personal testimony of Jesus Christ, and that she knew beyond any doubt this was *His* true church on the earth. Miriam listened, she asked questions, and more than once they both shed tears. The Spirit hovered strongly around them while they talked and talked with no comprehension of time or hunger. Eleanore found sweet fulfillment in simply being able to verbally express all that she'd held in her heart. She'd written her experiences and feelings to Sally, but she'd only spoken a small degree of her beliefs and feelings to her husband. And she'd spoken them to no one else. Just to allow them through her lips felt glorious! And Miriam was even more receptive than Eleanore might have ever expected. Her spirit had been ready and waiting, just as Eleanore's surely had been when she first found the book. They both agreed that she needed to study and search and pray for her own answers, but she took everything in as eagerly as if she had been spiritually starved.

Eleanore loaned Miriam her Book of Mormon, which she agreed to read discreetly and take very good care of. She also promised not to keep it too long, since Eleanore would miss it very much. But Eleanore was more than happy to share the gift of this great book, and she knew she could indulge in reading more from the Bible in its absence. Miriam felt anxious to share these things with her husband, and Eleanore agreed that a woman should not keep secrets from her husband. But Miriam promised not to utter a word to anyone else, and promised that they would talk again in a few days.

While driving the buggy home, Eleanore felt so overcome with happiness that she had to stop for a few minutes and just cry. She thought of the babies she'd lost and didn't feel nearly so empty as she had before talking to Miriam. She marveled that God would be so merciful, that His hand would be so evident in their lives. Then she arrived home to find James in the kitchen helping the children with their lessons while Amanda was out in the summer kitchen working on dinner, with Ralph helping her. And on the kitchen table was a package from Sally. Apparently Frederick and James had gone into town together with the wagon for some animal feed and supplies, and they'd picked up the mail. And this had been there as well.

"Are you going to open it?" David asked eagerly, touching the cardboard as if he could sense what might be inside. "See, it has your name on it." He pointed to the fact that it was addressed to Mrs. Eleanore Barrington.

"I wonder what it is!" Iris said, touching it as well. It was evident they'd been watching very closely for her to come home in order to satisfy their curiosity.

"Maybe it's a puppy," James said. Eleanore snorted an unfeminine laugh, and the children giggled. "A friend for Jack."

Iris said frankly, "It's not wiggling or making any noise." If not for that she might have believed him.

Eleanore caught concern in her husband's eyes as she kissed him in greeting. He whispered, "How did it go?"

Eleanore said to the children, "You're going to have to wait just a few more minutes. I need to talk to your father. Keep working on your figures and we'll be back soon." She took James's hand and led him from the room.

They groaned with disappointment but did as they were told. Eleanore took her husband to the library and closed the door. She immediately said, "It was a miracle, James." She quickly repeated the gist of the conversation while he listened, expressionless.

Once she'd told him everything, he said, "That *is* amazing. Why am I not surprised?" He shook his head. "Everything to do with you and this religion turns out amazing one way or another."

She just smiled and said, "That's because it's true." Again she took his hand. "Come along. I've got a package to open."

In the hall he said, "So you gave her your Book of Mormon. Whatever will you do?"

"I've got the Bible."

"Yes, but . . . you and that book are practically inseparable."

"It's only temporary," she said and smiled from his teasing.

The children jumped off their chairs when James and Eleanore walked into the kitchen. James helped Eleanore cut the string that was carefully tied around the folded cardboard in several directions to hold it firmly in place. When the cardboard was pulled away, Eleanore's eyes blurred with tears the moment she realized it was a lovely pieced baby quilt. She blinked the tears away in order to see, and found a note pinned to it that simply read, *Someday*. She felt as grateful for her friend's precious gift as she was for the message of hope that came with it. While she touched it with tenderness, she was grateful to hear James explaining to the children what it was and what Sally meant by the note. It then occurred to Eleanore that the package had been too heavy to have only a quilt inside. She unfolded it and gasped as several other items came into view. The children squealed over the candy, and James told them they could each have one piece. With candy in hand they ran off to play while Eleanore could only stare with disbelief at the most prominent item: a new copy of the Book of Mormon. She reached out to pick it up just as James said, "Apparently God doesn't want you to be without it."

"Truly amazing," she muttered.

"Like I said . . ." He laughed softly.

Then Eleanore realized there were *two* copies of the book, and also a hymnbook. "Oh, it's wonderful!" she said, thumbing through it. "But I know nothing of music."

"I do," James said, taking it from her. Eleanore eyed him skeptically; she'd never heard any such thing from him. "A little, anyway. I was forced through some piano lessons in my youth. I could probably manage to pick through them . . . the melody at least."

She stated the obvious. "But we don't have a piano."

"Well, maybe we should get one."

Eleanore gave him another skeptical glance and took the hymnal back. Even *if* he ordered a piano, she couldn't even imagine how long it might take to get it. And she had a hard time picturing James Barrington being able to play it.

Included in the package, besides books and candy, was a

letter. Eleanore sat down there in the kitchen to read it while James put the candy in the jar where he kept the candy he regularly bought when he went into town.

In the letter, Sally wrote that she'd finished the quilt and felt she should send it with the promise that it would come to good use someday. Sally didn't want it to upset Eleanore or make her sad, but rather wanted hope to come with it. Eleanore would write back that it certainly had. Sally also wrote that she'd had a feeling Eleanore might need some extra copies of the Book of Mormon, and she felt sure she would make good use of them. And she knew Eleanore would enjoy the hymnbook. Sally mentioned which hymns were her favorites, and added that she hoped the entire family would enjoy the candy.

In the middle of writing a letter to thank Sally for the wonderful gifts, Eleanore told James she would like to send Sally a gift as well, but she didn't know what. "I don't know how to *make* anything," she said. "I never learned to sew, or anything like that."

"I don't think you need to send Sally a gift just because she sends you one. Perhaps that defeats the purpose in gift giving. So, I would suggest giving it some time. And I'm certain you'll think of something you can give her that will show appreciation for your friendship."

"I'm sure you're right," she said and finished her letter, telling her in detail of her sharing the gospel with Miriam, and of the timely arrival of more copies of the Book of Mormon. She promised to let Sally know how Miriam felt after reading the book, and thanked her again for her warm generosity.

Once the letter was ready to mail, Eleanore ate two pieces of candy from Nauvoo and sat with the quilt over her lap, pondering the beautiful handiwork and longing for the day when it could be used. But she felt more hope than sorrow. God's presence in her life was readily evident.

Miriam came to see Eleanore the very next day with the Book

of Mormon in hand, tearfully telling Eleanore that she knew it was true. She and Andy had stayed up late reading and praying together; they considered this newfound knowledge a miracle. Eleanore's happiness was close to bursting. She took back her old Book of Mormon and gave Miriam a new one to keep, sharing with her the added miracle of its timely arrival. Miriam thanked her with a tearful embrace, then went home saying that she would write Sally a letter as well, thanking her for this wonderful gift. They had been neighbors at one time, and Miriam had been vaguely aware of the Jensen family participating in different religious beliefs, but she'd known nothing more. Now they too had a marvelous connection. Eleanore felt deeply grateful for these friendships that God had sent into her life. Barring her wish to have a baby, she couldn't possibly have been happier.

* * *

James was pitching clean straw into the animals' stalls in the barn when Andy Plummer walked in, wearing a smile. Of course, he was usually smiling. This neighbor and friend was shorter than James—in fact, not much taller than his wife, with a bristly beard and a balding head. And his kindness made him one of the finest men James had ever known.

"Good morning," Andy said. "Miriam's in talking with your wife. I thought I'd see what you're doing out here."

"Nothing terribly exciting, as you can see," James said.

He was unprepared for Andy's next statement. "So, this church you belong to is apparently rather amazing."

James stopped and stuck the pitchfork into the ground while he considered what had just caused his chest to tighten. He covered his feelings coolly and stated, "I don't belong to this church; my wife does."

Andy looked surprised. "Oh, I'm sorry. I misunderstood."

"But from what I hear . . . it *is* amazing." He doubted Andy

noted the subtle sarcasm on that last word, but he knew
Eleanore would catch it if she were here. He quickly added what
he felt was most important to such a conversation. "I assume
Miriam told you why we need to be very careful."

"She made that explicitly clear, yes. I had no idea."

"Of what?"

"Why the Jensens left, that people around here—or
anywhere—could be against something that's so . . . amazing."

That word again. James attempted to remain objective and
appropriate. "Clearly there's something great about this church,
and I'm willing to respect and support Eleanore's beliefs. But we
do need to be very careful."

"Of course," Andy said with contemplation in his eyes.
James wondered what exactly he was contemplating until he
said, "May I ask . . . why you support her beliefs but don't
embrace them?" James bristled at the question but nonchalantly
began pitching straw again. When he didn't answer right away,
Andy added, "Is there something about this religion you
disagree with or—"

"Truthfully, I don't know that much about it," James said
and realized how pathetic that sounded even before he glanced
at Andy, who looked surprised. It wasn't the first time he'd
considered that it wasn't typical in his relationship with his wife
to not share every detail of their thoughts and feelings on any
given matter. He just didn't want to know any more about it, for
reasons he didn't care to analyze. He stuck to answering the
question. "From what I know of their beliefs, it's Christianity,
possibly more pure in some respects than other religions.
Everything Eleanore has told me makes sense as far as I can see.
I have nothing against what she believes in. I'm not terribly
fond, however, of the attitude that others have taken against
Mormons."

"So, it's really as bad as Miriam told me?"

"If she told you there are some people who will even kill

Mormons to be rid of them, then yes, it's that bad. They've been driven and persecuted everywhere they've gone. That's why we haven't told anyone."

"Well, I'm certainly glad she told *us.*"

Again James stopped working, if only to be assured of his friend's genuine enthusiasm. "I've never encountered anything so wonderful as that book and the way it makes me feel."

"You've only had it one day."

Andy laughed with a ring of perfect joy. "Oh, my friend, when something's right, it's right. I've never been one to dawdle over such things. I knew the moment I looked into Miriam's eyes we were going to be together forever. And I felt the same way not ten minutes after Miriam and I started reading together last night." He shook his head in disbelief. "It's incredible, simply incredible." He patted James playfully on the shoulder and added, "Maybe you should try it sometime." He chuckled. "I'll leave you to your work. Have a grand day."

James actually cursed under his breath, then he had to ask himself why he felt so cynical about these good people discovering something that brought them such joy. It had brought Eleanore joy. Why not them? The answer was quickly apparent. He felt afraid—afraid that these good people would find as much sorrow interlaced with their joy as the Jensens had. He was afraid of people he cared for being discovered and hurt by those with evil intentions. He trusted Andy and Miriam to be discreet and careful, but he couldn't deny that the more people who knew—the more people who became a part of this—the more likely it would be for something to go wrong.

James tossed the pitchfork and leaned his head against a post with an audible groan. "Help me," he prayed aloud. "Help me to be free of this fear and give these people the support they deserve. And my wife. Help me to be everything to her that she deserves. Help me." He continued to pray silently while he completed his work, and then he went into the house to find

Eleanore glowing with happiness. How could he not be thrilled to see her so happy? She told him eagerly of her visit with Miriam, and how she'd gotten back her old Book of Mormon and had given them one they could keep. He told her that was wonderful, and for a moment he was tempted to ask if he could take the third copy and give it a serious read. Instead he kissed her and went in search of the children to see if he could intrude on their playing.

The following Sunday when the Plummers came to dinner after attending the usual church meeting, their visit turned into something of *another* church meeting. Since Miriam had some experience in singing and reading music, they picked out the melody of one of the hymns in the book Sally had sent, and sang it together with a zeal that compensated for their lack of musical abilities. The singing drew the attention of everyone in the house, and they all stayed while Andy, Miriam, and Eleanore read aloud from the Book of Mormon and discussed its concepts. They also talked about Joseph Smith and the things Eleanore had learned of him through Sally's letters. The children started asking questions, and so did Lizzie and Frederick. Eleanore gave them the other copy of the Book of Mormon, and they accepted it with nearly as much pleasure as the house that James had had built for them. The *meeting* was concluded with prayer, then the Plummers invited everyone to their home the following Sunday after church. And the pattern began. Every Sunday they all went to the usual meeting, not wanting to draw any attention to themselves by suddenly not being present for the standard religious service. Afterward they gathered either at the Plummer or Barrington home for dinner, and then the unofficial church meeting in the parlor. James just sat and listened, wondering whether to feel thrilled or concerned with the overt enthusiasm from everyone else present—even his children. They were full of questions, loved to sing, and took in the stories from the book with great eagerness. After a few weeks of alternating homes each Sunday, Amanda and Ralph joined them. Apparently Lizzie had been sharing with Amanda what she'd read and how she felt about it. Now she and her son were equally enthused. Eleanore sent some money to Sally in a letter telling her about this new little congregation, and some weeks later more Books of Mormon arrived, along with more hymn books and some other printed materials that stated doctrines and beliefs of the Church. David and Iris started reading from their own copies of the book, and they wanted to read from it more than anything else during reading time each day. James had always taught his children to trust their feelings and honor them; he could hardly back down on that admonition now due to his personal concerns over aspects of this situation that were frightening. So he listened, and supported, and remained on the perimeter of the growing craze in his home.

James had rarely seen Eleanore so happy. Her ongoing desire for a baby came up occasionally, but her love of the gospel and the opportunity to discuss it openly with people she loved left her often beaming. He wondered if he was letting her down in that capacity. Should he have given her the opportunity to more openly discuss her beliefs a long time ago? Did his lack of interest cause her sorrow? But she was too sharp to be patronized by his pretending to have interest in it simply to humor her. Perhaps it was best that she'd found others to bond with in this way. He just remained passively involved, present but not participating, supportive but not engaged.

As autumn settled in deeply and the harvest was winding down, James was struck with the passing of seasons and the fact that Eleanore hadn't yet become pregnant after losing their second baby months earlier. They were both doing well at ignoring the problem and appreciating all that was good in the life they shared, but he couldn't help but think of it and wonder when or if it would ever happen. But he was grateful to note daily that Eleanore was happy, not dwelling on her desire for a baby. While he was hesitant to embrace her religious beliefs, he would be amiss not to thank God for bringing them into Eleanore's life and to the lives of those who surrounded her, if only for the way it compensated for what she *didn't* have.

In the middle of a particularly noisy supper, a loud knock came at the front door.

"I'll get it," James said, appreciating the cooler air he felt as he stepped into the hallway. While they were on the late end of autumn, the last few days had been especially warm. He pulled open the door to see two gentlemen standing there, hats in their hands. Their attire was clean but humble. One man was older with graying hair, the other near James's own age.

"May I help you?" he asked, not recognizing either of them even remotely.

"We're looking for Mrs. Eleanore Barrington," the younger one said, and James felt decidedly uneasy.

"I'm her husband," he said, then repeated, "May I help you?"

They both smiled, and his nerves eased simply by sensing something good in the countenance of both these men. The older gentleman said, "There's no need to be alarmed, sir. We've come from Nauvoo."

The other said, "We're friends of Mark and Sally Jensen."

"Come in then," James said, opening the door wide. "I'll get my wife and . . ." Eleanore appeared in the hall, and he added, "Ah, there she is."

"Sister Barrington?" the men both said at the same time, prompting her expression to shock. Then one of them added, "Brother Joseph sent us." Eleanore's hands went to her face, and tears rose in her eyes even before he added, "It came to his ears that you have a little congregation here, and that we might be able to provide you with some things you stand in need of."

"Such as?" James asked, straining to keep any defensiveness out of his voice. But both men turned toward him as if they'd sensed it anyway.

Still, they both smiled, and the older one said with humble confidence, "The keys and authority of the holy priesthood, of course, so that you can live the gospel more fully, even if you need to live it privately."

James made no comment as he closed the door. Eleanore laughed and threw her arms around each of these men with a welcoming embrace, causing them to chuckle with mild embarrassment. She welcomed them zealously and asked them questions faster than they could answer. Between her and Lizzie they were both immediately seated at the table with the family, graciously accepting the supper they were offered. By the way they ate it, James could imagine they were nearly as starved as the missionary who had baptized Eleanore. Had these men traveled all this way with practically nothing to eat and little more than the clothes they were wearing? Apparently. James marveled at their conviction and at the same time felt wary of their presence. It wasn't that he didn't trust them. Their integrity and sincerity were readily evident. He was more concerned about what they'd meant exactly by saying they'd brought with them the keys and authority of the holy priesthood. He had a feeling that the changes in his household were only beginning.

The men introduced themselves as Brother Greeley and Brother Campbell. And once supper was over and cleaned up, they sat in the parlor visiting and answering questions that were asked by everyone but James, who just sat and listened. Even the children were full of questions, not only about Nauvoo but also about the Prophet, and they even asked questions regarding gospel principles that left James stunned by their understanding and eagerness. When it was time for the children to go to bed, the visitors promised that they could all talk some more tomorrow. They were settled into the guest room with all that they needed before James was alone with his wife in their bedroom.

Eleanore's first comment was, "It's so wonderful, James, I can hardly believe it."

"It's not so difficult to believe," he said. "Miracles have a way of following you around in regard to this church."

She looked at him skeptically. "Is something wrong?"

"No," he said when he couldn't come up with an answer that didn't sound stupid.

"Are you uncomfortable with this?" she asked. In that moment he would have preferred that she wasn't so perceptive.

"If you're happy, I'm happy," he said, "I just prefer to remain . . . uninvolved."

He saw sadness in her eyes but chose to ignore it. He also saw that she wanted to question him over the reasons; he was relieved when she didn't. "Of course that's up to you," she said. "I appreciate your support of me in this, as always."

"I doubt it would do our marriage much good if I were *not* supportive."

She made no comment on that. Instead she said, "You know, James, whatever happens . . . wherever this my lead us, you will always be most important to me."

He gave her a wan smile. "No, my dear, God will always be most important to you. But I knew that about you before I married you. I always knew that's the kind of woman you are. And I wouldn't want it any other way."

A short while later he was trying to sleep with Eleanore close beside him, reminding himself that what he'd told her was true. He truly *wouldn't* want her to be any other way. Still, it frightened him.

The following morning James found the two men chopping wood and feeding animals, and repeatedly asking both him and Eleanore if there was anything at all they could do to help. James thanked them and assured them that everything was fine. Soon after the breakfast dishes had been washed—mostly by Brother Greeley and Brother Campbell—the entire Plummer family arrived in response to a message that Frederick had delivered to them a few hours earlier. A version of the typical religious gathering ensued with the two missionaries explaining the power of the priesthood and then offering to baptize and confirm all who wanted to officially become members of the Church. They were also prepared and able to ordain the adult men with the power of the priesthood, which they boldly declared was the same power that had been present on the earth in biblical times, which had been restored through the Prophet, Joseph Smith, who had in turn ordained many to actively use that priesthood and confer it upon others. Unlike in other churches, all worthy male adult members were entitled to hold that priesthood authority, which made it possible for nearly every home to have the presence of that power within its walls. James felt increasingly uncomfortable with what he was hearing. Asking himself why, he had to admit that he didn't doubt that these men were telling the truth. He found what they were saying to be logical in a bizarre kind of way, and even his instincts told him it was true. Or perhaps it was the way these people he loved and respected were so confident in its truth that it left him trusting that it had to be so. But he didn't *want* to be baptized into this church, and he didn't want to have priesthood authority. He couldn't imagine himself being worthy of any such thing. He finally declared that he had work to do and left them to their discussion.

The visitors did well at earning their keep throughout the remainder of that day, and James couldn't help but be impressed with their kindness and humility. And they knew how to work hard. As insistent as they were about being given something to do, James put them to work whitewashing the porch on the house. He and the children worked with them, and they visited comfortably about many things other than religion. They both asked many questions about England and the circumstances that had brought their family to America. James enjoyed hearing how much his children remembered of their previous home, and especially how evident it was that they far preferred their new one.

That evening after supper there was more discussion in the parlor until it was time for the children to go to bed. Soon afterward, everyone else went to bed as well. James entered the bedroom to find Eleanore sitting at the dressing table, taking her hair down. He barely had the door closed before she said, "David wants to be baptized." James met her eyes and saw evidence that she was nervous over bringing this up. "He's afraid you won't want him to."

"And Iris?" he asked, sitting on the edge of the bed to remove his boots.

"She wants to as well. But she's too young. When children turn eight, they're considered old enough to be accountable for their actions. She won't be eight until next spring."

James thought about it for a long moment before he gave the only possible answer. "David needs to do what he feels is best. I just want him to do it for the right reasons."

"He's not doing this simply because everyone else is, if that's what you're wondering. He knows it's true; he's known for a long time."

"He's never said anything to me about it."

"He knows you're not interested."

James couldn't deny that. "Still," he said, "am I so difficult to talk to? Even when you were his governess, he talked to you more than he did me—especially about things that were difficult."

"Perhaps it's just something maternal in a woman that connects better with a child."

"You mean like his mother?" James countered with sarcasm, then added contritely, "No, I think it's more than that." He sighed. "David may do whatever he chooses so long as it doesn't break any rules. He should know that."

"He needs to hear it from you. And Iris needs to hear it too. Even though she'd not old enough, she still needs to know that when the time is right . . . you trust her to make the right decision." He put his head into his hands and sighed. "You're not comfortable with this," she said. He looked up at her. "If you don't want your children to—"

"They're *our* children, Eleanore. And if I tell them I won't support them in this decision, then I will surely look like a hypocrite in accepting your participation in all of this."

"Is that what you're worried about? Looking like a hypocrite?"

"No! I'm . . . I'm just worried, Ellie."

"That's understandable, James, but the children have been present while we've discussed the persecution and danger. They understand how careful they need to be."

"I know that. I do. There is no good reason for me to stand in the way of any of this, so I'm not going to. How can I not admire my children for having such insight and conviction at such a young age? They're willing to do what God asks of them. How can that not be a good thing?"

"And what about you?" she asked while brushing through her hair.

"What *about* me?" he countered, again sensing that she was nervous. Was the topic so difficult between them? Acknowledging his own defensiveness, he had to admit that it was.

"Clearly you prefer to remain . . . uninvolved, but . . ."

"But?" he pressed.

"I only want to understand your reasons. This is obviously becoming a more prominent aspect of our household. If you're unhappy about it, or have feelings against it, I think we should discuss it."

"Eleanore," he said and stood behind her, meeting her eyes in the mirror, "I have never stood in the way of what you've wanted, and as long as this family stays together and is not exposed to harm, I never will."

She stopped brushing and turned in her chair. "As always, you do what's right and appropriate in supporting me as your wife in every possible way, more than most men would ever consider. And as always, I am grateful for the way you honor me, James. What I want to know is how you *feel* about what's happening. Except for a rare moment here and there, you have shown absolutely no interest in even *talking* about my beliefs, or trying to understand them. As much as you read, you've never read the book, when you know it means more to me than any other. It's not a Jane Austen novel, James. It's the Book of Mormon—Christianity in its truest from. You are one of the most devoutly Christian men I have ever known, and yet you *avoid* this. You respect my beliefs and where I stand, and I'm willing to do the same, but I would like to understand why."

"It doesn't matter why."

"It matters to me. It matters to the children. Do you think they won't ask you?"

James blew out a long breath and put his hands on his hips. She had a point, but he didn't like it. He had to admit, "I'm not sure I know why."

She turned back toward the mirror. "Well, perhaps you should figure it out."

James considered the subtle bite in her voice and attempted to soothe it. He put his hands on her shoulders. He couldn't give her reasons he didn't begin to understand himself, but he could assure her of one indisputable point. "I love you, Eleanore. Please tell me you won't let this ever come between us."

She stood to face him. "Of course not; never." He put his arms around her, and she rested her head against his chest. "If you could have foreseen this day," she asked quietly, "would you still have asked me to marry you?"

James drew back to look into her eyes, needing assurance that she was serious. "How can you even wonder over such a thing?" he demanded. "The life we share is far better than I had ever imagined it could be. How would I possibly regret any of it?" She didn't comment, and James considered a deeper implication in the question. "If *you* could have foreseen this day, would *you* have accepted my proposal? If you had known that I would never embrace your religious beliefs, would you still have become my wife?"

"Of course," she said with conviction, then tears welled in her eyes, and she looked down abruptly.

James tilted her face to his view and asked, "Are you telling me the truth, Eleanore?"

"Of course!" she said again, alarmed.

"Then why the tears? What are you *not* telling me?"

He saw courage come visibly to her eyes and prepared himself to hear that while she loved him and appreciated their marriage, she *did* have regrets. Her chin quivered as she said, "If you had known that . . . I couldn't have children . . . would you have married me?"

James felt both relief and sorrow to realize her deepest emotions were not tied into their difference of opinion on religion. He wiped his fingers over her cheeks. "Oh, my darling, we do not need babies for what we share to be complete."

"I'm not sure I agree with that."

"Then you need to reconsider the vows we exchanged, my dear. Nowhere in the promises we made were there provisions or exceptions. I did not agree to love and honor you *except* in cases of medical challenges or disappointments. The ceremony did not exclude changes we might endure, struggles we might face, or differences of opinion—even in religious matters."

She laughed through her tears and took his face into her hands. "I love you, James Barrington."

He smiled and kissed her. "I love you too . . . Eleanore Barrington."

"When I married you," she said, "the best I hoped for was a lifetime of mutual respect. I thought we could be friends, that we could take care of each other, keep each other company."

He smiled again. "I imagined the same." He pressed a loving hand over her face and into her hair. "I never believed that you would love me . . . that I would love you . . . so completely."

She smiled, and he kissed her again, while any difference of opinion melted away.

Chapter Six
EXCLUDED

The following morning James went to David's room before the child was even awake. He sat on the edge of the bed and watched his son sleeping while he pondered how dear this boy was to him. And he was such a good boy. James knew he would love the child no matter what, but added to his love was a deep admiration over the tenderness of his son's spirit and his genuine desire to have integrity and do all that was asked of him. When David woke up and saw him there, he immediately smiled and sat up, wrapping his arms around his father.

"Good morning," James said with a smile.

While he was considering how to broach the subject that he'd come here to discuss, David ended his hug and looked up at him with timid eyes. "Papa," he said, "I want to be baptized."

"Yes, I know. Your mother told me."

David bit his lip for a moment, then asked, "Is it all right?"

"Of course it's all right . . . if you're sure that's what you want. I don't want you to do it just because others are. You need to follow your own heart. We've talked about that, about listening to your feelings and trusting them. If you feel you should do this, then that's what you should do."

David nodded, his relief evident. "Oh, I do!" he said.

James smiled and tousled his already mussed blonde hair. "Then you should do it."

"Will you be there?"

"Of course I will. I was there when your mother was baptized. I wouldn't miss it."

"Are you going to be baptized?"

He swallowed carefully. "No, David, I'm not."

"Why?" he asked, just as Eleanore had predicted.

"It's difficult to explain," James said. "All you need to know is what I've already told you." He changed the subject and talked to his son for a while longer before he left the child to get dressed for the day.

James went to Iris's room and found her already dressed and pulling a brush through her thick hair that was exactly the same color as her brother's. Eleanore had taught her how to brush her own hair, and she was very diligent about doing so each morning before her mother braided it to keep it in place. She smiled when she saw him, then gave him a hug that was even more eager than David's. He chuckled, then sat beside her on the edge of her bed and took the brush. "May I do this?" he asked. "Your hair is so beautiful, just like a princess." He brushed in long strokes for a minute before he said, "Your mother tells me you want to be baptized."

"I'm not old enough," she said, sounding only mildly disappointed. "But when I'm eight I can."

He spoke quietly to her of trusting her feelings and following them. She too asked him why he didn't want to be baptized, and again he gracefully skirted the question.

Later that day James stood on the bank of the river while Iris stood by one side of him, and Eleanore the other. He held their hands and watched as Frederick and Lizzie were both baptized, then Amanda and Ralph. And his son, David. The entire Plummer family was baptized as well, and all were confirmed members of the Church. James felt a growing warmth inside of him as he observed all that transpired, and he heard the silent question in his mind: *If you believe it's true, James, why do you not embrace it?* He couldn't answer that question any more than he'd been able to answer the ones Eleanore had posed to him the previous evening. He didn't know *why*, and he wasn't sure he wanted to dig too deeply for the answers.

After supper, Andy and Frederick were both ordained to the holy priesthood, and were instructed on what exactly that meant and how to use it properly. James was privy only to a small portion of the conversation. He knew this meant that their private meetings would now include partaking of the sacrament, and these men would be able to give special blessings for certain reasons that he didn't fully understand. But Brother Greeley and Brother Campbell gave such a blessing to everyone but him— only because he firmly declined the offer. Wonderful promises of great blessings were spoken to each individual, without repetitiveness and with a personal aspect that in itself seemed to make clear that the words being spoken did not come from these men, but rather through them on behalf of God. It all seemed too marvelous to be real, and yet too real to discredit. James was especially intrigued by his wife being told that God was mindful of her desire to gather with the Saints, but that her place was here, and her path was different than others who shared her faith. She was told that in time, as she remained faithful, the greatest desires of her heart would be answered. He wondered if that meant that she *would* bear children. Or if there were desires of her heart that only God knew about. James was also struck by hearing them tell his son that he had an especially noble and courageous spirit, and his mission upon this earth had been known by his Father in Heaven long before his birth. He was also told that the span of his life was known only to God, and was measured according to the fulfillment of his purpose. James wondered what that purpose might be, and he imagined his son as a man one day, doing great things with a courageous and noble spirit.

The following morning Brother Greeley and Brother Campbell left to go back to Nauvoo, and everything returned to normal.

But it wasn't the same. James couldn't help noticing that something had changed in his home; something felt different. But he had to admit that it was good. He continued his quiet support, finding a certain fulfillment in the evidence of his wife's happiness. It was as he'd often told her: if she was happy, then he was too. Even if he had excluded himself.

* * *

Eleanore found joy beyond description in being able to more fully participate in living the gospel. Their Sunday gatherings now felt more official and definitely more sacred with being able to partake of the sacrament, which gave them the opportunity to renew their baptismal covenants weekly. Her husband was always present for their meetings, but said practically nothing, and he was the only one who didn't actively participate. But he was there, and he never complained.

As months passed, Eleanore felt herself more readily accepting all that was good in her life while she tried not to even consider the desires of her heart that eluded her. James made a point of teaching her to ride, an experience she'd never been exposed to at all until he'd asked her to marry him. Once she gained some confidence in handling her own horse, they rode together every few days, just for the sake of getting some fresh air and being together. Eleanore always looked forward to the experience and loved the way James always found ways to enrich her life more all the time.

Eleanore also found great joy in the children, and took pleasure in sharing the simplest of moments with them. She loved braiding Iris's thick blonde hair and watching her preen with perfect femininity in front of the mirror each day after her hair was in place. The child was as beautiful as a doll, and she loved it when Eleanore shared her perfume or allowed her to sit at Eleanore's dressing table while she brushed her hair. Eleanore also loved pretending that the baskets of laundry were too heavy for her to carry so that David, clearly pleased with his own masculine strength, would carry them for her. Iris liked to hand Eleanore the clothespins when she hung the laundry, and then she loved to run between the linens blowing in the breeze. Sometimes Eleanore played hide-and-seek with the children amidst the clotheslines or in the woods, reminded of the garden mazes at their home in England. Eleanore loved the way David was always so eager to please his father. She felt sure that David would do almost anything just to earn his father's praise. Thankfully, James was mindful of his son's admiration and did well at setting a good example in word and deed.

In the months that were not too cold or too hot, the children loved to play in the attic, a place that had quickly become storage for a number of odd things that had nowhere else to go. But the children had arranged the trunks that had come with them from England so that it was rather cozy. Occasionally Eleanore went up there with them, and they would read together or play guessing games. It was also a favorite place for the children to write in their journals. Eleanore had given the children journals when she'd first become their governess, and she'd encouraged the habit ever since. And since she kept a journal herself, it was rare for a day to pass when they didn't have journal time. With Ralph around a great deal of the time, Eleanore had given him a journal as well, and he often joined them for journal writing as much as any other activity. James had told Eleanore more than once how pleased he was that she had initiated journal keeping with the children and that it had become a habit.

The children grew, and months passed. Eleanore began to wonder if God was sparing her from getting pregnant in order to protect her from the pain of losing yet another baby. But each day she prayed and thanked God for her blessings and asked Him to give her the strength to accept His will, whatever it might be.

Eleanore found an added bonus in her friendship with Miriam when she started taking advantage of some skills that Miriam was proficient at, things that Eleanore had never learned. With Miriam's help she knitted some rather uneven mufflers for the children, and then she made a pieced quilt, much like the one Sally had sent her, except that Sally's work showed evidence of much more practice and agility.

Eleanore continued her exchange of letters with Sally, and she sent her friend a package containing some treats for the children and some scented soap and shampoo for Sally. The idea had come to her when she'd been soaking in a bathtub scented with expensive bath salts that James had given her. Until she'd become engaged to him, she'd never worn perfume or had the money for such luxuries as scented bath commodities. Like her, James was a scent-oriented person, and he kept her well supplied in perfume and other such luxuries. But Eleanore felt certain that Sally wouldn't have the allotment for such niceties. And so she had sent her some with the explanation that she wanted her friend to feel a little bit pampered and feminine in the midst of whatever else she might be doing with her days. Sally wrote back with ardent appreciation, and the letters continued, often with the sharing of gospel principles and concepts and their feelings concerning them. Sally was especially excited with the organization of what was being called the Relief Society, specifically for the women of the Church. Joseph's wife, Emma, had been selected to be president. Eleanore longed to be in Nauvoo and be a part of such things, but in her heart she knew the time wasn't right.

Late in the spring Iris was baptized soon after her eighth birthday. Frederick told Iris he was honored to do this for her, and was grateful for the authority that had been given to him so that he could. Eleanore kept to herself her wish that James might have taken upon him such privileges so that he could be the one to baptize their daughter. Frederick teased James about following his daughter's good example, and James took it in stride, never being offended but always declining any well-meant offer to take steps that everyone else in the household had taken.

In early summer, Eleanore received a letter from Sally in which she recounted having attended the funeral of a child where the Prophet had spoken great comforting words regarding the death of infants and children. He spoke of how they were spared the wickedness and misery of this world. Sally had felt deep comfort from his words in regard to losing her own daughter. Eleanore found comfort in his words as well, especially on Sally's behalf. And while losing her babies had been difficult, she prayed that she and James would never be faced with the death of a child.

Near the end of June, following the usual Sunday meeting, David and Iris went upstairs to play, and everyone else went their separate ways except for Andy and Miriam Plummer. Andy had told James before dinner that they needed to talk. James had whispered this to Eleanore over the dinner table, and she'd felt on edge ever since, sensing that something wasn't right according to the somber mood of their friends. Once the four adults were alone together and the parlor door had been closed, Andy took Miriam's hand, then looked directly at James and Eleanore. "We've made the decision to move to Nauvoo."

Eleanore heard their explanations as if through a heavy mist. How could she dispute the spiritual promptings that had preceded their decision? How could she argue with their desire to be among the Saints? And how could she deny the piece of her heart that longed to go with them, the same piece that would break to see them go? She'd found such great delight in having the Plummer family adding numbers to their little congregation, and she reveled in the simple joy they'd shared in their private worship services. And now they were leaving. She told them she understood, she wished them well, and she covered her shock when they said they would be leaving in a few days. And after they left, she took the tears she'd been carefully holding back upstairs to her bedroom, where she set them free. She wasn't there long before James appeared beside her and took her in his arms, and she cried harder. When her tears had run dry she held tightly to him and wondered what she would ever do without him.

Out of the quiet he said, "You want to go with them."

"Yes," she admitted readily, "but I know we're meant to be here . . . at least for now." She hesitated a moment and added, "You *don't* want to move there."

"No," he said, "I love it here, and . . . I can't deny some fear related to being among the Saints. The stories of persecution haunt me, Eleanore."

"Yes," she agreed.

"But I'm going to miss our friends. Perhaps for different reasons than you will, but still . . . I'm going to miss them very much. It will be a difficult adjustment." This prompted more tears, but Eleanore felt his arms tighten around her.

The following week felt almost as hard to Eleanore as losing a baby. She felt touched by her husband's efforts to keep her distracted, but that first Sunday without the Plummers around was almost unbearable. She kept her tears behind closed doors and offered a brave face over the departure of her friends, except for the moment when she actually said goodbye to Miriam. She sent some gifts for Sally, and had fond thoughts of the Plummers and the Jensens seeing each other again. They'd been neighbors long before Eleanore had come to America. The irony was amazing, and miracles were evident. But still, Eleanore couldn't deny her sorrow in being left behind.

A couple of weeks after the Plummers had left, the children left the supper table the moment they'd finished eating, wanting to continue some game they'd been playing when they'd been called in to eat. Iris ran after David and Ralph, hollering a little too much like a boy. Once they were gone, James said, "It's a good thing she has her mother's influence."

"Perhaps Iris will be a good example to Mary Jane," Lizzie said.

"Or a bad one," James said with a smile, then he became especially serious. Eleanore felt mildly nervous even before he added, "There's something I need to say." He looked directly at Amanda, Lizzie, and Frederick—then at her, as if to offer some silent warning. What did he need to say that he'd given her no forewarning of? "I just need to make it clear that . . . if you feel that you should go to Nauvoo . . . I don't want you staying here out of some obligation to us."

Eleanore sucked in her breath and held it. If these people who were such an integral part of her household chose to leave, would she be able to bear it? It only took a moment's thought to understand why James might feel the need to clarify such a thing, and she could even understand why he'd chosen not to warn her. He'd likely not wanted her to stew over the matter. Now she held her breath, waiting to hear what they might say. Would God make it clear to her and James that they needed to stay in Iowa and then inspire these people to go?

Frederick spoke quickly and firmly. "We're family, James. We're not going anywhere without you." Eleanore felt such relief she almost moaned audibly. She saw Lizzie take Frederick's hand across the table and smile at him. It was evident they'd discussed this previously. He smiled at his wife, then turned to James and added, "I'm certain we could make a living there if we had to, but that's not the most important issue. We *work* for you, yes. But we're family. Perhaps eventually God might give us a different answer. For now, we stay where you stay."

Eleanore saw her husband's relief and knew he'd been troubled by the possibility. He turned to look at Amanda just as she said, "I echo that completely. We belong here . . . at least for now."

"Well then." James sighed loudly, then chuckled. "I'm glad that's settled." He stood up to start clearing the table, and the others rose to help. Nothing more was said about the matter, but that night Eleanore thanked God profusely for letting these people stay. If nothing else, considering even for a moment the possibility of them leaving had helped her with the perspective of the Plummers leaving. It could always be worse.

The following week James initiated a little vacation, and they took the children to stay in the little city on the Mississippi River where she and James had gone once before. They all had a marvelous time, and she returned home determined to find peace and contentment in her life. She bought some fabric and started another quilt, recalling Miriam's tutelage as she worked on it. She kept busy around the house and found joy in being with the people who shared her home. And it was a bright day when she received letters from Sally *and* Miriam. The Plummers had arrived safely and were staying with the Jensens until they could find more permanent accommodations. They were all doing well.

Eleanore was pleased to hear that someone had purchased the Plummers' home and they would be getting new neighbors. But it turned out to be a somewhat cantankerous man, who was much older than James, and his two grown sons, none of whom proved to be friendly. They invited the newcomers over for dinner on the Sunday after they'd gotten settled in, but the three men did little but complain, and occasionally they even became crude or vulgar in their conversation. James told Eleanore after they'd left that he would never be inviting them back, and she was relieved. She soothed her frustration by writing letters to both Sally and Miriam to tell them of the dreadful experience, doing her best to make the situation sound humorous. The tactic worked when she found herself laughing as she wrote. Rather than repeating the same details in both letters, she wrote different things in each one and told them they had to read each other's letters in order to get all of the news.

Summer eased gracefully into autumn, which was swallowed abruptly by winter. And winter ushered them into a new year. On a particularly cold morning in late January, Eleanore made an amazing discovery. Three days later she was snuggled up close to her husband in bed, loving the way each day came to its close with his arms around her, making her feel perfectly secure. When she knew he was relaxed but not yet sleeping, she said in little more than a whisper, "I'm pregnant, James."

She watched his face in the firelight, not surprised by the way his eyes came open in startled surprise, then he leaned up on one elbow in order to see her better, as if doing so might convince him she wasn't teasing. Before he could say anything, she added, "I don't want anyone else to know, at least until . . . if . . . I get farther along than when I lost the last one. The children were so disappointed; maybe it's better if they don't know."

"You sound as if you're accepting now that you *will* lose it."

"I'm . . . trying to be hopeful but . . . it's hard." Tears came, but she forced a smile.

"I know," he said, touching her face. He smiled as well. "Maybe this will be the one."

"Maybe," she said and held him closer. He relaxed again, and Eleanore fell asleep in his arms, praying that this *would* be the one, the baby that would go full term and come into the world strong and healthy.

Eleanore was proud of herself for her diligence in keeping her pregnancy secret. She often declared herself to be under the weather, and took to staying in her room more in order to keep the nausea and fatigue from being so obvious. James did well in conspiring with her, even though he told her he didn't entirely agree with keeping the situation from other members of the household. But Eleanore didn't want to contend once again with having the children grieve over the loss of another baby. When, or if, she became far enough along that she began to show, then there would be no choice. Until then, she preferred keeping it between her and James.

She was nearly three months along when a wave of nausea caught her off guard while she and Lizzie were doing laundry.

After she'd thrown up, she turned to see no concern on Lizzie's face, but some measure of disgust. "You're pregnant, aren't you," she said. "I'm certain you think you've been very clever in trying to hide it, but it's as plain as the nose on your face. Amanda's seen it too, so why don't you give up the pretense and let us help you?"

Eleanore swallowed her pride and admitted quietly, "I don't want the children to know."

"They'll figure it out eventually."

"Not if I lose it. They'll never have to know."

"And what makes you so sure you will? Maybe it will go better this time."

"And maybe it won't," Eleanore said and changed the subject.

The following week James left one morning after breakfast to take the children into town for an extended outing that would include several errands and lunch out. Not long after they left Eleanore began cramping and bleeding. The little grain of hope inside of her that had resisted her belief that she would likely lose this baby was quickly smothered. She felt resigned. And grateful for the timing that had James and the children out of the house. David and Iris would never have to know, and James would be spared the ordeal. She saw no need to send for the doctor. She knew what to expect, and Amanda and Lizzie were there to help her. By the time James returned, it was over.

James walked in the house with the children and started toward the stairs until he heard Amanda say, "James. Wait a moment." He stopped and turned just as she said to the children, "You two run outside to play. I need to talk to your father."

They quickly obeyed, not seeming concerned. But James was. "What is it?" he asked.

She turned back to face him and said with a cracking voice, "She just lost the baby, James."

"What?" he gasped and put a hand out in search of the wall to steady himself. "No!" His chest and throat burned and he felt dizzy. He pressed both hands to the wall and hung his head, struggling to breathe. "Tell me," he murmured.

"It was . . . the same as last time. She's going to be fine."

"In a manner of speaking," he said. It wasn't her physical health that concerned him. "I don't know what to say to her, Amanda." He turned to lean his back against the wall and wiped tears from his cheeks. "I don't know what to do."

"Just keep loving her. That's how we got through."

He looked hard at her, recalling what she'd told him more than once. "How many did you lose?"

"Five," she said gravely, and he took a sharp breath.

We're up to three now, he thought and struggled to accept it as a fact. "How did you survive?" he asked.

"God gives us strength, somehow," she said. "My Ralph is a miracle."

"I pray we are blessed with such a miracle, especially for her sake." He looked up the stairs, wondering how to face his sweet wife who had just experienced yet another loss.

"I'm confident all will be well with time," she said. "She'll have heard you come in. I'm certain she needs you."

James nodded and swallowed hard. Amanda returned to the kitchen. He took a long moment to compose himself, then hurried up the stairs. Once alone in the hall he was assaulted with such intense emotion that he leaned back against the wall, then slid to the floor, grateful to be alone as a torrent of sobbing rushed out of him. He lost track of minutes while he cried like a frightened child. Then he remembered that Eleanore might be wondering where he was. He forced himself to composure and dried his face before continuing on his path to the bedroom. He paused at the door, uttered a silent prayer and took a deep breath before he opened it to find Lizzie sitting near the bed. She stood when she saw him. They shared an embrace that expressed silent sorrow, then she slipped out of the room and quietly closed the door. Eleanore was lying with her back to him, the covers up to her neck. He wondered if she was asleep until he moved to the other side of the bed and found her staring at nothing with dazed eyes—eyes that frightened him.

Eleanore gazed at the wall, feeling nothing. A stark shock surrounded her every nerve, her every emotion, not allowing the reality to penetrate. The pain of grief seemed to hover around her at a close distance, circling her, threatening to close in, while a blanket of stupor held it at bay, like a bear holding off a pack of wolves. She felt startled by her husband's touch, his fingers on her shoulder, when she hadn't even known he was in the room. She looked up at him, and there was no mistaking the anguish in his eyes. He'd been crying, long and hard. And this sad evidence urged the wolves in for the kill; the pain threatened to smother her. He sat on the edge of the bed, saying nothing. But she saw his chin quiver as he touched her face. Their longtime emotional connection reached into her, and she sat up, wrapping her arms around him as if he might save her from the inevitable torment. He lay close beside her, and she felt as if they were reliving some kind of mutual nightmare while she held to him and wept inconsolably. And he wept with her.

When the blanket of shock settled back over her, she murmured with a hoarse voice, "I'm so sorry, James."

"Why would you apologize?" he demanded gently.

"Because . . . I can't . . . give you . . ." She couldn't finish.

"Eleanore," he murmured, "your having a baby is not about giving *me* something. It is something we share. And we are in it together, no matter what happens." He kissed her brow. "I only wish I could ease your pain, my darling. I know this is so much harder for you."

She only shook her head and succumbed to more tears, grateful at least to have his acceptance and love. If she had a husband who treated her with disdain over her inability to give him children, she would be utterly devastated.

A child's knock at the door interrupted their grieving. Eleanore sat up and frantically wiped at her tears, whispering, "I don't want the children to know."

James went to the door, and she heard him speaking quietly to Iris, telling her that Mama didn't feel well. He left the room with her to help her with something and was back in a few minutes. Again he held her, but there was nothing to say.

That night David came to their room declaring he'd had that dream again, of him holding a baby brother. James found it just a little too eery, especially considering that David and Iris didn't know their mother had been pregnant, and therefore didn't know another baby had been lost. James ushered him back to bed and tucked him in, but thoughts of David's dream hovered with him.

James got out of bed the following morning with little sleep behind him, deeply concerned for his wife while at the same time contending with the growing hole in his own heart over yet another baby lost. For the next three days Eleanore hardly got out of bed and rarely said a word. He had the doctor come and check her to make certain she was well physically. He assured them the ordeal had been minimal due to the early stage of pregnancy, and there was no reason she couldn't be about her normal activity. On the fourth morning while James was getting dressed for the day, he said to Eleanore, "If you don't want the children to know, you're going to have to do some pretty good acting." She gave him a sharp glance but said nothing. She did, however, show up for breakfast, almost appearing normal except for the barely disguised anguish in her eyes. James wondered if it might be a blessing for her to want to spare the children from any grief over the matter. Perhaps it would bring her around to herself more quickly.

More than a month after the miscarriage, James had to admit that his wife was barely existing. She did well at putting on a brave act for the children, although they were often asking her if she was all right. She would always smile and say that she was just tired, but he felt certain they were suspicious of something more. When the children were absent, Eleanore barely spoke, wouldn't smile, and hovered close to her bedroom whenever she could get away with it. The doctor had told them that a woman's emotions could typically create some melancholy following even the birth of a healthy baby, but that combined with the loss would naturally generate some depression. He felt confident that with time she would come around, but James felt deeply concerned in ways he could never define. He'd made himself available, regularly encouraging her to talk and grieve if she needed to. But for the most part she'd turned inward, showing little emotion at all beyond her initial response on the day of the miscarriage. The only real connection he felt to her was at night when he'd hold her close while she drifted off to sleep. Few words passed between them, but just being near to each other soothed something in him, and he sensed it soothed her as well, even though she never admitted to it.

On a moonless night he held her close and prayed silently to be able to reach her, to find the vibrant woman he knew existed somewhere beyond her broken heart. She snuggled a little closer, and he tilted her face upward to kiss her. There had been no passion between them whatsoever since she'd lost the baby. It had been common between them for a simple kiss or even a glance to hold some measure of passion. But he'd seen or felt no hint of it for many weeks now. Impulsively he kissed her cheek, behind her ear, her throat, hoping that perhaps initiating some intimacy might help them connect in a way that could bridge this horrible chasm between them.

"Please . . . don't," she said, and turned her back.

He felt tempted to just let it drop and go to sleep. But he felt more strongly compelled to ask, "Why not?" She didn't answer, and he pressed further, feeling a desperate need to get her to talk. "Do you not feel well?" Still she said nothing. "Can you not answer a simple question? An honest answer would be preferable."

"I feel fine," she said.

"Then perhaps I've become repulsive to you." He tried to ward off his emotional residue in relation to his first marriage. Caroline had barely tolerated his touch and continually discouraged any intimacy between them. And then he'd discovered that she'd been having a long-term affair with a man she'd loved long before she'd married him. He reminded himself that Caroline was dead, her betrayal in the past. This was Eleanore, the woman he'd always been able to talk with about anything. They'd shared a warm and tender relationship since the day they'd been married. They'd overcome many challenges together. Surely they could get through this one.

"Don't be ridiculous," she said.

"If my assumptions are ridiculous, Eleanore, then you need to give me a reasonable explanation. And please be honest with me."

"I've always been honest with you."

"Yes, but you've also omitted telling me the whole truth more than once. And you're doing it now. I need to know what's wrong." He touched her face and softened his voice. "Eleanore . . . what we share . . . here . . . together . . . has always helped us get through our struggles in the past. Let me . . . be with you. Let me share your pain." She only curled up, retracting farther away, and he added, "What's wrong, Eleanore? Talk to me. I'm your husband, and I have never given you any reason not to trust me."

Eleanore couldn't deny that was true. She didn't want to speak her thoughts, but she knew she had to. She'd dreaded this moment for weeks now, ever since she'd accepted that she could never go through this again. She closed her eyes and just forced herself to say it. "I . . . don't want . . . to get pregnant . . . ever again."

"What are you saying?" James asked breathlessly, wishing he hadn't sounded so astonished when she turned to look at him, her eyes bordering on anger.

"I'm saying I don't want to get pregnant. I can't go through this again, James. I can't . . ." She sobbed, but it was the first evidence of emotion he'd seen in weeks. "I can't . . . put hope into this and . . . see it fall . . . again. I can't." She sobbed again. "Surely you can understand that."

"I understand how difficult this is for you, but what you're suggesting would surely doom this marriage."

"I love you, James." She sniffled. "I need you, but . . ."

"But?" he pressed and turned her to face him. He touched her face and saw her wince slightly. He kissed her cheek and she did it again. Clearly this was much deeper than the issue she was discussing. "Is there something about what I'm doing right now that makes you fear getting pregnant?"

She moved away abruptly and stood, grabbing the robe she'd left at the foot of the bed. She wrapped it tightly around her and stood at the window, keeping her back to him.

"So . . . what?" he asked. "Would you prefer that I sleep elsewhere?"

"No, of course not."

"Oh," he said, his tone acrid, "I can sleep in your bed, but . . . what? Don't get too close? Because it might lead to something that could possibly get you pregnant? You're trying to solve one problem by creating an even bigger one."

"Bigger for whom?"

"For both of us!"

"A man's needs are different from a woman's."

"Don't make this about my male needs. It's *never* been about that! Our intimate relationship has *always* been equal and tender, and at least as emotional as it ever was physical. I kept separate beds with my first wife for years once I knew she wasn't being loyal to me. I've lived celibate and I can do it again. I am certainly capable of sleeping in the same bed with you and keeping our relationship platonic, but the strain it would put between us is something I won't tolerate. Do you think you can just remove this part of our marriage and have everything else be the way it's always been? Can you start pulling threads out of a tapestry and not have it unravel? You and I both know that the physical intimacy in a marriage is an integral part of it. What a man and woman share in that regard strengthens the bonds between them. We've talked about it, and both admitted it, over and over. The ability to create life is only one aspect of a wide spectrum of its purpose in marriage."

"But still . . . I could get pregnant, and . . ." She didn't finish.

James knew it wasn't just about getting pregnant. She was closing herself off for reasons he had trouble understanding, but he wasn't going to let it stand. "Yes, you certainly could," he said, more calm. "But life is about taking risks; it's about trusting. So tell me this, Mrs. Barrington. You call yourself a Christian woman." She looked toward him sharply. "I know that you believe Jesus Christ paid the price for all suffering. Why not this? Is this . . . grief . . . this loss of yours . . . somehow . . . exempt?" She looked away again, but not before he saw her eyes turn brittle. "Do you put yourself above His atoning sacrifice by condemning yourself to let go of your deepest wish to have children? If you shut yourself away from me and the children will that make it better? It sounds like hypocrisy to me, Mrs. Barrington. Either you're a Christian, or you're not. Either you trust Him or you don't. And why would He bless us with more when we can't find happiness and peace with what we've already been so richly blessed with?"

She made no comment, and James felt anger building inside of him. But it only took a moment's thought to find its source in a deep sense of hurt and betrayal. How could she turn him out of her life this way when they needed each other more than they ever had? He wanted to ask her but sensed that she was closed. He wondered if she'd heard anything he'd said. Or if she had, would she allow it to penetrate her heart?

Eleanore heard James leave the room, and the moment he was gone the tightness gathering in her chest burst out of her in a rush of tears. She staggered to the edge of the bed, then sank to her knees there, unable to pray while her husband's accusations of hypocrisy echoed through her mind. But he was right. She had studied, absorbed, believed Christian principles. And now, when she believed the burden was too great, she had completely ignored those principles. She finally found the will to pray, begging forgiveness, and for the pain to be lifted from her enough that she could find joy in her life, that she could press forward, that she could trust in God to guide her path. And that she could mend all that was wrong between her and her husband. She knew she'd been unfair, and she'd certainly not considered fully the implications of her fear of getting pregnant. But now that she'd said what she had, she wasn't certain how to undo it.

Chapter Seven

CITY BEAUTIFUL

James sat on the side porch, staring into the darkness until he felt cold, and then he went into the office and lay down on that ugly couch to do more of the same. He woke up cold again and wondered how long he'd been sleeping. He felt mildly panicked, not wanting to have left Eleanore alone so long. He lit a lamp and read one-forty on the clock before he crept up the stairs and into their room. His panic increased when she wasn't in the bed, but he soon found her on the other side of it, asleep on her knees, her face pressed into the bedcovers.

"Eleanore," he murmured and lifted her into his arms. She opened startled eyes. "You fell asleep," he said and tucked her into the bed.

"I was praying," she whispered.

"I could see that."

He kissed her brow and eased away but she grabbed his arm. "Wait," she said. "We need to talk."

He sat on the edge of the bed. "Yes, we do. And I'm going to start by apologizing. Forgive my anger, Eleanore. I can't possibly know how difficult this is for you, but I will be here for you, no matter what. No matter how hard it is, no matter how long it takes to come to terms with it. I will be here. Do you understand?" She nodded with tears in her eyes. "And if you need some time . . . some distance . . . so be it. We can wait for that, Eleanore. But I'm not going to sleep elsewhere and I'm not going to leave you alone, because I need you, and you need me. And we're going to get through this together, and we're going to be happy, no matter what might befall us. Do you understand?" he asked again. Again she nodded, and more tears came.

"Oh, hold me," she said, and he eased into the bed beside her. "I need you to hold me." Her weeping came in torrents while he kept his arms around her. "Oh, it hurts!" she cried. "It hurts . . . so badly."

"I know," he said and held her more tightly, crying with her.

Their tears settled into silence until she said, "You were right, James. I just . . . became so caught up in the pain that I . . . completely forgot everything that truly matters. I need to trust in the Lord. I need to accept His willingness to give me peace." She sniffled. "What is that scripture in Proverbs?"

"'Trust in the Lord with all thine heart, and lean not unto thine own understanding.'"

"That's the one. It came to me while I was praying. I asked God to forgive me . . . for being so blind. I hope you can forgive me too."

"Your pain is understandable, Eleanore. I've let pain distort my thinking in the past; you know that well enough. You certainly suffered for it."

"No, I never suffered," she said. "You were always good to me. You still are." She leaned up on one elbow to look at him. "Do you think there is some greater purpose to this, James? If we trust in God, and He is all powerful, does that mean there is purpose in . . ." her voice broke, "losing our babies?"

"I don't know," he said and touched her face. "Perhaps it's simply . . . to trust in God, to not lose faith—in Him or in each other. I suppose we have a choice to allow this to make us bitter and afraid, or to be happy in spite of it."

"We have so much to be grateful for," she murmured.

"Yes, we do."

"I need to remind myself of that."

"For as long as I've known you, Eleanore, you have never taken your blessings for granted. You mustn't be hard on yourself now for struggling with this. It will take time to heal, but it will never happen if you won't talk to me . . . or to God."

"You're right. I know you're right." She sighed and put her head on his shoulder. "You were right about everything, James. I need you. I can't get through this without you. I just . . . let my fear get the better of me, and I lost my head." Again she looked at him. Tears came as a preamble to her confession. "I *do* want to get pregnant, James. I want to have your baby. I just . . . don't want to lose another one. I don't know how I could live through it again. But it came to me while I was praying that we have to keep trying, and I can't let my fear come between us." She touched his face. "Forgive me."

"It's all right," he said. "I understand; truly I do."

Eleanore relaxed in his arms and tightened her hold on him. James listened to her breathing become even and he prayed while she slept. He woke to daylight and found her gone. A glance at the clock told him he'd slept much later than normal, and he wondered why she hadn't wakened him. He hurried to get dressed and went downstairs to find that breakfast was being cleaned up and that the children had gone outside to do their chores. Amanda told him she was keeping his breakfast warm to eat whenever he was ready. He thanked her but first went searching for his wife. He found her in the office, sitting at the desk.

"Good morning," he said. She glanced toward him with a glimmer of the real Eleanore showing in her eyes. "Are you feeling better?"

"I believe so; a little," she said.

"You should have wakened me." He crossed the room and bent to kiss her cheek.

"You looked tired. There's nothing that couldn't wait an hour or two."

"What are you doing?" he asked.

"Writing to Sally . . . and Miriam," she said. "I never told them I was pregnant, but now that it's over, I thought they should know. If either of them had such a thing happen I would want them to tell *me.*"

"That's what friends are for," he said.

"Will you go with me into town to mail the letters?"

"Of course," he said and went to the kitchen for his breakfast.

The remainder of the day felt more normal than a day had since Eleanore had lost the baby. James couldn't say she seemed happy or vibrant, but there was an absence of the tangible pain that had radiated from her for weeks now. He hoped it was truly a sign of healing, that she had been able to wade through the anguish and tap into the inner strength that he knew she possessed—a strength that was undoubtedly linked to her faith in God.

After the children were tucked into bed that night and the house was quiet, James found her on the side porch, leaning against the rail, looking up at the stars, wrapped tightly in a shawl. Spring was bringing warmer weather, but it still felt cold. She turned to look at him as he closed the door, then her eyes crept back to the sky.

"It's a beautiful night," she said.

"Yes, it is." He stood beside her and leaned his hands on the rail. "You seem to be feeling better."

He heard her sigh deeply and hoped he wouldn't regret bringing it up. He didn't want to remind her of grief she was likely trying not to think about. "I'm working on it," she said and turned again to look at him. She put a hand to his face, then lifted her lips to his, surprising him with a hint of passion in her kiss. Keeping hold of her shawl she wrapped her arms around him, and he drew her as close as humanly possibly while he kissed her on and on.

"Oh, James," she murmured close to his lips. "When you kiss me like that . . . I'm so . . ."

"What?" he whispered and kissed her again. "You're so . . . what?"

"So . . . glad that I'm your wife," she said and initiated another long, savoring kiss.

"Oh, so am I," he said and ended their embrace abruptly, only so that he could take her arm and guide her into the house and up the stairs.

As they walked she said, "Do you remember our wedding night?"

"How could I ever forget? You were terrified."

"Not for long. You were so sweet . . . so gentle. You always have been." At the bedroom door she hesitated and touched his face. "It was amazing. It's always been amazing."

"Yes, it has," he said and urged her into the bedroom, closing the door behind them.

* * *

A few days later Eleanore received a letter from Sally. She was grateful for the decision she'd made not to share the news of her pregnancy until it was over. She was glad not to have to read about Sally congratulating her on her pregnancy or asking how she was feeling or when the baby was due. And Sally had clearly not yet received the letter that Eleanore had written with the latest difficult news. But for the moment that was all the better. Sally's letter was filled with the usual trivialities of life that Eleanore loved to read about. The temple walls were growing higher, life in Nauvoo was thriving, and newcomers flocked there regularly. Eleanore wanted to be among them, but she knew in her heart that the answer hadn't changed. She needed to stay where she was. Until the Spirit prompted her otherwise, she felt no need to even ask the question again. In her heart she just knew.

Eleanore was surprised to read in Sally's letter, *You asked me a long time ago if I wanted you to send anything that had been left with the house. I meant it when I said that I didn't. I truly had no trouble leaving those things behind, and what we have here now is more than adequate. I must admit now that I've changed my mind. I would be most grateful if you could send the china. I know it won't be easy to pack it adequately to keep it from breaking, but it would be so dearly appreciated if you could do that. You did say that you don't use it, and if that's the case, I got thinking that it could likely be put to use here.*

Eleanore finished reading the letter and immediately took the china down from its resting place in a high cupboard in the kitchen. With Amanda's help they carefully wrapped each piece in tissue and then in old newspaper, and packed it into a box, but Eleanore still couldn't help being afraid that it would arrive in Nauvoo damaged. She was carefully arranging the last few pieces when James came into the kitchen and sat down to remove his muddy shoes.

"What *are* you doing?" he asked, grateful to see her up and doing *anything*.

"I'm sending Sally her china, but I'm worried about it getting there without breaking. I can't even imagine how packages must be handled when they're sent so far."

James hardly realized what he was thinking before the words came out of his mouth. "Why don't we just take it to her?"

Eleanore's heart pounded, and she turned wide eyes toward her husband, certain he was teasing. He looked serious enough, but she had to say, "Surely you jest."

He shrugged and noticed Lizzie smiling. "I hadn't really thought about it before now, but . . . why not? Maybe it would be good for the two of us to get away together. And maybe it's time you and Sally met each other. And we could see Andy and Miriam and the kids and see how they're coming along. I bet

Lizzie and Frederick would be happy to look after the children while we're gone."

"We'd love to," Lizzie said enthusiastically.

James winked at her and said to his wife, "We could go up the river."

Eleanore's sudden breathlessness matched her quickened heart. How clearly she recalled the beautiful riverboats going back and forth when she and James had taken a belated honeymoon in a little city on the Mississippi River after she'd lost the first baby. And later they'd taken the children to the same place. She knew the boats carried passengers and cargo up and down the river, but she'd never considered actually going on one.

"Well?" James asked and stood up, certain the idea had been inspired by the way it had come seemingly out of nowhere, and with such confidence. The theory was strengthened by the stunned pleasure in her expression. Perhaps they *did* need to get away together, just the two of them. He recalled when they'd done it before, following the loss of the first baby; it had given them generous opportunity to talk through their feelings and examine their grief without the busyness and distractions of everyday life. A part of him felt a little hesitant to take her to Nauvoo, not wanting to offer any encouragement for her desire to move there and live among the Saints. Perhaps that's why the Spirit had kicked the words out of his mouth before he'd had a chance to think about them too deeply. But he felt certain the trip would do them both some good.

"Well?" he repeated more firmly when she didn't answer. "Do you want to go or not?"

Eleanore threw her arms around his neck and held to him tightly, murmuring close to his ear, "Of course I want to go. It would be so wonderful. Thank you."

Arrangements were quickly made over the next few days. Eleanore packed her things for the trip and repacked the china into a trunk with some quilts and blankets placed on every side to offer more protection. Eleanore added some gifts for Sally and her family, and for Miriam and her family as well. She promised David and Iris that she would bring them gifts from Nauvoo, which eased their disappointment in not being able to go. She and James had discussed the possibility of taking the children, but after weighing all aspects of the situation and the purpose of the trip, they both felt it would be best to leave them behind. And there was no question that Frederick and Lizzie would take very good care of them.

On the day they were leaving, Eleanore got out of bed feeling the excitement of a child at Christmas. After consuming a quick breakfast and sharing appropriate farewells, Frederick drove them into town where they caught a stagecoach that would take them to the river. Soon after their trunks were loaded onto the steamboat, they boarded and were soon moving south down the wide and gracious Mississippi toward Nauvoo. Eleanore loved the calming effect of the river and recalled the same feeling when they'd crossed it on their initial journey to Iowa. The journey was both relaxing and rejuvenating. The unhurried nature of the riverboat soaked into Eleanore, leaving her content just to be with her husband and immerse herself in the passing scenery while her anticipation of arriving in Nauvoo heightened hourly.

It was afternoon when the boat docked in Nauvoo, Illinois. Eleanore was so full of jittery excitement she could hardly breathe. She stood for several minutes while James arranged for transportation, just observing the bustle of activity and the many people coming and going. A warmth in her heart brought tears to her eyes as it occurred to her that the vast majority—if not all—of these people shared her religion. She'd become so accustomed to hiding it, keeping it secret, surrounding herself with people who didn't know and wouldn't want to. And now she had stepped off a boat, and everything was different.

"Come along," she heard James say as he took hold of her

arm. He guided her to where a kind man was loading their trunks into a wagon.

The man introduced himself as Brother Smith, and immediately added, "No relation." as if they should clearly know what he meant. And they did. Even the simple, indirect reference to Joseph Smith quickened Eleanore's heart. This was the city where he lived!

While James and Eleanore were sitting next to Brother Smith on the seat at the front of the wagon, headed toward the center of town, he asked, "So, are you folks new here, or just visiting?"

"Just visiting," James said firmly, while Eleanore uttered a silent prayer that his heart might be softened toward moving to this place. Of course, he'd been willing to consider it before, and they'd both received undeniable answers that they needed to stay in Iowa. But perhaps that had changed now. Perhaps the time had come that God would guide them to the opportunity to live in this beautiful place.

While Brother Smith chatted about trivial matters, Eleanore listened to the subtleties interwoven in his words that indicated he was a Mormon; his religion was a part of his life, and he spoke freely of it. She wanted to ask questions and engage herself more in the conversation, but she felt too much wonder. With the fascination of a child she took in the lovely houses, thriving businesses, neatly groomed yards and streets, and people coming and going while a spirit hovered in the air that urged tears to her eyes. They were in Nauvoo! The City Beautiful. And it *was!*

Brother Smith drove directly to the address that James had given him. But he said, "I'll wait and make certain we've got the right place."

"I'd like you to wait anyway," James said, jumping down from the wagon and then helping Eleanore. "Once we let them know we're here, we should find a hotel room."

"I know just the place," Brother Smith said and got down as well.

Eleanore noted that the home was lovely, though not as large as the one the Jensens had sold before coming here. It was constructed of the same red brick that was prominently displayed throughout the community. The yard was spacious and fenced in, with signs of children scattered over the lawn, and a little black dog tied to the porch. The dog started to bark at their arrival. But James was apparently unintimidated as he took the trunk that held Sally's china to the porch, set it down and quickly won the dog's favor by allowing it to smell his hand, and then by scratching its furry little head. Eleanore was barely through the gate when James lifted a hand to knock just as the door came open. A woman stepped onto the porch, apparently coming to investigate the dog's barking—or perhaps its subsequent silence. Excitement surged through Eleanore as she wondered if this could be her longtime friend. She'd wondered a hundred times what Sally might look like. This woman was average height with a well-rounded figure, and hair so blonde it looked almost white. Most of it was pulled back into a bun, except for the ringlets that hung at the sides of her face. She wore a dress of red calico and a white apron. Eleanore hovered near the fence and watched as James turned his focus from the dog to the woman who smiled at him and said, "He's not much of a watchdog when he makes friends so quickly." James chuckled, and she added, "May I help you?"

"Might you be Sally Jensen?" he asked, brushing his hands on his breeches.

"I am," she said. James tossed a quick smile toward Eleanore, but Sally apparently missed it.

Eleanore put a hand over her quivering stomach and suppressed the urge to giggle. James said, "I have a delivery for you, Mrs. Jensen." He motioned toward the trunk on the porch. Sally looked at it and furrowed her brow. Before she could ask any questions, James added, "Oh, that's only part of it." He motioned toward Eleanore, and Sally turned to look at her. As their eyes met across the yard, James said, "I thought your china might be more likely to arrive safely if Eleanore brought it herself."

She shot wide eyes toward James and put a hand over the center of her chest. Eleanore heard her mutter, "You're James Barrington?" She said it as if he was nothing like she'd expected.

"I am," he laughed.

Sally laughed as well and put both hands to her face as her eyes turned toward Eleanore, at first inquisitive, and then filled with wonder and excitement, all in the breadth of a second. And then she ran off the porch and down the walk, letting out a squeal of laughter. Eleanore moved toward her and they met with an immediately tight embrace while both of them laughed and cried.

Eleanore heard Brother Smith say with a chuckle, "Apparently we found the right place."

"Apparently," James added with pleasure.

Sally drew back and took Eleanore's shoulders. "It's really you?"

"It is. I hope it's all right to surprise you like this."

"Of course," Sally said and laughed again, wiping at her tears. "You're so much younger than I expected."

"I am?"

"It's just that your letters are so . . . wise and insightful. I expected you to be older."

Eleanore took that as a compliment. By Sally's smile that was clearly how she'd meant it.

"Oh, I can't believe it!" Sally said and laughed, hugging her again. "It's the most wonderful surprise I've ever had."

Eleanore became aware of James beside her when he said, "We wanted to deliver *that*," he motioned to the trunk on the porch, "and make certain we could find you. Now we'll have Mr. Smith here take us to a hotel, and then we can come back and—"

"Oh, no!" Sally said with such vehemence that Eleanore was startled. "I won't hear of it! You're staying here with us. All that going back and forth to a hotel is just a waste of time when we could be visiting, and it's certainly a waste of money."

"But . . . you had no idea we were coming," Eleanore said. "We can't impose on you this way and—"

"Nonsense," Sally said. "Surprise company is the best kind. Besides, since Andy and Miriam moved into their new home, we're feeling so spacious we're almost lonely. It will be grand." She said to James as if she'd been ordering him about for years, "You can tell Brother Smith to go, Brother Barrington."

"I'll do that," James said with a subtle smirk toward Eleanore. He added directly to Sally, "Please call me James."

She smiled at him but turned her attention to Eleanore. Brother Smith retrieved the other trunk they'd brought with them that contained their belongings and carried it to the porch. James paid him generously and thanked him while Sally guided Eleanore to the porch, muttering again that she couldn't believe it and that Eleanore was younger than she'd expected. Eleanore found her friend to be very forthright and talkative, but she preferred that to silence. It was odd to realize how well they knew each other through written words, when being with her felt so strange. Sally's husband, Mark, was working at his job at the mill and would be home shortly, but they met the children before one of them was sent to let the Plummers know that the Barringtons had come to visit.

The awkwardness dissipated somewhat as they went inside and sat to visit. The children gathered around as Eleanore opened the trunk and brought out gifts for everyone, as well as some candy. Some things for Andy and Miriam and their children were set aside. Then Sally cried when she unwrapped one of the china teacups. Eleanore could well imagine how it might represent everything she'd abandoned when they'd left in a frantic hurry to come to Nauvoo. While Sally was tearfully expressing gratitude for the china, and especially for them bringing it personally, the entire Plummer family came in with a flurry.

"I can't believe it!" Miriam said, crying herself as she wrapped Eleanore in her arms. "We came the moment we heard you were here." Hugs and greetings and laughter were exchanged all around, then Sally's husband, Mark, arrived, and introductions were made. He seemed almost as pleased to have them there as Sally was. They all hovered in the parlor for a long while, chatting and getting to know those they'd just met, and renewing acquaintance with friends they knew well.

Sally finally declared that it was past suppertime, and with a little help in the kitchen it would be no trouble to cook more vegetables and add more dumplings to the broth she had simmering. James insisted they didn't want to be any bother, but she insisted more firmly that their surprise visit was cause for great celebration, and they would all enjoy supper together. Apparently the Jensens and the Plummers still shared meals on occasion, even though they now had separate households. Eleanore had to remind herself that until recently both families had been living under this roof. They were obviously accustomed to working well together in the kitchen, and used to accommodating everyone.

James left Eleanore helping her friends, looking happier than he'd seen her in a long while. He walked out to the backyard with Mark and Andy where they all made themselves comfortable on some chairs left there in the shade. Mark and Andy talked for a few minutes about happenings of the city, and things going on at their places of profession. The building of the temple came up, and they talked of their personal efforts in helping with the project. James learned that each person had been asked to tithe their time, that one day in ten they would dedicate their work to the completion of the temple. James enjoyed just listening and comparing how different his life was from that of these men, and it gave him a new perspective. They had each lived in the area where he now lived—Mark in the same home. But now they'd come here, and their lives had changed a great deal. James preferred his own life and prayed that it would remain as it was.

"So," Mark said to James, "how was your trip down the river?"

"Very nice," James said, wanting to say that it wasn't necessary for them to make diplomatic effort to include him in the conversation.

"I've rarely seen Sally so happy," Mark said. "It was truly good of you to come all this way."

"I doubt Sally could be any happier than Eleanore. I'm certain meeting Sally is likely to be one of the high points of her life. Sally's letters have meant a great deal to Eleanore."

"As Eleanore's have meant to Sally," Mark said. He then added, "Your wife is very charming. She's much younger than I expected. She must have been *very* young when you married her."

James interpreted the comment as an implication of the age difference between him and Eleanore, as opposed to Eleanore having been unusually young when she'd married. He simply said, "Yes, I suppose she was. She's rarely seemed young to me. She's wise beyond her years."

"Yes, that's evident," Mark added. "An amazing young woman."

"Indeed," Andy said and went on to talk about Eleanore bringing the gospel into their lives. He spoke of her spiritual strength and emotional maturity with great admiration. James wholly shared their esteem, but he couldn't account for the mild uneasiness he was feeling. Then Andy chuckled and playfully slapped James on the shoulder, saying, "How *did* an old man like you catch yourself such a lovely and remarkable young bride?"

James forced a soft laugh in return and tried to ignore the way the question pricked him. "That is an excellent question, my friend," he said and changed the subject by asking Andy how his children were doing here in Nauvoo.

Though the remainder of the day was enjoyable, James found himself distracted by Andy's question, or more accurately, he wondered *why* he felt bothered by it at all. Late that evening after the Plummers had gone home and everyone else had gone to bed, he and Eleanore were settling into the spare room where they would sleep. James became so preoccupied with the matter that he was barely aware of his wife taking down her hair while he eased the curtain aside and looked toward the starlit skies over Nauvoo.

"Why did you marry me?" he asked.

Surprised by the question, Eleanore turned to see James holding a piece of worn hair ribbon. Absently he pressed it to his nose then returned it to the pocket of his waistcoat, apparently unaware that she'd even noticed. She'd become aware a long time ago that he discreetly carried a piece of hair ribbon sprayed with her perfume. But she'd not seen any evidence of it for months and had forgotten all about it, or perhaps she had assumed that with as long as they'd been married he no longer indulged in such a silly, sentimental habit. Recalling that he'd asked her a question, she turned back toward the mirror and said, "What brought this up out of nowhere?"

"Just . . . wondering." James closed the curtain and looked at her directly. "Why did you marry me? And don't say it was because you loved me."

Eleanore turned in her chair and regarded the somberness in his eyes that wasn't typical of any discussion regarding the circumstances behind their marriage. Generally it was treated with matter-of-fact acceptance, or perhaps humor. His present attitude left her especially alert. She answered firmly, "No, I certainly couldn't say that; and I wouldn't. You know I would never be anything less than completely honest with you."

"I know that. So I need you to tell me why you married me."

"But you *know* why, James. I don't understand the relevancy of the question."

"Yes." He sat on the edge of the bed and heaved a loud sigh. "I suppose I know the answer. You were given a perfectly practical proposal, and you accepted it for perfectly practical reasons."

"You *did* make the practicality of the arrangement very clear at the time of your proposal. Have you forgotten or—"

"No, of course not, but . . ."

"But?" She sat beside him, still brushing through her hair. "What's wrong, James?"

"Nothing is . . . *wrong*. I've just been . . . thinking about it; about how we came to where we are. And now that we've come this far, I can't help wondering why you married me. I know for a fact that you weren't even slightly attracted to me. So it must have been my money." He said it with no sign of humor, and Eleanore attempted to consider what might be lurking beneath such a comment.

"The reasons are irrelevant now, James," she said. "All that matters now is that I *am* attracted to you, and I *love* you. And you love me. What we share is more than I could have ever hoped for."

His eyes turned inquisitive. "Perhaps that's part of the point, Eleanore. It *is* more than you ever hoped for; more than either of us ever expected. What if we were living with what we'd expected?"

"But we're not."

"What if we were? What *did* you expect, Eleanore? Why *did* you marry me? That's what I want to know."

Eleanore stopped brushing and looked into her husband's eyes. She was stunned by the question. But she was even more stunned by what she saw. James Barrington had always been a dignified, self-confident man. When vulnerabilities had surfaced, they were always cloaked with a certain amount of maturity and decorum. But what she saw in his eyes now reminded her of David, back in England, when he'd run away from home, and she'd found him, frightened and helpless. She felt afraid herself. She wanted to demand that he tell her what had induced such feelings and concerns in him. And why here in Nauvoo? Was it coincidence? Not likely. She realized in that moment how much she depended on his natural strength, how just a hint of the absence of it quickened her heart with dread. But she kept her composure and resigned herself to answering the question, hoping it would provoke a conversation that clearly needed to take place.

"I married you because I knew it was the right thing to do. I knew it was the course God wanted me to take for my life. I believed then and I know now that decisions should be made according to a tried-and-true formula. It is a combination of gathering information so that you can logically assess a situation, then asking God to guide you through your thoughts and feelings. That's what I did. I absolutely knew beyond any doubt that marrying you was the right thing to do. I was not and never would be the kind of woman to marry a man for his money. You offered me security; you promised to provide for my needs. Any woman would be a fool not to consider those factors in a proposal of marriage. Still, that was only a portion of my reasons for believing you would be a good husband. May I remind you, however, that you put a great deal of effort into pointing out the advantages of my marrying a wealthy man. As I recall, you were very convincing."

He looked down, sheepish and embarrassed, and that aura of uncertainty heightened. "Yes, I did, didn't I."

"You told me that you believed we were compatible at the deepest roots of ourselves, and you believed we could follow the same dream and find fulfillment and contentment together."

He sighed loudly. "I did say that, yes. But . . . what if you had never grown to love me? How would we be living?"

"We would be comfortable and content."

"Would we?"

"I don't know," she said with suppressed exasperation. "What if you had married Lucy the nanny?"

"I never would have."

"Exactly." She set her brush on the bedside table. "This conversation is irrelevant. It's impossible to know the course of something that simply isn't or never would be. We love each other. This is the life we share." She pressed a hand to his face. "I love you, James. I *need* you."

She saw relief in his eyes that intensified when he said, "Oh, I need you too, Eleanore." He wrapped her tightly in his arms. "I *need* you."

Eleanore just held him close, wondering where this apparent desperation in him had come from. Sensing that any further attempt to talk about it at the moment would be pointless, she simply prayed that he would find peace over whatever might be troubling him, and that he might know in his heart the full depth of her love for him, and never have cause to question it. She drew back and took his face into her hands, repeating with fervor, "I love you, James Barrington. I always will."

He showed a soft smile and pressed his lips to hers. His kiss began tenderly, then became passionate, and Eleanore eagerly became lost in the joy of being his wife. Long before she'd come to love him, she'd taken on his name and become his lover. There was little in life so sweet as the experience they shared alone together this way, when nothing else in the world mattered. Even whatever might be troubling him seemed temporarily forgotten in the midst of one of the greatest gifts given to man and woman within this earthly experience. It didn't matter *why* she loved him, or he her. The love they shared was manifested in all they gave to each other, day in and day out, hour by hour, in the commitment and mutual respect of daily life that all culminated in such blissful moments.

Chapter Eight

THE PROPHECY

Later, they lay close together in contented silence. James threaded his fingers between hers and pressed a lingering kiss to her brow before he whispered, "I love you, Eleanore. Don't ever leave me."

Eleanore leaned abruptly onto one elbow to look at his face. "Why would I ever *consider* leaving you? Why would you even *think* such a thing?"

Eleanore wanted him to laugh it off and tell her he was being silly. But his intensity remained as he said, "Just tell me you'll always be here, and I'll believe you."

Eleanore had to consider the timing of such a comment, especially when the only other time he'd expressed concern over her leaving him had been upon his discovery of her interest in finding the Mormon Church. Whatever his concerns might have been, she'd had no trouble setting them straight. "I told you before we ever came to America that I could never leave you. *Never!* Not for anything. The vows we exchanged are most important, above all else. Why are you bringing this up now?" He said nothing, and she ventured a bold guess. "Now that we are among people who share my religion, did you think I would choose being with them over you?"

"Would you?" he asked far too quickly.

"Do you have any idea how ludicrous a question that is? I've said it before and I'll say it again. What value would any religion have without family? Do you know me so little as to think that I would make such a horrific choice? Do you think God would condone such a choice? For me to leave a good husband and dishonor my marriage vows?"

"Are you saying you would never leave me under any circumstances?"

She let out a sardonic chuckle, appalled at the absurdity of the question. "If you were drunk all the time and beating me, I would steal David and Iris and run away and you would never find us. Clearly that is not an issue, and again, even bringing it up is ridiculous."

He lifted a hand to touch her face and said gently, "I just had to know."

"So, you know," she said. "Now you can kiss me and try to remember that we're on holiday."

"So we are," he said and kissed her with renewed passion. Eleanore felt grateful to find no trace of his apparent fears, and she prayed that they would never show up again.

The following morning Eleanore was pleased to see that James was more like himself. At breakfast Mark asked him questions about the happenings in Iowa City, and they chatted on and on. When they'd finished eating, Sally said, "I still can't believe you're here. Bringing yourselves is so much more exciting than getting the china."

"We considered bringing that couch you left in the back room," James said with a sideways smile.

"That old thing?" Mark said with a laugh. "My mother gave that to us. I always thought it was hideous."

James exchanged a humorous glance with Eleanore. Sally said, "That was the only thing I was truly glad to leave behind. I must apologize for the grief it's given you."

They all laughed, and James said, "It's tolerably comfortable. I do sleep there on occasion when Eleanore has need to put me in my place."

"Oh?" Eleanore said. "I thought you slept there when you needed to put *me* in *my* place."

"That too," James said and took her hand across the table. He saw her smile and hoped the tension of the previous evening was gone.

The children scattered to finish chores that hadn't been completed before breakfast. Eleanore set to work helping Sally in the kitchen while James went outside with Mark to help him as well. When all was in order, the adults set out for a day on the town, since Mark had taken some time off to spend with them. He assured them it was not a problem, and James hoped that it wasn't. It was evident the family got along all right financially, but he saw no evidence of abundance, and he felt concerned that their visit might put a strain on the food budget. And now Mark was taking time off his job at the sawmill. They were kind, generous people, and he prayed that they would be blessed for being such.

While Mark was driving the buggy toward the center of the city, he said to James, "I don't believe you ever told us what exactly you did in England."

James shifted slightly and cleared his throat, wondering how to admit to these people the uselessness of his upbringing. And he wondered if he wanted to. Eleanore glanced discreetly at him, and he knew she sensed his discomfort. He was glad Mark and Sally were in the seat in front of them, oblivious to their expressions. While he was struggling to remember what he'd told other people who had asked, Eleanore said, "He managed an estate with many farms."

"A business man, then," Mark said. "I believe Andy told us you'd owned land and made a good sale of it before coming here." *So that's what he'd told others.*

"That's right," James said.

"You certainly arrived in need of a home at just the right time for us," Sally said, then she pointed out the Seventies Hall as they drove past.

Eleanore felt as if she were in a dream as they took in the sights, and even the feeling, of the city. They saw the printing office where the newspapers that Sally had sent Eleanore copies of were printed, and nearby was the post office where Sally and Miriam mailed their letters. They saw many shops of all kinds and did some shopping. Eleanore purchased gifts for everyone who had remained at home, and purchased some souvenirs for herself. With all the people they encountered, she couldn't help wondering if they might actually see the Prophet. She hesitated to even ask Sally if such a thing were possible, not wanting to sound silly or impertinent. Surely every visitor or newcomer to Nauvoo had curiosity over Joseph Smith. And the city was huge—nearly the biggest in Illinois, apparently. Surely the odds of seeing him were slight, if not impossible. Still, she prayed that it might happen. She wanted so badly just to see his face, if only from a distance, perhaps just so she could have a mental picture of what he really looked like when she heard stories about him. And while she prayed repeatedly for such a privilege, she countered her prayers with telling her Father in Heaven that she knew it was likely a silly wish, but she wished it nevertheless. And she kept her wish to herself, certain her disappointment would be easier to swallow if no one else knew about it.

Following their shopping they all went out for lunch, which James insisted on buying. Then they did more shopping, doing more looking than actually purchasing anything. In the middle of the afternoon they went to see what Sally declared was the highlight of the tour—the rising walls of the temple. They were actually able to get close enough to touch the gray limestone, and Eleanore felt as if she had touched a piece of heaven. While they wandered about the site, staying clear of the many workers who were busily engaged, Mark and Sally talked of the sacrifices being made in order to see that the temple was built. But they spoke of it eagerly and with joy, as if they would gladly give far more than they already were. They spoke of their own efforts as if they were nothing. Talk of sacrifice blended into their sweet anticipation of the temple's completion and the work that would be done there on behalf of their eternal welfare. Eleanore imagined herself coming back here when she might enter the temple and partake of those blessings, whatever they might entail. She imagined James going with her, but wondered if such a thing would ever happen. Taking hold of his hand, she exerted some faith on that account. Surely he *would* embrace the gospel so that they could share its sweetest eternal rewards.

James said very little as Mark and Sally talked on and on about the temple, its purpose—concisely and simply explained—and the unfathomable work and sacrifices taking place to see it built. He felt respect and amazement, but doubted that he could ever engage himself in such sacrifice. He couldn't deny that the comfort of his life was highly important to him. He wondered how these people could be so happy and at the same time so utterly poor and thoroughly exhausted with strenuous work.

Walking away from the temple while Mark remained behind to speak with someone he knew, James glanced over his shoulder to take another look. *Why?* he wondered. *Why would they commit so much to such a project?*

"Oh, look," Sally said. "It's Brother Joseph. I was hoping you could meet him."

James thought nothing of it until Eleanore replied with quiet glee, "The Prophet?"

Eleanore's heart quickened as Sally hailed this man and got his attention. Dressed as he was, he'd obviously been working personally on the construction of the temple. She couldn't believe she was actually going to meet Joseph Smith. She thought of the first time she'd become acquainted with the name. It had been printed in the front of the book she had found in England. She had immediately come to treasure the book, and to wonder about this man who had translated it. And now they were standing face-to-face at the side of the road as Sally said, "You

must meet my dear friends, James and Eleanore Barrington."
She added eagerly, "Sister Barrington found the Book of
Mormon in the road in England and came to America as
quickly as she could, looking for us."

Eleanore saw the Prophet's eyes fill with intrigue, perhaps
contentment. And they *were* a prophet's eyes. She only had to
look into them to know as he took her hand and shook it with
gentle firmness. "How good to meet you, Sister Barrington."

"And you," she said. At just that moment, Sally became
distracted by seeing someone else she knew, and she moved a
few steps away to exchange greetings.

"Brother Barrington," Joseph said, shaking James's hand as
well. Eleanore took the two of them in, how they met almost
exactly eye to eye. And she couldn't help noting the way Joseph
looked into her husband's eyes, as if he could see into his soul.
And James looked boldly back.

"I'm not a member," James said.

Brother Joseph showed a warm smile and a sparkle of humor
in his eyes as he asked, "Why *is* that, Brother Barrington?"

James had no desire to answer the question, but it took him
a moment to speak. He couldn't deny the presence of this man.
There truly was something extraordinary about him. "My sweet
wife is a member," he finally said. "This church of yours means
a great deal to her."

"It's the Lord's Church," Joseph said. "And surely the Lord
has led you here to His beautiful city."

"We're only *visiting* Nauvoo," James said.

"And why is *that*, Brother Barrington?" Joseph asked, again
with a sparkle in his eyes and a faint smile.

"God has led us to Iowa," James said, and Eleanore could
almost believe that Joseph could sense the resistance of James's
heart. "And until He tells us to leave, that's where we're staying."

Joseph's smile broadened, and he immediately replied, "Then
surely He will eventually see you gathered with the Saints, in

His own good time." Eleanore felt something swell in her heart, as if this great man had truly spoken prophecy and her heart had felt the truth of it. Without waiting for further comment, Joseph took hold of Eleanore's hand again, holding it between both of his while she could almost literally feel his power creep into her. The spirit of prophecy intensified in his countenance and in his voice as he looked into her eyes and stated with firm tenderness, "You will be greatly blessed for your faith, Sister Barrington, and shall be the means for doing much good." She already felt breathless, even before he added, "You shall bear and raise many fine children who will settle in Zion and carry forth God's kingdom on the earth."

Eleanore was attempting to catch her breath against the burning in her chest when he let go of her hand, saying, "A pleasure meeting the both of you," as if nothing profound or out of the ordinary had just taken place. Eleanore could only nod, utterly speechless. James did the same, apparently struck dumb as well. "Good day, Sister Jensen," Joseph added. Sally said something to him that Eleanore didn't hear. Misty-eyed, she turned to watch him leave, then she looked up at her husband and saw the glisten of moisture in his eyes as well. He put his arms around her as if to silently share the wonder of the promise they had just been given.

The moment ended when Mark approached and they all got back into the buggy to head for home. Eleanore listened to Sally chattering as if from a distance while the Prophet's words, and his eyes, and his presence lingered in her spirit and left her silent. James held tightly to her hand, remaining quiet as well, and she knew he was affected, but it was hard to tell how deeply.

"Are you all right?" Sally asked when Eleanore was slow to answer a question.

"I'm fine," she insisted and made an appropriate comment before her thoughts wandered back to Joseph's promise. Could it possibly be true? Would she bear and raise many children? If she believed he was a prophet, then it *had* to be true. She wanted to shout for joy and cry like a baby. Instead she just leaned her head against her husband's shoulder and cried silent tears, thanking God for answering her prayers, for giving her the rare privilege of coming face-to-face with this great man, and for the added privilege of being given a personal promise. And she prayed that it would, indeed, come to pass.

The excursion ended at the Plummers' new home, where the men worked together in the garden and chatted, while Sally and Eleanore helped Miriam hang her laundry. In her forthright way, Sally said to Eleanore, "Your husband seems as good a man as you've told me in your letters."

"He is, yes," Eleanore said readily.

More lightly Sally added, "But he's so austere, isn't he?"

"Is he?" Eleanore asked.

"Forgive me," Sally said with a girlish giggle. "It's just that . . . you're so much younger than I expected; I guess that makes him older than I expected. And to see the two of you together, I wouldn't immediately think you're well matched. He's so . . . formal."

"Not like he used to be," Miriam said with a little laugh. "He was much more so when they first arrived from England."

"Yes, he certainly was," Eleanore agreed. "But you must understand, we did come from dramatically different backgrounds, and his was nothing like the life we're living now. Although he's much more suited to this life than that one."

"Different, how?" Miriam asked, and Eleanore realized that with all the talking they'd done, she'd really told her friend very little of their situation in England. Miriam added what she already knew, "You told me that you had worked for him, caring for his children after his first wife died, but . . . does that make your backgrounds so different?"

"Immensely," Eleanore said. "Although, I must tell you in confidence, James prefers to leave all of that behind and not have it discussed. One of our reasons for coming to America was to be free of ridiculous social distinctions." The women both looked overtly intrigued, and she added, "Many people in England were highly critical of his choice in a wife."

"But . . . why?"

"He was a lord, and I was a governess."

"Truly?" Sally said. "An aristocrat, then?"

"That's right."

"I never would have dreamed," Miriam said with a little laugh.

"People were really critical over your marriage?" Sally asked.

"Indeed. A friend of his mother's practically accused him of committing treason by marrying me. But he stood by me without question, always treated me as his equal."

"That is so sweet," Miriam said dreamily. Eleanore knew her to be a romantic. "He *is* a good man. Andy tells me often how he misses his friendship. And perhaps one day James will take the gospel into his heart."

"Perhaps," Eleanore said, fighting back the sting of tears.

"I'm certain of it," Sally said as if she'd seen it in vision. "I sense that he knows it's true. I'm certain that with time he'll come to accept it."

"I'm sure you're right," Eleanore agreed, grateful to hear someone else voice what she believed of her husband.

That evening they all shared supper at the Plummer home and had a wonderful visit, except for when the conversation wandered into matters of ongoing persecution from those who would prefer that the Mormons settle elsewhere. They were vague in sharing details of things that had happened to Saints living in Nauvoo and the surrounding settlements, as if it might be too horrific to say aloud. Eleanore preferred it that way. She didn't want to hear details that might haunt her, but even so, her imagination could run rampant thinking about atrocities that might be occurring. She noticed her husband looking as disturbed as she felt, but they all relaxed when the conversation eased into more pleasant topics.

The following day they all went to church together. Eleanore felt weepy all through the service. She wondered if her emotion was residue from her encounter with the Prophet, or her joy at simply participating openly in a Mormon Church meeting. Oh, how she longed to worship this way each and every Sunday! But she felt certain James had no interest in moving to Nauvoo. And just the thought of bringing it up left her extremely uneasy; she doubted she could even broach the topic—especially after hearing about the negative aspects of living here. For her, the positive would far outweigh the risks, but she felt certain James didn't share her sentiments in that regard. She didn't bother thinking about it too deeply in that moment, but chose instead to just enjoy the experience while it lasted, and to appreciate this grand opportunity.

On Sunday evening, Eleanore was overwhelmed with mixed feelings. She missed the children and wanted to go home, but the spirit of Nauvoo had woven its way irrevocably into her heart, and she never wanted to leave. She found herself praying that James's heart would be softened, that he might be willing to sell their home and move here to be among friends where they could live their religion openly. She felt certain that if James lived here among the Saints, it would only be a matter of time before he embraced the gospel himself. And then her joy would be full.

* * *

James found his thoughts dwelling on a certain matter that he knew needed to be addressed before they left Nauvoo. He prayed about it and weighed it carefully before he took a few minutes to be alone and go upstairs to get his checkbook. Then he sought out Mark and asked if they could talk privately.

In the backyard James handed a check to Mark, who asked, "What is this?"

"It's for the temple . . . on Eleanore's behalf. I'm certain you can see that it gets to the right person."

"Of course," Mark said and glanced at it; then his eyes widened. He looked at James as if to be assured this was not a joke.

James kept his expression firm as he said, "I trust you will be discreet."

"Of course," Mark said again. "Your sacrifice will surely bless your life, James."

"It's no sacrifice, Mark. If it were, I'm not certain I'd be willing to do it."

He sensed Mark's mind mulling over the underlying messages. Enlightenment showed in his gaze. He looked at James with new eyes. He said straightly, "When you gave us more than the asking price for the house, I assumed you had ample financial resources. But you have more than ample, don't you? Apparently what you left behind in England was rather significant."

"What we found in America is far better, I can assure you. The rest doesn't matter. But since you know that my resources are more than ample, I trust you won't be too proud to accept this." He stuffed a second check into Mark's pocket. "It's what we would have spent on a hotel. I know you can use it, so don't argue with me. Staying in your home was a great privilege, and we had a marvelous time. But we don't want you going without because of your generosity." Mark opened his mouth as if to protest. James lifted a finger and said, "I felt strongly that God wanted me to give this to you. Consider it from Him; you don't turn down blessings from *Him,* no matter through what means they might come."

Mark closed his mouth and gave an exasperated sigh. "Thank you, my friend. You and your sweet wife have been a great blessing in our lives; and the money is the least of it."

"I can say the same of you and Sally." He shook Mark's hand firmly. "Thank you for opening your home to us. Perhaps one day you can come and stay with us, although it might feel strange to visit a home that was once yours."

"It would be delightful. We'll have to do that one of these days."

That night in bed Eleanore cried. James just held her, relieved that she didn't want to talk about the reasons. He knew them well enough. She didn't want to leave Nauvoo. She didn't want to leave her friends. She felt torn, and he felt scared.

The following morning they left early to meet a riverboat heading north. Mark drove them in the buggy, and Sally rode along. Goodbyes were difficult, and once they were aboard and headed home, James noted that his wife had become very quiet. The little cabin they were sharing felt close and strained while he tried to read as she did nothing. After many hours with far too much silence between them he finally said, "You want to move to Nauvoo, don't you?"

Eleanore felt startled by the question. Her heart quickened with hope until he added, "Well, we're not going to."

"I wasn't going to suggest it," she said, but she still felt angry that he would be so immediately unyielding over the matter.

"Good. I'm glad we're clear on that."

She knew he would never bend, but she felt compelled to make a point. "And you won't even consider it? Just like that?"

"No, I won't," he said, but it was the way he said it that got her attention.

"You're upset. You've been stewing over this a great deal."

He gave her a sharp glare. "Yes, I suppose I have. To be truthful, I was concerned that if I took you to Nauvoo you'd never want to leave."

"Then why *did* you take me?"

"It felt like the right thing to do; I knew it would make you happy."

"But you wouldn't move there for the same reasons?"

"How happy do you suppose we would be if our home was burned or we were living in fear for our safety? I understand your desire to be among people who share your beliefs, Eleanore. Truly, I do. But it's not worth the risk."

"You can only say that because you have no comprehension of what it means to have these beliefs fill your heart and soul, to know that you would do *anything* to live them freely."

"Freely? These people don't live them *freely,*" he countered. "They live in fear. It's only a matter of time before they will be driven out again, homeless and wandering."

"No! Nauvoo is thriving; their numbers are great. They won't be overcome this time."

"I'm not so sure." He shook his head. "And I'm not going to risk it. We're staying where we are, Eleanore. You're right. I have no comprehension of how you feel about your beliefs, but I'll not risk your well-being, or that of the children. I won't."

Eleanore wanted to cry so badly that she felt sure tears were running backward into her head. She fought to keep her composure and her dignity while she pressed what she considered to be an important point. "You've always made decisions according to what you believed God wanted you to do; always. Why not now? If God wanted us to move to Nauvoo, would you do it? Do you not trust Him? Will you not even ask Him?"

James felt so angry he wanted to shout at her. He swallowed hard and forced his anger behind the fear at its source. Committed to honesty, he had to say, "I don't want to ask Him, Eleanore."

"Because you're afraid He'll tell you we should move."

"Yes," he snarled, too quietly to be overheard, "that's exactly what I'm afraid of."

"So, you'll . . . what? Hide from God the way Jonah did? Do you think we can expect His blessings in our lives if we live like that?"

James wanted to curse at her—but only because she was right. He shook his head again and resisted the urge to act on his exasperation.

"Just . . . pray about it," she pleaded gently. "If you can look me in the eye and tell me that you know in your heart God wants us to stay in Iowa, I'll not bring it up again."

"Very well," James said with reluctance, already seeing images in his mind of moving his family to Nauvoo—and then moving them again as part of some horrible mass exodus, fleeing the persecution of evildoers who were bent on driving the Mormons relentlessly. "I need some time." He had to admit, "I'm not certain God would appreciate my coming to Him in prayer with my present attitude. But I'll work on it." He left the cabin and went to the deck to cool off and calm down, hating what seemed the inevitable course of their lives. He cursed the day his wife had found that book in the road in England and wondered why they couldn't just live as ordinary Christians like the majority of Americans.

Eleanore watched her husband leave the room, then she sat down and cried. She *did* want to live in Nauvoo, in spite of the risks and the challenges. But she certainly didn't want this discord with her husband. Still, she felt certain that once he got an answer to his prayers, he would come to terms with it and find peace.

Nothing more was said over the matter through the remainder of the journey, but a subtle tension hovered between them as they returned home. It became lost in the excitement of being reunited with the children, but descended again as everyone wanted to hear all about Nauvoo. And Eleanore couldn't help showing her enthusiasm as she answered their questions. But James remained mostly silent.

Over the next few days Eleanore felt the tension dissipate, but she wondered if he was praying about the matter or ignoring it. And for the time being she preferred not to bring it up. She put the issue to serious prayer herself, knowing that she had to know beyond any doubt in her own mind and heart that it was right. She began making plans in her head of how they would pack and what they would take with them. She imagined the kind of house they would build in the same vicinity as Sally and Miriam, and how they would all grow old there together. A week after returning from Nauvoo, Eleanore was stunned to realize that God did *not* want them leaving their home. They needed to stay right where they were, and she knew it beyond any doubt. She wept heartily when she finally accepted the answer she was being given, and it took her another day and a half to find the courage to discuss it with her husband. They were preparing for bed when she gathered the nerve to say, "About moving to Nauvoo, I—"

"Yes, we need to talk about that," he interrupted and sat on the edge of the bed. He then reached in his pocket and pulled out a small piece of paper folded in half, which he handed to her.

"What is this?" she asked as she opened it. But he didn't need to answer. She recognized it immediately. When they'd been struggling over the decision of where to settle once they'd arrived in America, they had agreed to each write down three locations in order of preference, according to their feelings. They had each written down exactly the same places in the same order with no knowledge of what the other had written. The first place on the list was Iowa City, and that's where they had gone. The other two places written there in her own hand were Illinois and Missouri. She'd not given the matter any thought since that day, but now those other two locations felt significant, and she took a sharp breath.

"I saved it," James said. "The means by which we chose a place to settle is rather amazing, don't you think?"

"Yes, it certainly is."

"Of course, at the time neither of us knew anything about where the Mormons were, or where they'd been. Now we both know they had been in Missouri, and they were settling in Illinois. It must be significant, don't you think?"

"It would seem that way," she said, feeling saddened while at the same time chilled by his point.

"You were praying to find them, weren't you?"

"Yes," she said as if she'd been caught stealing.

"We know we were meant to come here, but I look at this now and I can't help wondering if God wanted you to know that, in spite of His leading us to *this* place, He had heard your prayers." He sighed. "I believe He always hears your prayers, Eleanore, but I don't think He's hearing mine."

"What do you mean?"

"I've been praying, Eleanore, I have. But . . . maybe I need more time."

She sat beside him. "What do you mean?" she repeated.

"I'm just . . . not getting the answers, at least not the ones I think I'm supposed to get. I'm sure it's me. I admit to being stubborn over this. I'm probably just . . . not seeing what's right because I don't *want* to move, but I can't do it if I can't *know* and I . . . guess I . . . just need more time."

Eleanore became too emotional to speak. His willingness and humility, especially in contrast to the last conversation they'd had about this, were unmistakable evidence of the reasons she loved him so dearly. When he became aware of her crying, he demanded gently, "What's wrong?"

She shook her head and held up a finger to indicate that she needed a minute. He put his arms around her and she held to him tightly until she was able to say, "You *are* getting the right answer, James; at least you're getting the same one I'm getting."

He drew back to look at her, his eyes wide. "What are you saying?"

"We're not supposed to go. I know it beyond any doubt." She sniffled loudly. "It wasn't your desire to stay that got in the way of God's will for us; it was my desire to go. We need to be here. I don't know why, but we do."

James felt so relieved he wanted to cry himself. Not only was the discord gone from between them, but he also hadn't been nearly so far removed from feeling God's guidance as he'd begun to believe. And they would be allowed to stay here in this beautiful place that had become home. No, they were not with friends, but neither were they alone. And they didn't have to live in fear.

Within a few days, as the tranquility and beauty of their surroundings settled into her, Eleanore found peace with the decision to stay. This place truly felt like home, and she was grateful for the people here who *did* share her beliefs. She was not entirely alone in them as she had once been. And while she desperately longed for James to embrace them and share this aspect of her life, she could not deny his support and encouragement.

Eleanore wrote a detailed account of her visit to Nauvoo in her journal and savored the memories, holding them close to her heart. She felt grateful for the opportunity and looked forward to going back one day to visit again. Perhaps by then the temple would be completed.

Eleanore was thrilled to receive letters from both Miriam and Sally. They both wrote of how good it had been to see her and James, and how grateful they were for the visit. Miriam wrote of how she'd missed her, and how the surprise visit had felt like a gift from the Lord. Sally wrote of how good it had been to finally meet her and to put a face with her letters. Eleanore was surprised, even startled, when Sally told her that she'd donated the china to the building of the temple. Apparently that had been her intention all along. Eleanore certainly understood. She was simply left in awe of this woman's willingness to sacrifice. It occurred to Eleanore that she would like to make a donation to the temple, and she wondered why she hadn't thought of it before. Then she read on and was surprised to have Sally thank her for her generous contribution.

Eleanore found her husband pulling weeds in the garden. She stepped carefully over the rows of vegetables until she was beside him. He brushed the dirt off his hands as he stood straight to face her.

"Hello," he said and kissed her.

"I got letters from Miriam and Sally. Frederick picked up the mail when he went into town."

"And how are they?" he asked.

"Fine. They were both very grateful that I'd been able to come to Nauvoo. I'm grateful too. I wanted to thank you for that."

"For what?"

"For taking me to Nauvoo."

He smiled and put his hands on his hips. "It was nice. We'll have to go again one day; we could take the children."

"I'd like that," she said. "Sally also thanked me for my generous contribution to the building of the temple."

He looked down and cleared his throat. "I was going to tell you about that."

"How generous was it?"

He lifted his eyes. "That doesn't really matter, does it?"

"No, I suppose not. I only wish I had thought of it myself. Thank you."

He shrugged and returned to his work. "It seemed like the right thing to do."

Eleanore said nothing more. She just moved down the row and started helping him pull weeds.

Chapter Nine
SOCIAL DISTINCTION

James was sitting in the kitchen helping Iris with an arithmetic problem when Eleanore came in from her ladies club meeting, sparkling with unusual excitement. She'd been attending the regular meetings nearly as long as they'd lived in Iowa, but he'd never seen her return with so much enthusiasm.

"You must have had a good time," James commented and rose to greet her with a kiss.

"I did, yes," she answered, then kissed Iris on the cheek. "Oh, it's coming along well, I see," she added, taking a moment to inspect the child's work.

"I couldn't do it without Papa telling me every step," she said.

"You're doing just fine," he said. "We'll keep at it. But I think you've done more than enough for today. Perhaps you should go read a book or something."

"With pleasure," Iris smiled and hurried from the room.

"Well?" James said after their daughter was gone.

"Well, what?" Eleanore asked with feigned innocence.

"You can't keep secrets from me, Mrs. Barrington. What is it that you can't wait to tell me?"

"You know Mrs. King."

"I know more *of* her," he said. "You've talked of her a great deal, but I think I've only met her once."

"She's a fine lady, likely one of the finest in Iowa City. Very influential."

"Yes?" he drawled, not impressed.

"Her home is large and very elegant."

"Yes," he said again, even less impressed.

As if she sensed his attitude, Eleanore added, "Insignificant in comparison to your home in England, of course, but—"

"I have no need to compare *anything* to *our* home in England, my dear." He motioned with his hand. "Go on."

"Well, she's going to host a ball, and we're invited."

Eleanore saw her husband's brow furrow and his eyes widen, as if she'd just told him the sun might not come up tomorrow. "What?" she asked, wondering over his thoughts.

"I'm just trying to understand why you're so excited about this."

"Why are you *not*? It's a marvelous opportunity to become acquainted with some influential people in the community and—"

"Is there a reason we *need* influence in the community?"

"No, of course not, but . . ."

"But what?" he pressed when she hesitated.

"Well, surely it could be . . . fun, nice to have a reason to get dressed up and go somewhere besides church."

She saw James smile, and again she asked, "What?"

"Now, that's the honest answer; that sounds more like you." He took her hand. "If you want to get dressed up and socialize with your lady friends, I would be more than happy to accompany you."

"I wasn't worried that you wouldn't."

"Weren't you?"

"No. You're generally rather agreeable."

"Generally," he echoed with only a slight tinge of sarcasm.

Eleanore's excitement continued throughout the remainder of the day; however, when James went to the bedroom to change for bed, he found her sitting at her dressing table, staring at the floor with a scowl on her face.

"Where's your happiness gone to?" he asked, pulling off his boots. She sighed loudly, and her expression faltered further. "It must be serious," he said.

She sighed again. "I really have nothing to wear to a ball that would be suitable."

James laughed. It was nice to have her worry about something so trivial, especially in contrast to the loss of her babies. His first wife had *never* worried about anything *but* trivialities; for Eleanore, it was a refreshing contrast.

"We can have something made, my dear," he said. "I assure you we can afford it."

Eleanore wanted to ask questions, but they would all bring more attention to her own naiveté over such matters. Was there time to have a dress made? Would the dressmaker be able to do something that wouldn't look like what all the other ladies would be wearing? Was it really worth the trouble for a dress she would likely only wear once? And how would she possibly know where to begin to choose what was suitable for such an occasion? "Yes, I suppose we could," she said, "but . . ." She honestly couldn't think of a way to finish the sentence that didn't sound silly.

"However . . ." James rose and opened the wardrobe, as if something might magically appear. He rummaged through her dresses to reach into the back. And something *did* magically appear. There in his hands was an exquisite gown made of rich purple taffeta. She'd completely forgotten about its existence. When she'd officially become engaged to the lord of the manor, he'd purchased her an entirely new wardrobe, most of which had been practical and appropriate for traveling to America and the simple life they'd be embarking on. But an evening gown had been included. At the time she recalled thinking that it would never get used. But the dressmaker had insisted that it was necessary, and that Mr. Barrington had requested she have something suitable for an evening occasion.

"Oh, my," she said as he urged her to stand up and face the mirror, holding the gown in front of her. "It's beautiful," she had to admit.

"Once Lizzie airs it out and presses it, you'll look stunning in it."

"I don't know about that . . . but it *is* a beautiful gown. Why *did* you insist on my getting this? There was never any occasion to wear it."

"There's an occasion to wear it *now*."

"Oh," she laughed softly, "so you foresaw Mrs. King's social and thought I should be prepared?"

He laughed with her. "Truthfully, at the time I'd been thinking we might have an engagement party or something, or there was the possibility that we might have been invited to something social prior to our leaving England. But it didn't happen. There wasn't time for parties, what with planning the wedding and preparing to come to America."

"Just as well. I would have been scared senseless over such an event. I barely survived the wedding." Her own comment brought to mind her other source of concern over this event. Holding the gown against her she turned to face him and said, "Maybe this isn't a good idea. I'm not certain I'll know what to do, or if I'm even capable of socializing this way without standing out like a sore thumb, or—"

"Nonsense. I have proof that you are perfectly capable of being a complete lady in any situation."

"Proof?"

"I've lived every day with you for years now, and—"

"That is hardly any indication of—"

"It *is!* You are a lady in every respect."

"Not in England, I wasn't. I was a servant in your household. Or have you forgotten?"

"Yes, I *had* forgotten, actually. Such social distinctions were left behind with our old life. This is America."

"And clearly social distinctions still exist."

"Yes, but they're different. You don't need to have a title or wealth to be respected."

"Not a title, perhaps. But surely wealth and profession still create social distinctions."

"Of course they do; that's simply the way of the world. *However,* Mrs. King would not have invited you based on any such thing."

"How do you know?" Eleanore saw his eyes turn skeptical.

"What *does* Mrs. King know about us?" he asked, his voice bordering on angry.

"Practically nothing," she insisted. "She's asked questions about our background, our life in England. And I have graciously skirted around them. I told her you owned some land that you had managed, and you sold it for an excellent profit, which makes it possible for you to be a gentleman farmer."

He snorted a laugh. "Gentleman gardener, more like."

"It doesn't matter."

"No, it doesn't. We'll go to the ball and have a marvelous time. It will be nice to get out and do something different."

"Yes, it will," Eleanore agreed, turning again to admire the dress in the mirror.

"And you will be exquisite," he added and put his hands to her shoulders, meeting her eyes in the reflection. "I well remember our wedding day. No lady or duchess would be any more refined than you were that day. There is no reason for concern. And this is not about impressing anyone, Eleanore. If I believed it was, I'm not certain I'd go. We'll go to meet people and have a good time."

"I wish Miriam and Andy were here to go."

"Yes, that would be nice," James said, knowing Miriam had also attended the ladies club meetings. But he wondered if Mrs. King would have invited them. Andy and Miriam were simple farm people with hardly a dollar to spare. James had never spoken more than a hello to Mrs. King, and he reminded himself not to judge. Perhaps he was cynical about the kind of people who hosted these things. Were the Kings people who would simply throw a party and invite anyone, no matter what they could afford to wear or what their professions were? Or had she invited Eleanore because she knew there was money in the family? And if Mrs. King were sharp, she might have deduced from Eleanore's cryptic information that his being a landowner in England might have broader implications. He told himself to stop being paranoid and think of it exactly as he'd just told Eleanore. They would go and have a good time. Simple as that.

When the evening came to go to the Kings' ball, Eleanore was full of flustered excitement while Lizzie put the finishing touches on her hair. James stood in front of the mirror, tying a cravat he'd not worn since he'd left England. In fact everything he was wearing hadn't seen the light of day since they'd come to America. He felt as if a different man were looking back at him; a man who was remotely familiar, but not necessarily someone James wanted to see again. He'd put that life behind him, and he'd been glad to do it. He reminded himself that he was doing this for Eleanore. If only to prove to her that she was indeed a lady, he would see this through. But he could already feel himself bristling with cynicism. He couldn't count how many such socials he'd attended in his life, and he couldn't think of a single one that he'd actually enjoyed.

James was grateful for the distraction of seeing how utterly beautiful and happy his wife looked once she was ready to go. She'd not had her hair done up so intricately since their wedding day, and she positively glowed in the purple gown, which was far more feminine than the simple frocks she wore to go about her everyday life. He wondered for a moment what it might have been like if they'd stayed in England. He felt sure that some people would have quickly forgotten that she'd ever been a servant girl. She would have melted hearts and proven her own refinement. But he knew there were other people who would have *never* forgotten. And he was grateful she didn't have to be subjected to such disdain.

Eleanore felt decidedly nervous during the drive into town. Arriving at the Kings' home, all lit up for the festivities, her nerves increased. "It's just a party," James said, taking her gloved hand into his as they approached the door. "Think of all that dancing we've done in the kitchen this past week. It will be fun."

"I'm sure you're right," she said. "Although . . . dancing with you in the kitchen might be more fun. We shouldn't stop doing it just because this night is over."

"What a pleasant thought," he said and caught a smile that indicated her nerves had been soothed somewhat.

James observed his wife as they milled into the crowd and she introduced him to her friends, and they both met the ladies' husbands. She was clearly amazed and overcome by the lavishness of such a gathering. Her nervousness quickly subsided, however, and she seemed to be genuinely enjoying herself. They chatted and danced and enjoyed hors d'oeuvres while they avoided the champagne and drank the punch instead. While Eleanore relaxed and managed to fit in even better than he'd anticipated, James felt prickly and out of sorts. He overheard snatches of conversation that clearly indicated the attitudes of the people in attendance, and memories came rushing over him. The loud chattering combined with the stuffiness of the little ballroom, and the smell of sweat mixed with that of expensive perfume. It all came back to him, and he hated it. He fought to keep a smile on his face, and he engaged in appropriate conversation with arrogant businessmen and landowners, while Eleanore flitted around like a butterfly just emerged from her cocoon. He felt a little afraid that she would become addicted to such social events and want to be a part of them, the way Caroline had. She'd thrived on such gatherings and the attention she would get from both men and women alike. He told himself that Eleanore had nothing in common with his first wife, and even if she were going through a phase, he doubted it would last long.

James was more grateful to finally leave than he could ever express. The fresh air felt especially invigorating; he could breathe again. While he drove the buggy toward home, Eleanore sputtered with excitement over the evening and how wonderful everything had been. He just listened until she said, "You're not saying much."

"What do you want me to say?"

"Well . . . did you have a good time?"

"I had a good time watching you in that dress," he said with a smile.

"And that's it?"

He had to be honest. "That's it."

"Didn't you find anyone to talk to that you . . . well . . . did you have no stimulating conversation?"

"No, not really." She looked astonished, and he added, "Eleanore, this kind of thing is old for me. Different country, different society, same attitudes and conversations."

"I see," she said, looking away.

"Now, don't go all sullen on me. This is new for you, and you have a right to enjoy it. And I'm willing to come along once in a while to such events if that makes you happy. But I have to be honest. It's not really for me."

"So, if you go again it would be simply to do me a favor."

"Is there something wrong with a man making a compromise on behalf of his wife?"

"No, of course not," she said, "but . . . I'd simply hoped that you would meet someone that . . . well, perhaps you could find some new friends or—"

"My life is full, Eleanore. It's not lacking in any respect, I can assure you."

"But in England . . . you used to go to a gentleman's club; I know you did."

"Rarely, if you must know. I more often used the excuse of going to the gentleman's club in order to go riding or walking without being regarded as some kind of reclusive hermit by my household."

"I see," she said again.

"Did *you* have a good time?" he asked. "Now, be honest."

"I did, yes."

"That's good, then. I'm glad. Perhaps you should order a new dress to have on hand the next time something like this comes up."

Eleanore was quiet the rest of the way home until James started talking about what a beautiful night it was; then they shared conversation that was more typical of their relationship. She *did* order a new dress a few days later, and the very next week they attended a similar social at someone else's home. After five in less than a month, James felt compelled to say, "I know you enjoy this, my dear, but could we perhaps compromise and keep it to one or two events a month?"

"You really don't like going, do you?"

"No, I don't."

"Why?" she asked with an unnatural exasperation. "I don't understand."

"It's hollow, Eleanore. It's like biting into a piece of fruit that looks perfect on the outside, but once you get past the peel, it's barely this side of rotten and completely without flavor."

"That's a horrible metaphor for people I've grown to like."

"I'm sorry. That's how I see it. I think you're caught up in something because it's new and unique. I think it will lose its appeal, because it doesn't really seem like the woman I know would truly care about such things as climbing a social ladder."

"That's not what I'm doing!" She sounded downright defensive.

"It most certainly is," he countered, adding a chuckle in an attempt to keep the conversation light. "You feel included in a world that was beyond your reach in England. And it feels good; admit it."

"So, what if that *is* the case? Is there something wrong with that?"

"No, nothing at all—as long as it doesn't become excessive and you don't lose perspective." He took her hand. "I don't want you to get hurt. I'm not saying there aren't some kindhearted people there, Eleanore. But there is a certain type of people drawn to this kind of thing; it's all very garish and phony. And I've heard way too much there to indicate that there's also a lot of selfishness and backbiting. And even some bigotry." She looked astonished, and he added, "I can't see you getting too chummy with such attitudes."

"I've heard no such thing."

"Well then . . . it seems you're associating with the right people; either that or they're very good at keeping their unfavorable opinions to themselves."

"I've never known you to be so cynical."

"Realistic, Eleanore. I know this world."

"That was England."

"Same world. True, it's America. It's wonderful that your having once been a servant does not exclude you from their social circles, but you're still there because you have money."

"How so?"

"Did you see anyone there who couldn't afford to be wearing the latest fashion?"

She couldn't answer that.

"Don't worry about it. Just go and enjoy yourself. I simply . . . would prefer to attend less often."

Eleanore thought about that and couldn't deny that he was being more than fair. "Very well," she said. "I suppose twice a month is plenty."

"Indeed. Thank you."

"Maybe," he said a few minutes later, hoping he wouldn't regret it, "you like having a social group to be involved with because you can't be among the Mormons." She scowled at him but said nothing.

They didn't attend any social gathering for nearly three weeks. Eleanore turned down a couple of invitations and James made a point of taking her out of the house a couple of times to make up for it. He took her on an evening picnic. And another evening after supper, he took her into the library and read to her from her favorite novel, the type of book that he generally avoided. For that reason she was especially delighted by the activity.

As they arrived together at another social event, in a home that was larger and more elaborate than any they'd been in so far, James prayed that Eleanore's eyes would be opened to the shallow nature of what they were doing. He pondered his reasons and couldn't deny that he preferred not to have to attend these tedious functions. But he also had to admit that he was genuinely concerned for her. She had a tender heart—and a good one. But she wasn't afraid to speak her mind. He feared that she might end up getting hurt by women who were taking her under their wings so long as she agreed with everything they said. Maybe he *was* cynical. Maybe there were women surrounding her who had good hearts in spite of their social shallowness. He hoped so.

This particular event included dinner with ten other couples who were all seated at a ridiculously long table set with excessive lavishness. Eleanore leaned over to James and whispered facetiously, "The table in your home in England was at least this long; I know because I polished it once a month." He frowned at her, not appreciating either comment.

Gathered together as they were, it was impossible to mill around and avoid certain topics of conversation, or certain people. They were stuck at the table and forced to endure it all. James found his mind wandering with fantasies of reasons they would have to leave early. Perhaps Eleanore might feel suddenly ill, nauseous and dizzy perhaps—due to pregnancy. That would be nice. And perhaps if she were pregnant and not feeling well, she wouldn't be up to attending such ridiculous events, and life could get back to normal.

James felt more uneasy than usual as the conversation turned to slave trade, which was especially common in the southern states. He'd been as appalled to learn that Americans kept slaves as he'd been to realize that it was legal to kill Mormons. But he kept his opinions to himself, longing to just walk under the stars with his wife, or read by the fire with his children. He tried to block out the conversation while the issue of slavery was discussed as if people of color had been born for the purpose of being purchased and used like animals. And apparently animals were treated better. James forced his mind to wander, wondering if his wife was hearing the underlying messages of bigotry and ignorance among these people. And then he heard his name.

"I'm sorry, pardon me?" he said. "I'm afraid my mind was wandering."

"I simply asked," a balding man said, with a name James couldn't recall, "about England's stand on the matter. I understand they did away with slavery quite some time ago."

"They did indeed," James said and felt Eleanore squeeze his hand tightly beneath the table, as if to warn him against saying anything that might threaten their social position among these people.

"That certainly must have been difficult on the economy," someone else said, and James bristled.

He took turns looking into the eyes of every man at the table as he said, "Slave trade was abolished throughout the British Empire many years ago, due to its gross inhumanity and the unspeakable suffering inflicted upon our fellow human beings." He heard subtle gasps, saw eyes go wide. But he couldn't deny enjoying this moment. "I must say I was surprised upon our moving here to learn that a country that fought so hard to gain its independence from the crown would condone such an atrocity as this." The gasps became louder, and Eleanore squeezed tighter; her expression became alarmed. "If we are one nation under God, then surely God would want us to acknowledge, as it says in the Bible, that all men are created in His image." James chuckled comfortably. "I was sure I'd heard that the freedom of this country was based on the concept that . . . all men are created equal." He chuckled again. "Perhaps I misunderstood." He raised his glass toward the hostess and added, "A lovely meal. I've never tasted pork so sweet and tender."

Eleanore felt horrified by the silence that followed her husband's declaration. While she completely agreed with him, she felt sure it would have been more appropriate to simply answer the question he'd been asked and keep his opinions to himself. She was prepared for them to be thrown out and never invited again. But the conversation moved awkwardly into the best places to travel abroad these days, and then more smoothly into the fluctuating prices of imported goods from Europe and the Indies. And somehow that merged into matters of religion. Some friendly banter broke out over the fact that three different denominations were represented at the table, including the one that James and Eleanore attended on Sundays for the sake of keeping up proper appearances. But there seemed a healthy respect among them with the common belief that they were all Christians and proud of it. One man praised the opportunity to have diversity in religion, then another said that it was going too far, that anyone could start a church these days, and religion could turn into a cult while people were oblivious to evil happenings right in their midst.

"Like what?" a woman asked as if she couldn't comprehend any such thing.

"Like the Mormons, for instance," a man said.

More gasps. "Surely we don't have *Mormons* among us," another said as if it were leprosy.

Again Eleanore squeezed her husband's hand, even more tightly, while she fought to keep a straight face. He leaned over and whispered, "Laugh quietly as if I've just whispered something alluring and we are completely oblivious to the conversation." She hesitated and he added, "Go on, do it." He did just such a laugh as an example, and she followed his lead, grateful for his insight and strength. She noticed a few glances their direction, some subtle implication that they were being rude, while others just pressed forward with the topic as Eleanore's heart threatened to pound out of her chest.

"I'm afraid we do," Mrs. King's husband said. "Or at least there have been. From what I hear they've all been driven out, and we're the better for it."

"Very good," James whispered over the top of the conversation. "Now pretend perfect indifference. We've never heard of Mormons, and we don't care. Do you understand?"

She nodded, then met his eyes and smiled as if he'd just reminded her of their first kiss. He drew her hand to his lips, then played with her fingers as if his mind were only on her, and it kept her distracted as well. Eleanore could imagine the others in the room being disgusted by the way they were behaving like newlyweds. But she felt so terrified of being discovered that she didn't care. She could only be grateful for her husband's clever tactics of diversion while conversation whirled around her concerning the heretic beliefs of the Mormons and their cultish ways. They spoke of Mormons in the same way they'd spoken of slaves, as if these people at the table were somehow superior and entitled to abuse and demean other human beings for differences in religion or the color of their skin. Eleanore felt herself drowning in some kind of evil whirlpool, while memories of James's description of these social circles came back to her. *It's hollow . . . barely this side of rotten and completely without flavor.* How could she have been so stupid? How could she have not sensed the underlying shallow nature of these people? Now she felt trapped. She wanted to get up and rush out of the house, knowing her husband would follow. But to do so in the middle of a conversation about Mormons would surely invite suspicion. So she swallowed carefully and focused on her husband's playing with her fingers while she listened with pretended indifference to the ignorant beliefs of people who despised Mormons and everything they stood for, having no idea what they were talking about. The conversation finally flowed into something else, which happened to be the quality of liquor according to age and origin. Eleanore was appalled to hear how much these men spent on a bottle of drink, then they laughed and one of them compared it to the amount of money they spent on their wives' clothes and jewels and "these ridiculous parties." And he was right. It *was* ridiculous. And Eleanore told her husband so on the way home, once they'd been able to graciously escape. She cried and apologized for being so blind and told him she never wanted to go back. He just kept his arm around her and dried her tears, and not once did he even imply that he'd told her so.

In the days following Eleanore's cruel lesson on the shallow nature of society, the only real good she could find out of the experience was a deeper appreciation for all she had in her life that was not shallow at all. She sent a note to Mrs. King saying that she would no longer be attending her ladies club, and that she and her husband would prefer not to be invited to any more social events. In the note she wrote that they simply could not tolerate such bigoted views on slavery and other such issues that placed some human beings above others. James smiled when she showed it to him, then she sent it off, knowing their social standing in this city had just been slaughtered. But she felt rather pleased at the thought.

Chapter Ten
GOING BACK

James went into town to do some errands, stopping last at the post office. He returned to the wagon while he absently sorted through the small stack of mail until a letter appeared that quickened his heart. A closer examination showed that it had come from England. He'd received only a few pieces of mail since he'd written to notify a couple of people of where they had settled, just to let them know all was well. One had been his solicitor, the man who had handled all of his business and legal matters, and the other had been Mrs. Bixby, the head house-keeper of the estate he'd sold and left behind. This letter was from her. James opened it, expecting some friendly correspon-dence and perhaps trivial details of the life and people he knew there. Instead he found a disconcerting report of the difficult situation that she and the rest of the household were now in as a result of the indiscretions of their employer, the new owner of the estate. James felt literally ill as he considered what he was reading. He knew Mrs. Bixby to be a woman of strong integrity, and also one who was not a complainer. She surely wouldn't have taken the trouble to write such a letter if the situation were not dire. Once James recovered from the shock of such a report, he felt decidedly angry. The man who had purchased the estate had wholeheartedly agreed to treat the remaining staff with kindness and respect, and to continue with the policies and salaries that had been in place. In fact, the matter had been included in the contract. But clearly he was not adhering to his end of the agreement. Mrs. Bixby apologized in her letter for bothering him with this matter, and simply asked that he might write to the solicitor, or perhaps anyone else he might know of who could have some influence over the situation. She had attempted to appeal to the solicitor herself without success, for reasons she did not specify.

James felt sick and angry and confused as he drove home. He couldn't believe it! All this time he had imagined that life in his previous home was going on as it always had. He'd thought of those who had worked for him with pleasant musings over what might be going on in their lives. And now his tender thoughts had been shattered with news that people he had felt responsible for were being ill treated as a result of his selling his estate and leaving. And to make the matter worse, he knew it had taken Mrs. Bixby's letter a couple of months to arrive, and it would take the same for any letter from him to return to England. He wondered how long the problem had existed before she'd finally reached the point of writing to him. He wondered why his solicitor would not have done something to remedy the problem, when he had given his word to make certain James's affairs were well represented in his absence. James had worked with the man for many years and trusted him completely. Only something seriously wrong in his life could prevent him from taking steps to correct such a problem. Beyond his solicitor, James honestly couldn't think of a single person he might trust to follow through on this situation and take some appropriate and ethical action.

By the time James arrived at home, he had thought the matter through so intensely that his head hurt. No solution seemed feasible. He felt helpless and even more angry. And frustrated beyond words.

The moment he entered the kitchen, and before any other greetings were exchanged, Eleanore asked, "What's wrong?"

Amanda focused on the dough she was kneading, as if she were deaf and blind to the problem, determined to remain discreet and stay out of it. James said nothing. Eleanore set down the knife she was using to cut potatoes and wiped her hands on her apron as she moved toward him. James just motioned her out of the room, and she followed until they were in the office with the door closed.

"What is it?" she asked. He just handed her the letter. Eleanore's heart thudded as she stared at him, then at the letter, then at him again before she took it as if it might burn her hand. She sat down near the window where the sunlight made it easier to see, and she suppressed an involuntary shiver when she saw whom the letter was from.

James watched Eleanore's brow furrow as she began to read, then her hand went absently to her heart. She lifted her eyes to look at him, as if he might tell her this was some kind of joke. When he only returned a level gaze, tears welled in her eyes. She dabbed at them with the handkerchief he handed to her, then she continued to read.

"But what can possibly be done?" Eleanore asked when she'd finished reading Mrs. Bixby's words.

"I don't know," James admitted. "I simply . . . don't know what to do."

She listened patiently while he recounted every idea he'd thought through during his ride home from town. She matter-of-factly stated what he hardly dared put to words. "You must go back. As I see it, there's no other option."

"Go back?" he echoed, unwilling to admit he'd already thought of it but didn't want to face it. "How can I?"

"How can you not?" Eleanore countered. "What if *I* were still working there?"

Her question struck deeply. Through her he had come to see the other side of life in the manor house, and he'd gained a strong perspective of the challenges of servitude. He felt responsible for these people, and for good reason. She was right. He couldn't leave their care to chance, and he couldn't wait for months to have his letters received and answered and sent again.

"You must come with me," he said, while visions of contending with the enormity of the ramifications stormed through his head. "I can't do this alone."

"Very well," she said without batting an eye, and he wondered how she could be so courageous when thoughts of the journey alone made him cringe. "And the children?"

"They would be better off here, don't you think? The trip will be long, arduous, and boring. We must travel as quickly as we can."

"Of course," she said. "Shouldn't we pray about it?"

"I don't need to," he said, quickly reaffirming the peace he felt concerning the matter. "I already know it's right."

"As do I," she said and left the room, heading for the stairs.

"Where are you going?"

"We need to speak with the household, tell the children. We must pack. We should leave right away."

"We'll need to take some of our best clothes," James said, following her.

"Why?" Eleanore asked and stopped walking, alarmed.

He answered frankly and without apology. "The people I must contend with need to face a man who has the necessary power and influence to put the matter in order. If I show up looking like a farmer, I'll never be able to do what needs to be done."

Eleanore understood the principle, but she didn't want to admit he was right. In fact, she didn't want to talk about it at all. She'd grown comfortable with her husband, the farmer. She'd been relieved to leave the lord of the manor behind in England and really had no desire to face that part of their lives again. So she said nothing and simply dug out some of her finest clothes, hoping they would be adequate.

Saying goodbye to the children was more difficult than Eleanore had anticipated, made worse by James's obvious hesitancy to leave them. Frederick and Lizzie assured them all repeatedly that everything would be fine, and Eleanore reminded James in the hired carriage that no one would take better care of their children than these dear friends who were like family.

By the time they arrived on the east coast, they were both thoroughly exhausted, having slept very little and poorly with the rationalization that they could rest once they were aboard a ship that would take them to England. As James took Eleanore's hand to escort her aboard, he felt her resist and turned to her, his eyes questioning her silently. The fear in her eyes took him off guard.

"What is it?" he asked.

"I don't know," she admitted. "I just . . . I suppose that . . . I don't know." She looked over her shoulder at the bustle of activity on the pier, then up at the sails lying stagnant against the masts of the ship. "This is our home now. I suddenly feel . . . afraid . . . to leave it behind. I don't know why."

James sighed and took her shoulders, looking squarely into her eyes. "You told me you absolutely know that taking this journey is right for us, for both of us. Our children are in good hands. We must trust that all will be well."

Eleanore took in his words and nodded firmly. "Of course. I'm just being silly. It's just that . . . so much has happened since we left England, and I . . ."

"What you're suffering from is mostly nostalgia, my dear," he said, taking her arm to guide her aboard. "We'll talk later. I'm certain you'll feel better once we set sail and you get some sleep."

Eleanore *did* feel better once she was rested. And devoting some serious time to prayer helped as well. However, she found it difficult to relax, considering how long the journey would take and how impatient James was to get there and solve the problems. Once they arrived in England, Eleanore knew the time it would take them to travel from Liverpool to the manor house would be minuscule in contrast to how long it had taken them to get from Iowa to the ocean.

* * *

Apart from the low roar of carriage wheels that synchronized with galloping horses' hooves, silence reigned for many miles. Eleanore finally mustered the will to ask her most pressing question. "So . . . what exactly are we to do once we get there? Do we just . . . knock at the front door and demand to speak with the lord of the manor so that you can argue with him—threaten him perhaps?" James glared at her, and she added, "Have you thought this through, James?"

"I've thought it through until I want to scream. But . . . no, I really don't know what to do when we get there." He glanced at her more humbly. "I'm open to suggestions, Mrs. Barrington."

"Well, I do have *one* thought. Perhaps my personal expertise could help." He looked confused but intrigued. She laughed softly and proceeded to tell him about Nephi in the Book of Mormon, and how he went into a difficult situation, not knowing what he would do, but trusting in the Spirit to guide him. She was pleased with her husband's reception of the idea, even though he didn't say much as the carriage took them closer to the place they had once called home.

They stayed that night at the same inn where they'd come with the children on their journey to America years earlier. James sent word to his solicitor's office immediately, with careful instructions to the courier that if the man who had once represented him was not available, he needed an immediate response from someone else capable of helping him with the situation. In the message, James included a generous offer to more than adequately pay for the services of a qualified professional.

That night Eleanore drifted in and out of sleep, while memories mingled with dreams and her concerns for what might lay ahead. She felt as if she were a completely different woman from the one who had left here as a new bride to James Barrington, and she felt unnerved to think of once again facing the life she'd lived here. Along with her own restlessness, Eleanore was keenly aware that her husband was also having difficulty sleeping. Finally she whispered in the darkness, "Are you thinking what I'm thinking?"

"And what might that be?" he asked, turning toward her.

"That we're different people now, going back to a place that could never be the same as the life we knew there, in spite of how much a part of our lives it was . . . for so long."

She heard him exhale slowly. "You do have a way of putting my feelings into words, my dear."

"So, you *are* thinking what I'm thinking?"

"I must be."

"Still," she said, "I was only a servant there. It was *your* home, your *family* home. You spent forty years there. I only lived there for about ten."

James wrapped his arms around her. "Still, it was as much home to you as it was to me, and I fear what we will find. I think I would prefer to keep my pleasant memories intact."

"I agree," she said, lapsing into contemplative silence.

"I miss the children," he said.

"So do I." She wiped at the corners of her eyes, surprised at how quickly tears surfaced simply to hear them mentioned. "I'm sure they are well," she added, trying to sound positive.

"I'm sure they are," he agreed, and nothing more was said before they both rose at dawn to face the difficulty before them.

While they were eating breakfast in the dining room of the inn, James was handed a message. He opened it anxiously, relieved to have gotten *some* kind of response from the solicitors' office. He scanned the written words, then reported to Eleanore,

"My solicitor has been very ill. He's doing better, but has gotten severely behind on his work. His partner, a Mr. Earl, is willing to meet me this afternoon." He looked up from the letter to say, "He says they've worked together for nearly twenty years; that alone tells me I can trust him. I do recall meeting Mr. Earl more than once. I'm certain he will serve us well. He also writes that he's notified the owner of the estate that he'll be coming to visit, with no mention of me or his purpose, and the owner has agreed to be there."

"Then there's nothing to worry about," Eleanore said tonelessly, but James's lack of comment left no doubt that he shared her skepticism.

Before leaving their room at the inn, Eleanore suggested they kneel and pray together. As they came to their feet, James felt surprisingly calm. He knew everything would be all right, and as the thought passed through his mind that solving this problem would be easy, he also felt keenly that it was not the most important reason they had come back to England. James kept this thought to himself and focused on the day ahead.

Riding in the carriage, Eleanore had expected to feel a certain nostalgia when the scenery became familiar. But looking out the window onto a view that had once been such an integral part of her life left her also feeling eery and lost somehow—chilled yet warm at the same time. The moors and hills had kept her company through much of her youth. She felt as if she were seeing an old friend, but now the friendship felt all wrong. The home she'd left behind in Iowa was now the only home she knew. She felt the moisture of tears on her face, and then her husband's fingers as he wiped them away.

"This will all be over quickly," he said, "and then we'll be on our way home."

"It all feels so strange," she said, still gazing out the carriage window.

"Yes, it does," he agreed, looking in the same direction.

"Do you ever wish you could come back?" she asked.

"No," he said without hesitation.

"Not even seeing how beautiful it is here and—"

"It's beautiful in Iowa, and that's our home now. This doesn't feel like home anymore, Eleanore."

"I'm glad to hear you feel the same as I do. Otherwise, we could have a challenge on our hands."

"So, you don't regret going to America?" he asked.

"Never!" she said, and he kissed her.

* * *

Eleanore left James to wait at the front door for Mr. Earl to arrive for their meeting. She went instead to the entrance near the kitchens where she had gone in and out hundreds of times in her life. She almost felt moved to tears as she entered the kitchen, and time stood still for a moment. There stood Miss Gibbs and Mrs. Bixby chattering near the stove while the former nonchalantly stirred something that simmered in a large pot.

"It's as if I've never been away," she said, and they both turned at once, astonished. Mrs. Bixby put her hands to her face and gasped. Miss Gibbs squealed and rushed toward Eleanore, wrapping her in a familiar embrace.

"Oh, my dear!" she said, taking Eleanore's face into her hands. "Look at you. You've become a real lady."

"Just older," Eleanore said and turned to embrace Mrs. Bixby.

"And all the more lovely," the housekeeper said. "But what are you doing here?"

"We've come in response to your letter," Eleanore said, and both women became speechless with tears for a long moment. "Come," she said, guiding them to sit at the table, "you must tell me all about it."

They repeated details of the atrocious behavior of their employer, who seemed to gain some distorted pleasure out of making ridiculous demands. The list of problems he'd caused was abhorrently long, and Eleanore's heart ached for these people she had once worked with.

Mrs. Bixby finally said, "Enough of that. You must tell us all about what you've been doing. What's America like? How are the children? Is Mr. Barrington—"

"One question at a time," Eleanore laughed. "Mr. Barrington is fine. He's meeting with your employer this very minute here in the house." The two women exchanged surprised glances and smiled. Eleanore went on. "The children are growing and loving their new home. It's beautiful there; different from here, but beautiful just the same." She went on to describe their home and the land around it, and gave a brief account of their journey to get there. They each got tears in their eyes when she told them of the babies she'd lost, but they also shared her joy as she related how very happy she was, and how much she had grown to love her husband.

"He's a good man," Mrs. Bixby said, dabbing at her eyes. "We've missed him almost as much as we've missed you. But it seems you made the right decision in going."

"Oh, yes," Eleanore said, "and I finally found what I'd been searching for."

They both looked baffled, bringing Eleanore to the realization that she'd never told them what she'd been looking for. She had kept her passion for the Book of Mormon completely to herself while she had lived in this house. She'd not even shared her feelings with James until after they were married. And now the words had practically stumbled out of her mouth, and she didn't know what to do with them. She quickly realized that she need not fear for her safety in telling anyone here about her religious beliefs. And since she was only staying for a short while, she certainly had no concern over disdain from the local clergy or anyone else regarding her beliefs.

"And what was that, dear?" Mrs. Bixby asked.

Eleanore pondered only for a moment how to answer the question. She said it firmly and with confidence. "I found the religion I was looking for. I know even more now than I did before I left here that it's true. Next to marrying James Barrington, it's the best thing that's ever happened to me."

Eleanore took in the silent response. Mrs. Bixby looked concerned to the point of being uncomfortable. She could well imagine the housekeeper considering ways to remind Eleanore that she should not question the religious beliefs she had been raised with. And she likely hoped to put Eleanore in her place if only for the sake of saving her soul. Miss Gibbs, on the other hand, had a sparkle of intrigue in her eyes that quickened Eleanore's heart. She was ready to start spouting off information in answer to this silent eagerness, but Mrs. Bixby abruptly changed the subject by asking more questions about Eleanore's new life. She commented more than once how much she admired Mr. Barrington, and how thrilling it was to see Eleanore so happy.

They chatted of trivial things for a few more minutes before other servants began filtering into the kitchen. Lunchtime was approaching, and the kitchens quickly became crowded and noisy. There were several people that Eleanore knew, and they exchanged kind greetings. Mrs. Bixby was called away, and Miss Gibbs had to get busy putting the meal on. Eleanore helped her for a short while, expecting James to find her at any minute. When he didn't, she began to feel restless and concerned about what might be going on. She told Miss Gibbs she was going out for a walk, just in case Mr. Barrington should come looking for her.

Beneath clouded skies, Eleanore wandered the familiar landscape that had once been home to her. She couldn't deny the beauty of her surroundings, so different from Iowa. But she missed her prairie home and ached to go back. Thoughts of the weeks of travel that would be required just to get there dampened her mood further.

Eleanore was surprised to come over a hill and see the local church in the distance. Apparently she'd lost her bearings, because she'd thought she was going in the opposite direction. But now that it was in front of her, she couldn't resist going there. While the distance between her and the steepled structure lessened, Eleanore's mind wandered through vast corridors of memories of this place. She'd attended services here every Sunday for many years, and had often felt frustrated with aspects of the sermons that hadn't made sense to her. She could see now that a seed of unrest had been planted in her spirit to guide her to the truth. And she was grateful to have found it.

Stepping inside the building, the memories became more tangible. She was glad to find no one else there, and she slipped onto a bench about halfway up the aisle, just to soak in the nostalgia. Then a memory caught her off guard, first making her gasp, then laugh. How could she have forgotten? This was where she and James had been married. She closed her eyes and pulled the memories closer, recalling well that she'd been far too nervous to fully appreciate what a profound and beautiful event it had been. She recalled the dress and veil James had bought for her, the finest to be had in the county. She'd felt like a queen, adorned in satin and lace that were delicately spattered with pearl beads and glistening sequins.

* * *

"You wook so pwitty," Iris said just before Eleanore scooted her through the doors to walk up the aisle ahead of her. Eleanore could hear her little voice so clearly, mingled with the organ music filling the church, and she could recall the sweet fragrance of the flowers she was holding as she moved slowly up the aisle herself. She recalled the way her heart had pounded when the image of James Barrington waiting with the vicar had brought home to her the reality that this was really happening. She was a servant girl about to be married to

the most powerful man she had ever known in the narrow realms of her life. Through the sheer netting that veiled her face she could see him watching her, and she wondered what might be going through his mind. He didn't look even slightly nervous, as if this were nothing out of the ordinary. And he looked terribly handsome in an elegant brocade coat. A month prior she'd never given a thought to him beyond his being her employer. Now she was about to become his wife. She wondered if this marriage of convenience would ever grow into anything beyond convenient. She wondered if his kind affection toward her during their brief courtship would continue once they were married, or wane entirely and become lost in the trivialities of everyday life. In her heart she knew this was the right course for her to take. If not for that conviction, she likely would have turned and run away. Eleanore felt as if she were dreaming and any moment she would wake up gasping, certain that James Barrington could not be marrying her, of all people. But she didn't wake up, and his hand slipping into hers was far too real to be imagined. She handed the flowers to Iris, who held them with visible pride in being part of this event. Eleanore glanced at David, who was holding the rings, and he looked equally proud. A gentle, reassuring squeeze from the groom brought Eleanore fully to the moment. And then the vicar was speaking. The words felt lost on her clouded brain, while the seriousness of their meaning sank deep into her heart. She was relieved to hear conviction in the groom's voice when he spoke his vows, and equally relieved to be able to speak her own vows with the same confidence. A quickening of her heart caught her off guard when they were pronounced man and wife, until death. And she could hardly breathe when James Barrington lifted the veil from her face. She felt warmed by the faint smile that touched his lips, and the tender sincerity in his eyes just before he closed them and bent to kiss her. Eleanore had never been kissed before, and it was far too brief to either anticipate or savor before it was done. He smiled again, the warmth in his eyes growing deeper, giving her an obscure kind of comfort. He took both her hands into his and lifted them to his lips in a gesture of overt devotion.

* * *

Eleanore's memories became so clear that she could almost see another version of herself standing at the front of the church, exchanging vows and a kiss with James Barrington. She felt a deeper appreciation for how wondrous that day had been. At the time, she'd been able to acknowledge that the wedding was beautiful; everything had been perfect. But she had taken those steps down the aisle mostly on faith, trusting that the man she was marrying would be a good husband, and believing that God would not have her do this if it weren't right. In her abstract visions of going with this man and his children to America, she never could have comprehended what the journey would entail, and how quickly she would grow to love him. Her baptism aside, James Barrington was the best thing that had ever happened to her, and she knew beyond any doubt that God had brought them together.

Eleanore heard the door open behind her, and she sighed. She was enjoying her solitary nostalgia and preferred to have the church to herself. She remained as she was, hoping to be ignored, surprised to hear a familiar voice say, "I've been scouring the countryside looking for you."

She turned to see her husband ambling toward her. "Forgive me," she said. "I didn't mean to worry you."

"I know. And I wasn't really *worried.*" He sat beside her. "I just want to know how you expect me to contend with any event in my life without you there at my beck and call to discuss the matter in pathetically analytical detail."

He smiled, and she laughed softly. "If you're trying to tell me you need me, I already knew that." Then she remembered what he'd been doing when she left. "Oh, how did it go? Are they going to—"

"It went as well as it possibly could," he said. "Our prayers have been answered."

"So, he's agreed to live up to the agreement and—"

"The agreement is null and void. He showed no apparent remorse for his actions and gave me no reason to believe that his behavior would change. But he has no recourse when the contract is perfectly clear. The estate has legally been removed from his ownership, and he has received an equitable refund, an amount agreed upon by both our solicitors."

"And now what?"

"The estate is mine again."

"What will we do?" she asked as it sunk in that the refund given would have come from James if he had taken back ownership.

"What do you mean?"

"Well . . . the money and . . . we obviously can't live here and . . ."

"Obviously we will be going back to Iowa right away. I've already seen to the arrangements. We'll be leaving tomorrow." Eleanore couldn't help but feel relief on that count. "And," he added with a weighty sigh, "the estate will remain in the care of the staff, who keep everything running smoothly all the time, anyway. The matter will be left in the hands of the legal firm. They know how to reach me and will be more than adequately compensated for their efforts on my behalf."

"And you trust these men?"

"Absolutely; you already knew that."

"I'm just making sure." He smiled, and she added, "And what about the money? I can't even fathom the enormous amount that—"

"It is a lot of money, yes. Be we will manage just fine."

"We will?"

"We don't really *need* the money . . . at least not for ten or twenty years." He chuckled. "If it doesn't sell by then I might have to get a job."

"What would you do?" she teased.

"I have no idea." He chuckled more deeply. "I was raised to be relatively useless. Perhaps Frederick can teach me how to farm the land. Or perhaps the estate will sell long before then. Either way, I'm certain God will watch out for us. He always has. I don't believe He'll stop now."

"You're right, of course," she said and squeezed his hand.

"Truthfully," he exhaled loudly, "it all went so smoothly that I've been wondering why we made the journey. I felt so strongly about coming."

"Yes, so did I."

"But I think Mr. Earl could have handled it. I almost feel as if the journey was a waste."

"Perhaps it wouldn't have gone so smoothly if you'd not been here," she suggested.

"Perhaps," he said but didn't sound convinced.

"How did you find me?" she asked.

"Well," he drawled and put his arms along the back of the pew, "after riding to all of the places I know you once frequented, I said a little prayer, and a few minutes later, that little voice in my head asked me if I'd bothered to check the church. And here you are."

"Here I am," she said. "Would that be the same little voice that told me to marry you?"

"I believe so."

"And to settle in Iowa."

"The very same."

"A voice worth listening to, then."

"Indeed," he said, then silence fell.

Eleanore's thoughts went back to the memories she'd been indulging in. She turned to look at her husband sitting beside her, and tears burned in her eyes. She blinked them back and said, "It was a beautiful wedding." He turned to look at her as if he didn't know what she meant. "*Our* wedding," she clarified.

"I know which wedding you mean," he said. "I just thought the fact that it was beautiful had been established long ago."

She knew he was teasing her, but she said quite seriously, "Perhaps it's more beautiful in actuality than it was in memory." His brow creased with intrigue, and she added, "Now that I know what I got myself into, I can see that it was a glorious wedding; it was perfect. One of the greatest moments of my life."

"And mine," he said, touching her face. "So, you'd do it again?"

"Absolutely!"

He stood and offered his hand. She took it and stood beside him, but rather than leaving the chapel, he put her hand over his arm and guided her slowly up the aisle. "What are you doing?"

"The same thing you're doing," he said. "Just reliving the past a bit. If you had it to do over, would you do it any differently?"

"No," she said eagerly.

"I would," he said, surprising her.

"*What* would you do differently?"

He looked down as they continued walking. "I withheld too much of myself from you, Eleanore. I should have opened my heart to you . . . right from the start."

They arrived at the front of the chapel, the very spot where they'd exchanged vows, and he turned to face her. "But James," she said, "you were always—"

"Hush," he said and took both her hands into his. "Now that we're here, there's just something I'd like to say." He smiled subtly and added in a hushed voice, "I, James, take thee, Eleanore, to be my wedded wife, and I give unto thee my whole heart." He smiled again. "I may now kiss the bride."

He kissed her in a way that would never take place in public, then he wrapped her in his arms. "I love you, Eleanore."

"I know," she said. "And you gave me your whole heart a long time ago. You didn't have to come here to do that."

"Well, I hadn't planned on it . . . but since we're here . . . it's all official now. And perhaps *this* makes the journey worth the effort."

"Perhaps," she said, and they both laughed.

They spent the night at the house while memories swirled around Eleanore, not allowing her much sleep. She rose just past dawn and left James sleeping. She knew they'd be leaving right after breakfast, and she felt anxious to return to her Iowa home and the children. By habit she wandered into the kitchen and found Miss Gibbs there alone.

"Good morning," she said and startled the woman.

"Oh, goodness, it's you." She crossed the room and stood directly in front of Eleanore. "I've been praying I'd have a moment alone with you before you leave." Tears rose along with an intense conviction in her eyes. "I have to know, my dear. This religion you found . . . I've been praying . . . I've felt uncomfortable at church services for such a long time now—well, soon after you left, I suspect." She took Eleanore's hands. "You must tell me!"

Eleanore couldn't hold back her own tears as she urged Miss Gibbs to the table where they had sat together hundreds of times to share trivial conversation. Knowing time was brief before the household would be embroiled in the usual morning flurry, Eleanore told her the brief version of her finding the Book of Mormon, how she knew it was true, and of her baptism. Miss Gibbs wept openly but said very little. She didn't have to.

Before Eleanore left that morning with her husband, she had given Miss Gibbs an extra copy of the Book of Mormon that she had tucked in her satchel before leaving home. She was glad she'd bought some extras when they'd been in Nauvoo. She also left Miss Gibbs their address in Iowa, and the promise that if she ever decided to leave England and join the Saints, Eleanore would do anything to help her. Climbing into the carriage,

Eleanore recalled their firm embraces and the gratitude and hope her visit had kindled in this longtime friend of hers.

A few miles from the estate, James startled Eleanore from her thoughts. "What *are* you thinking about?"

She smiled and took his hand. "Our journey wasn't wasted at all. It was the answer to someone's prayers."

"The servants all seemed very grateful for our intervention, but—"

"*Your* intervention; yes, they were. But that's not all."

Eleanore told him about her experience with Miss Gibbs. He listened attentively, then said, "You are amazing, my dear."

"It wasn't me. I'm just the messenger."

"Indeed," he said with a little laugh, while she wondered if her own husband would ever be receptive to the message.

Chapter Eleven
THE STORM

James and Eleanore were both glad to return home to their loved ones, especially the children. They quickly eased back into their comfortable routine. Months passed, and Eleanore settled into a deeper contentment than she'd ever known. They never heard from Mr. or Mrs. King or any of their friends, and never even encountered them on the streets, but Eleanore declared to her husband that if they did she would simply smile with confidence, say hello, and move on.

Eleanore's desire to get pregnant and have a baby certainly hovered with her, but she had come to believe in her deepest self that it would happen in God's time and that she needed to trust in Him and not allow her own impatience to destroy her peace and happiness. Her marriage to James became increasingly comfortable, and the love they shared was surely one of her greatest joys. He continued to be completely supportive of her religious beliefs, and he was always present when the household gathered for their private Sunday service following the usual church meeting they attended in town. But he never actively participated beyond occasionally offering a prayer, and he showed no interest in actually reading the Book of Mormon or any other materials that Eleanore had received from Nauvoo. Still, Eleanore had heard from her friends there about families that were divided over the matter of religion, and of spouses who were antagonistic and difficult. She appreciated the tolerant attitude her husband took and prayed that one day his heart would be softened.

Eleanore was completely shocked when a piano was delivered as an early Christmas gift for the family; it had been ordered and delivered early to avoid the inevitable harsh storms of winter. James had once admitted that he'd had some minimal music training in his youth, and once the piano was set up in the parlor and had been tuned, he started picking out the melody of some of the hymns in the book Sally had sent. Music then became more of an active part of their Sunday gatherings, and an aspect that James *did* participate in. Eleanore discovered he had a fine voice and carried a tune better than anyone else in the group. He purchased a variety of sheet music and started teaching her and the children how to read music, and then some basic piano lessons became a part of the daily routine, even though his knowledge was minimal. Eleanore loved the way that music, as simple as it was, began to fill the house during cold winter days. And she loved to hear the hymns come to life, even if it was only in their simplest form.

During the winter the children seemed to hit a growth spurt all at once, and James joked about how the food they'd been growing in the Iowa soil was making the children grow almost as quickly as the garden had grown. They all required a wardrobe change within a matter of weeks when clothes suddenly became too tight and too short. Mary Jane was talking and running around the house, full of wild energy. Iris was nearly ten and had lost her little-girl look. David had turned twelve and was behaving very maturely, although he was still small for his age in spite of his growth. James assured him that he'd been the same way and had gained his height in a sudden burst at the age of sixteen. Ralph had proved a good example of James's theory when he changed from a boy into a man almost overnight. At the age of seventeen he was strong and nearly as tall as James, gradually taking over more of the physical labor that required a man's ability. In spite of the age difference between Ralph and David, they remained as close as brothers and spent much time together. David's maturity meshed with Ralph's easygoing nature. They played less like children and were more likely to be found reading together or indulging in long conversations that occupied cold winter days. The maturing of the boys left Iris somewhat excluded, since she'd been accustomed to following them around, but she made up for it by playing with Mary Jane. Iris was gifted at keeping the toddler out of trouble and entertained. Iris loved to behave like she was Mary Jane's mother, and Mary Jane loved the attention, so it worked out nicely. Occasionally the children all bundled up to play in the snow, and once in a while the adults joined them. They made snowmen in the yard and had snowball wars. Then they would gather around the fire in the kitchen to warm up, enjoying hot soup and warm cocoa.

When spring came, James sought out a piano teacher for the children; he came to the house once a week, and Eleanore sat in on their lessons so that she could learn as well. The children progressed as well at the piano as they did with the rest of their studies. Their love of reading grew in proportion to their ability to do so. David had progressed to being able to read anything he chose from their growing library as they regularly purchased new books, sometimes ordering them from back east, or even Europe. Iris was not quite so advanced, but was doing well. Ralph was also improving in his reading, much more so than he'd ever done prior to sharing lessons with David and Iris, according to his mother. The children were also doing well with arithmetic, history, and other subjects that Eleanore taught them, sometimes with James's help. The children also made strides in their ability to work and help with various tasks around the house and yard. The boys were expected to help in the kitchen some, and Iris had chores assigned in the barn. James made it clear that he wanted them all to be capable of doing everything required to maintain the life they lived should the need ever arise. Eleanore loved the way James had learned all of those things himself, completely eradicating the man who had been raised to be waited on and pampered. And he expected his children to be strong and self-sufficient. He included Ralph with his own children very naturally, and even little Mary Jane, who was still too young to read or do chores, but was often found tagging along behind James or Eleanore. And in the same respect, Frederick and Lizzie were actively involved in guiding the children. Eleanore loved the life they lived, and while she looked forward to a time when certain desires would be met, she found perfect contentment and gratitude in all they shared that was good.

Late in the spring of 1844, Sally wrote Eleanore a letter that was good news mixed with word of ongoing difficulties and persecution for some of the residents of Nauvoo. Eleanore focused on the good. The temple was rising, and the Prophet had told the people that upon its completion, ordinances could be performed there for worthy members of the Church that would enable them to remain married eternally. Sally wrote of the peace she felt to realize that the child she had lost to death could be sealed to the family by proxy, and they could all be together forever. Sally's greatest desire was to see the temple completed and be able to partake of these rich blessings. Eleanore read the letter, then wept. More than anything she would hope to be with James and the children forever, to know that death would not end all that they shared. But what would happen if he never chose to embrace her beliefs? The very idea threatened to break her heart.

She was startled when the bedroom door came open and James caught her crying.

"What's wrong?" he demanded.

"Nothing," she insisted and quickly tucked the letter into a drawer.

"Don't lie to me," he said. "Say you don't want to talk about it, but don't tell me nothing is wrong when you're crying."

"Fine. I don't want to talk about it."

"Why not?"

Eleanore looked at him squarely, wondering for a moment if she *should* talk to him about it. But the impression came clearly to her mind that now was not the time. She simply said, "Because I have no reason to believe that you would understand."

He looked confused, then hurt, then enlightened. "It must be about religion."

"Yes," she said as she brushed past him to leave the room, "it must be."

Eleanore felt disappointed that he never brought it up again. She had hoped that his commitment to total honesty in their relationship would compel him to broach the subject and at least understand her emotion. But he didn't. Days passed, and Eleanore reminded herself to be patient and trust in the Lord. Her husband was a good man. He'd given her a good life, and he'd given her his heart. Perhaps one day he would fully open his heart to God.

Spring merged into the sticky heat of summer, but they'd all become accustomed to it and had learned how to cope. The garden kept them busy, the trees offered shade, and the nearby river gave them plenty of water to cool off in as much as they wanted. Letters from both Miriam and Sally came at regular intervals, often staggered, which spread the pleasure out more.

In midsummer, Eleanore rode into town with James for the usual errands. They picked up some things at the general store, some feed for the animals, and stopped to get the mail last of all. Eleanore waited on the seat of the wagon while James went into the post office to get it. He handed the mail to her as he sat beside her, then took the reins. She was thrilled to see a letter from Sally and nearly opened it as James drove toward home. But her hand halted in breaking the seal of the envelope as surely as if cold fingers had wrapped around hers to stop her. The cold filtered through her in a tangible dread.

"What's wrong?" James asked, taking note of her hesitancy.

"I don't know," she said. "I think it's bad news." She glanced at the people surrounding them on the busy street as they drove along. "Perhaps I need more privacy."

James felt chilled by her conviction as much as by the intensity of her expression. He'd learned long ago that the Holy Ghost spoke strongly to her at times. He didn't dispute it, but it could be unnerving. Long after they had left town, and after they turned off the main road onto the lane that led to their home, James stopped the wagon at the side of the road. "How about now?" he said. "If it *is* bad news, maybe it's better to read it here rather than at home with the children around."

Eleanore took in his words as if through a fog and looked down at her trembling hands holding the letter. She knew he was right. But she didn't want to open it at all. She could never explain how she just *knew* that what Sally had written would be life altering. She could feel the comfort of the Holy Ghost already in place, preparing her, warning her, seeming to tell her that even with Its power, the news would still be hard to take. But she had to open the letter. She had to.

"Very well," she said, and James helped her down from the wagon. He watched her step slowly into the trees, a short distance away. He remained nearby but not too close, watching her and waiting. Her hands were visibly shaking as she opened the letter, took out the pages and unfolded them. He saw her eyes scanning the written words. She sucked in her breath and put a hand to her heart. She made a noise of anguish and teetered. He rushed to catch her, fearing her legs would fail her. She sobbed and dropped the letter, clutching onto his shirt. James felt his own heart pound, and his stomach knotted. *Someone had died. Or worse!* The possibilities of what could be worse filed through his mind, and he felt nauseous.

"What?" he insisted quietly. She sobbed again. "Tell me!"

"The Prophet's been murdered." She gasped for breath. "And his brother with him."

James trembled from the inside out. "Heaven help us," he muttered. He felt horrified and sick. He marveled that such a thing could happen in a country that claimed freedom of religion. He felt terrified for the people of Nauvoo and what this might mean for them. What possible repercussions could be in store for the Saints now that their leader was gone, murdered no less? But most of all, James felt inexplicable, unfathomable relief—that his family was not among them. And then he felt guilty. Guilty for being safe and secure while others were surely struggling. He wanted to say something to console Eleanore and give her hope, but he could only urge her to pull herself together so that he could take her home. He offered her the option of some time alone in the bedroom while he looked after the children, and she eagerly took it.

Later they reread the letter together, taking in the few details Sally had known of the situation regarding the deaths of Joseph and Hyrum Smith. Apparently they had been wrongfully arrested in Carthage, Illinois, along with some other men who held significant positions in the Church. The word among the Saints in Nauvoo was that the jail had been stormed by an angry mob with painted faces. The Prophet and his brother had been shot in cold blood. Sally wrote of her own feelings of shock and horror, feelings shared commonly by family and friends and every resident of Nauvoo. She stated that she felt certain no man had ever been loved or revered by so many people, and for that reason the Prophet's death had brought unfathomable grief. But Sally also wrote of peace, and that too was a common opinion of the majority of the Saints. It was believed that Joseph and Hyrum had fulfilled their earthly mission and it had been their time to go. There was even talk that they had known the end was coming when they had gone to Carthage.

James stared at the words on the pages of Sally's letter while the images of her report huddled in his mind and left him a little queasy. Eleanore cried in his arms as if she'd lost a member of her own family. And he just didn't know what to say. She grieved deeply for days while he just felt horrified and scared without fully understanding why. He couldn't help wondering if the Church would disintegrate without its leader, but more letters came from Sally and Miriam, making it clear that the temple would be completed and the Church would go forth under new leadership. Miriam put it well when she wrote that it had not been Joseph Smith's church; it was Jesus Christ's church and it would stand no matter what effort evil men put into destroying it.

When Eleanore read of the strength and determination of the Saints in Nauvoo, she found added peace in her own grief over the Prophet's death. The Church would go forth, the members would press forward, and she would do the same. She set her mind to being a good example for her household, of having faith in spite of difficulties and heartache. She felt certain it had been time for Joseph and Hyrum to be taken home; otherwise God would have surely protected them. And now it was time for new leadership to step forward and continue to build the kingdom. Eleanore wanted to do her part, in her own little way, in her own secluded world. She felt certain the best way for her to contribute to building the kingdom would be to continue living her religion as fully as possible, and to teach her children to do the same.

On a beautiful Sunday morning, late in the summer, Eleanore took great pains with her appearance while getting ready for church. She believed it was important to put on one's best for the Sabbath. Once she was ready, she went to check on the children and fix Iris's hair, aware of James coming in from caring for the animals to get washed up and change his clothes. When she returned to the bedroom to get her gloves, he was standing in front of the mirror, straightening his tie. While she pulled on her gloves she couldn't avoid admiring him while her heart manifested an irregular beat. He wore an elegant coat and waistcoat that were remnants of their life in England. He'd never bothered to replace or update them to anything more fashionable, since he didn't wear them enough to wear them out, especially since he had more than one complete set. But no matter how many times Eleanore saw him dressed that way, it affected her. All that time she'd worked for him in England, she'd never once stopped to consider what a handsome man he was. Now it preoccupied her thoughts on a regular basis. And for some reason, he looked especially handsome today as he made certain his tie was perfect, then combed through his thick, dark hair, putting it neatly into place.

She wondered if his thoughts were in the same vein as he turned and eyed her up and down with a little smile. He took her hand, gloved in white lace, and pressed it to his lips. "I remember you," he said with mischief in his eyes. "You were that governess who used to work for that wretched, miserable old man."

She smiled back. "He was neither wretched nor miserable."

"You're not disputing old," he said with a chuckle.

"Old*er* than me, but certainly not *old*. Still. Wretched? Miserable? Hardly."

His eyes became startlingly somber for the nature of the conversation. "On the contrary, my dear, I was both wretched *and* miserable. I was just a very good actor."

They heard the children bounding down the stairs, which meant it was time to leave. He offered his arm with a sparkle in his eye that made her wonder if he'd been teasing. But she didn't think so. "Shall we, my dear? Once again we can sit through a tedious service while we mentally tally all of the ways this man at the pulpit has no idea what he's talking about and demonstrates that he clearly has not read the Bible nearly so accurately as he thinks he has."

"How delightful," she said sarcastically, hoping the comment was some indication that he believed in the religion she was living more than the one they were pretending to live.

Later in the day, still dressed in their Sunday best, everyone gathered in the parlor for the Sabbath meeting that was the highlight of Eleanore's week. She was grateful to have Frederick in their home, and the priesthood he held, so that they could fully participate in the sacrament. And while James remained passive over most aspects of the meeting, he enjoyed singing the hymns, and his rich voice added strength to the rest of them. Eleanore was moved to tears as she watched her husband at the piano bench, with David and Iris on either side of him, fluidly playing, if only with one hand, while they all sang zealously, *We'll sing and we'll shout with the armies of heaven, Hosanna, hosanna to God and the Lamb! Let glory to them in the highest be given, Henceforth and forever, Amen and amen!* That night while she lay in bed beside her husband, the song kept repeating in Eleanore's mind while a certain peace swelled in her heart and generated tears.

The following morning while Eleanore was getting dressed, she was struck with a wave of nausea so overpowering she could hardly stand. She sat bent over a basin for several minutes, expecting to lose her stomach, but she never did. Lizzie found her there and brought her a biscuit, which helped a bit, but the sensation hovered with her throughout the day. Surely it had to be pregnancy, although the symptoms had never been so dramatic. When James inquired over her not feeling well, she simply told him she was having a bad day and that it was no cause for concern. But the following day was worse, and the horrific nausea became too intense to ignore or hide, combined with exhaustion that made it difficult for her to do even the simplest tasks.

"Are you pregnant?" James asked, taking her hand as he sat beside the bed where she'd returned after making very little effort to begin her day.

"I think so, but . . . it's never been so bad."

"Perhaps we should have the doctor come here to check on you."

"Perhaps we should," she agreed, having no desire to make the trip into town, but wanting his assurance that something more serious wasn't happening.

The doctor came and assured them that Eleanore was indeed pregnant, and she appeared to be in good health. But during the following days she became more ill than she'd ever felt in her life. Even the pregnancy symptoms she'd endured while traveling by wagon to Iowa had not upset her life as this did. The worst was an absolute inability to keep her food down, which left her weaker every day. Days became weeks while she rarely made it out of bed, and she got beyond the walls of her bedroom even less. She missed being able to go to church on Sunday, but was grateful to have James carry her down the stairs for the family meeting.

Each day became increasingly difficult while she became more and more feeble. Instinctively she believed everything would be all right, but she sensed a growing concern in James that she didn't know how to console. Following her usual routine of throwing up in a bucket that Lizzie took outside to empty, James looked into Eleanore's eyes as he did every morning before leaving to do his chores, and asked if there was anything he could do.

"No, thank you. I'm fine, truly."

"You're not fine, Eleanore," he said with a low growl, making his concern more evident than he normally let on. "You've got me worried sick. Look at you." He appeared as if he might cry. "You don't have the strength to get out of bed. How are you ever going to get through this pregnancy and give birth in such a condition?"

"I'll be fine," she assured him, finding strength in the memory of Joseph Smith's promise to her, but she didn't want to bring that up right now, certain it wouldn't have the same calming effect for James. She sensed him suppressing his worry as he kissed her brow, then he hurried from the room, clearly upset. Eleanore closed her eyes in prayer, wondering how she might soothe her husband's fears. When the answer came it made her smile.

* * *

James went through the routine of his chores with extra vigor while he hoped working up a sweat might alleviate this stark fear that deepened each day on behalf of his wife. He wondered if his feeling that something wasn't right might only be a form of paranoia, or if he was somehow being prepared for tragedy. He was just finishing up in the barn when Iris ran in to say, "Mama says she wants you to come to her room when you can."

"Is she still really sick?"

"Yes. Lizzie is with her. But she said it's not an emergency."

"Tell her I'll be there in just a minute. Thank you, Iris."

James washed up in the kitchen and hurried upstairs. He entered the bedroom to find not only Lizzie but also Frederick sitting near the bed. Eleanore looked so weak and drawn it frightened him. He couldn't remember the last time she'd left this room unless he'd carried her. For the thousandth time he silently told God that he was not willing to lose her for the sake of trying to bring a child into the world, and he hoped his prayers were being heard.

He sat on the edge of the bed and took her hand. "How are you feeling, my darling?" he asked, forcing a smile.

"Awful," she said and smiled in return. "But Frederick is going to give me a priesthood blessing."

It took James a moment to perceive what she meant, then he glanced over his shoulder to meet Frederick's cautious eyes.

He seemed to expect James to be angry or protest. "I see," was all James said.

"I wanted you to be here," Eleanore said.

"Very well," James said and stepped away from the bed, figuring it couldn't hurt. As much as he trusted and admired his friend, he had difficulty believing that any significant power of the holy priesthood would be present in such an ordinary man.

Frederick stood beside Eleanore, saying gently, "You know it's more appropriate for two priesthood holders to do this, but I'm certain the Lord understands why we only have one available."

James looked at the floor and had no idea if Eleanore glanced in his direction as she said, "I'm certain He does."

Frederick then placed his hands on Eleanore's head and pronounced upon her a blessing by the power of the holy priesthood which he held. He told her that her Father in Heaven was pleased with the choices she had made in her life, and with her faithfulness. He told her that the child inside of her would grow healthy and strong and come into this world without any trauma or threat to its well-being. She was promised physical strength throughout the course of the pregnancy to do all that was required of her as a wife and mother, and that the bothersome ailments that were weighing her down would be tempered, that her body would become strengthened to bear the physical trauma that pregnancy would place upon it not only through bringing this child into the world, but with many more.

Even while he listened, James didn't know whether to feel angry or astonished. Clearly that would depend on whether or not he believed that the words being said were true. And he simply couldn't decide. At the moment he felt more prone to anger. How could this man dish out such wondrous promises in abundance and encourage Eleanore's hopes when past history indicated they would likely be dashed? Then Frederick went on with words that made James's heart pound. Eleanore was promised that her strength of spirit and her keen faith in the

Savior would become the rock upon which this household would stand as a storm of grief and heartache descended. But she was also told to remember that whatever occurred was in God's hands, and by trusting in Him, peace could be found in knowing that His plans were formulated with exactness, and His children were not left to chance. And she was promised that joy would abound for her and those she loved no matter what challenges they faced, so long as they turned to their Savior for strength.

James could hardly breathe as the implication settled in. Then he had to tell himself that if he didn't believe Frederick actually had any power, if he held no account for what was being said, then why should he be affected at all?

When the blessing was finished he watched as Frederick exchanged a tender smile with Eleanore and squeezed her hand while tears rose in her eyes. She turned to look at James with an expectancy he couldn't answer. What did she think he might say? Overcome with a sudden need to be alone, he rushed from the room and out to the barn where he mounted a stallion bareback and rode over the prairie at breakneck speed. His mind whirled with fears and memories until he almost felt sick himself. Mingled with the fear of losing this baby as they had the others, was an even deeper fear that he might lose Eleanore as he'd lost his first wife from complications related to childbirth. How could he ever survive it? He felt sure that he couldn't, and he told God so. He prayed fervently that whatever struggles she might endure, her life would be spared. When he realized how long he'd been gone he felt guilty to think how he might have worried Eleanore, and how he should have never left at all without saying anything. He returned and quickly removed the bridle, leaving the horse secured in a stall before he ran into the house and headed for the stairs. His usual quick glance into the kitchen caught his attention and he stepped back, certain his eyes had deceived him. But there she was, standing at the big worktable, rolling out a pastry dough.

"What on earth are you doing?" he demanded. "You should be in bed."

"I feel fine," she said. "Well, a little lightheaded now and then, but much better. It feels good to be up and about . . . now that you're back at least. I've been worried. Where have you been?"

He focused on his own need for apology. "I'm sorry about that. I . . . needed to be alone. I should have told you I was leaving. I just went riding and lost track of the time."

She looked mildly displeased but said, "Just so you're all right."

He glanced around. "Where is everyone?"

Frederick and Lizzie went into town and took the children. Amanda took Ralph home early; he wasn't feeling well. She left some soup on the stove, and I told her I'd finish this."

James glared at the task, then at his wife. "If this is some noble attempt to make me think you're doing better—"

"I *am* doing better." She glared back.

"Are you?" he asked, unable to avoid sounding skeptical. "Maybe you just think you feel better because all those wonderful promises made you *want* to feel better, and you're overdoing it without even realizing. Maybe you should be in bed."

Eleanore tried not to feel angry at the evidence of his cynicism, but it was difficult. "Maybe you should have a little more faith, Mr. Barrington."

"And maybe you should be a little more practical. You've been so ill you could hardly get out of bed for weeks, and suddenly you're better?"

"Yes, I am."

"Maybe staying in bed is best no matter how you feel. If you lose this baby too, then what?"

"This one will be different."

"How can you know that, Eleanore?"

"Weren't you listening?"

"Yes, I was listening, and I heard an ordinary man make promises he has no right to make."

"He was speaking on God's behalf."

"And how is that possible?"

"I don't know, but it is. I *felt* the truth of what he said, James. I *felt* it." She pressed a fist to her chest and left flour on the front of her dress. "The same way I felt it when the Prophet promised me that I would have children."

"You *have* children."

"He said I would *bear* children. And I was just told that this child would come into the world healthy and strong."

"And you truly believe that?"

"I truly do," she insisted.

"Then you must also believe that this household will soon be faced with a storm of grief and heartache."

Eleanore sat down. "Yes, I must admit I believe that too." She looked at her husband. "And so do you, apparently." His eyes darted away abruptly. "That's why you left. If you didn't believe what he said was true, you wouldn't have been upset."

James sat down as well. "Maybe I do; I don't know. I don't know what to believe." He leaned his elbows on the table and pressed his head into his hands. "I believe that we have a good life, Eleanore, and I don't want it to change. I don't want anything to go wrong." He dropped his hands to the table and looked at her. "As much as I want more children, I don't want them at the risk of anything happening to you. I treasure what we have, what we share. I'm not a man who takes my blessings for granted. I only ask that God will give us the privilege of keeping what we have."

Eleanore stood and walked around the table, putting her hands to his shoulders. He turned and wrapped his arms around her, pressing his face into the folds of her dress. "Everything will be all right, James. You'll see. I was promised peace and joy, no matter what happened. We must hold on to that."

James just held her tighter, wishing he could rationalize away this uneasy foreboding that had hovered inside of him long before Frederick had given Eleanore that blessing.

From that day forward, Eleanore didn't throw up once, and her nausea was eased immensely, then gradually went away. Strength and color came back to her as the pregnancy progressed. The holidays were blissful, and James chose to forget about any hints of future challenges. Instead he reveled in the goodness of his life.

The new year brought a sudden spurt of growth from their unborn child. Eleanore's belly blossomed almost overnight. By the time signs of spring began to appear, she looked ready to pop and could barely walk without difficulty. But in spite of her aches and pains she seemed to be in good health. Still, James regularly cautioned her to take care of herself, and he was often scolding her for doing any little thing that might cause her the tiniest strain. She always laughed off his concern and told him how nice it was to know he cared, but he found no humor in his fear that something would go wrong with her health, or that this pregnancy might come to a tragic end—or both. Knowing there was little else he could do, he prayed fervently and kept a close eye on his wife, counting the days until she would give birth to this baby and they could put this trial behind them. Having a strong, healthy baby and seeing Eleanore the same following its birth seemed a miracle beyond his comprehension, but he imagined it hourly and tried to keep the vision clear in his mind in order to soothe his own nerves over the matter. They'd been married six years, and still they'd not been blessed with a child. But he could never reconcile his longing for one with any risk to Eleanore's life. He prayed it would never come to that.

* * *

Eleanore hummed as she worked in the kitchen, occasionally pausing to endure a strong kick from inside her belly. Amanda and

Ralph had gone home, and Lizzie was out in the summer kitchen overseeing the stew Amanda had left simmering, while Eleanore put the finishing touches on an apple pie that would soon go in the oven. James and Frederick had gone into town on errands and had taken Iris and Mary Jane with them; David had declined going since he'd been in the middle of a project with Ralph. Now David was in the yard, throwing a stick for the dog to fetch. The spring day had been warm, which made the sudden rush of a cool breeze through the window feel especially good. Gathering clouds added to the cooling effect, and Eleanore felt certain it was going to rain. She glanced out the window to check the sky just in time to see David following the dog into the woods. She rushed to the door and hollered loudly, "David! Don't go too far!"

"I won't!" he called back.

"I want you to be back in twenty minutes!" she shouted even louder.

"I will be!" he replied, more faintly.

Eleanore looked skyward to see that the clouds were darkening quickly, and the breeze felt suddenly chilling. She felt tempted to run after David and insist that he come back immediately. If she weren't so pregnant, she might have. But under the circumstances, she never could have caught up with him.

Twenty minutes later, the pie was in the oven, and it was starting to rain. Ten minutes after that the family returned from town and she'd seen no sign of David. She went out to the barn to find James unharnessing the horses, and found herself confronting sleet before she got the door open.

"What's wrong?" he asked, as if her appearance in this weather indicated a problem.

"David went into the woods . . . following the dog. He should have been back by now. I'm sure he's just lost track of the time, but . . . the weather."

"I'll find him," he said, already bundled for the cold. "You get back inside and take it easy." She understood the deeper meaning, which was echoed by the grim concern in his eyes. And she didn't hesitate to do as he'd said. While she often teased James about his overt concerns, she couldn't deny that if she lost this baby due to even the smallest bit of overdoing, she could never forgive herself.

Inside the house, she resisted the urge to pace the floor and sat instead near the fire with her feet up, watching the clock too closely. Lizzie brought her a cup of warm cocoa, reporting that Iris was in her bedroom playing with her dolls, and Frederick had left a few minutes ago to aid in the search.

"I'm certain they'll be back soon, and all will be well," Lizzie said, but a howl of the wind followed her words, and a glance out the window revealed that the sleet had turned to heavy snow in a matter of minutes.

While the clock ticked, Eleanore's anxiety mounted radically. She had to will herself to remain seated and stay calm, and she appreciated Lizzie remaining close to keep her conscious of minding her own condition.

"There's the door," Lizzie said and bolted out of her chair. Eleanore came more slowly behind her, entering the hall to see Frederick holding the door for James, who had David in his arms. She rushed toward them, then moved aside to let him pass. The child looked almost dead with cold, and Eleanore's heart threatened to stop beating.

"I'm going for the doctor," Frederick announced and headed back out.

"How did you find him?" Eleanore asked, following James up the stairs.

"Angels, no doubt," he muttered breathlessly. "And a lot of praying. Help me get him out of these wet clothes." He sat the child in a chair, and they worked frantically with David barely conscious. She was aware of Lizzie stoking the fire and turning down the bed, then she shoved a clean nightshirt into Eleanore's hands and set a blanket within her reach. In minutes they had David wrapped up tightly beneath the covers and the fire blazing.

"This is like some kind of twisted nightmare," James grumbled, his voice low while he pushed David's damp hair off his face. "How many times has he done this?"

One time too many, perhaps, Eleanore thought but didn't dare say it aloud. She knew her memories were the same as her husband's. David's running off had gotten him into trouble once before. Prior to their leaving England he'd been caught in a storm and had become so ill that they'd feared for his life. He'd come through it unscathed eventually, but Eleanore wondered if they would be blessed with such a miracle twice. Her heart pounded with dread just to observe him; he was looking far worse than he had the last time this had happened. She felt a growing fear that threatened to burst out in volatile sobbing, but she forced it back, knowing she needed to remain calm. "Where was he?" she asked, sitting on the edge of the bed, noting that David had started to shiver, which at least gave more of an indication that he was closer to living than dead. Still, she didn't know if that was a good sign or not.

"Huddled by a tree," James said, his voice trembling with obvious fear, "apparently too cold to move. If I hadn't found him when I had . . ." He sat on the other side of the bed and touched his son's face. The child barely acknowledged him with a brief glance. "Heaven help us," James muttered and pressed his brow to David's, as if he could feed strength into him.

"You need to change your clothes," Eleanore said, trying to remain practical, "or you'll be ill as well." Their eyes met as their memories mingled almost tangibly. It *was* like a bad dream. She prayed they would be blessed with positive results once again. But her instincts told her this was worse—far worse.

When James didn't respond to her suggestion, she stood and moved to his side, putting her hands on his shoulders. "Go change into dry clothes," she urged firmly. "I'll stay with him.

There's nothing you can do for him now." He reluctantly left the room, and Eleanore leaned against the headboard, lifting her feet onto the bed, then wrapping her arm around David to hold him close to her. He moaned and eased closer. His shivering became violent. She just held him and whispered comforting words until her husband returned and sat on the other side of the bed. He lifted David, still wrapped in a blanket, into his arms and cradled him as though he were a much younger child. Eleanore put another blanket over him and pressed a kiss to his brow. "Everything's going to be all right," she whispered, but she found it difficult to feel convinced.

Chapter Twelve

MEASURING

By the time Frederick returned with the doctor, David's shivering had ceased, but he didn't look at all well. The doctor reported that it would take time to know how the trauma might have affected him. Lizzie fed the doctor stew and pie before he set out into the storm to make his way back to town. Thankfully the snow was letting up rather than becoming worse.

Lizzie brought dinner to David's room for James and Eleanore and insisted they eat it. She assured them she would take care of Iris and leave them to be with David, who was too lethargic to eat but showed no signs of misery.

Long after Iris had been put to bed and the Higgins family had gone across the yard to their own home for the night, James and Eleanore rested on either side of David, who was sleeping soundly. Eleanore felt sure they could go to their own bed, but she sensed her husband's hesitance to leave his son alone, and she wanted to be near them both. She noticed James looking distant and contemplative and was about to inquire over his thoughts when he spoke in little more than a whisper. "Did you know that I had a brother and a sister . . . who both died?"

Eleanore shifted in order to see his face better, not certain she liked such a thought in light of the present circumstances. "Only because I read their birth and death dates in the family Bible. You've never told me anything about your family."

He looked toward the ceiling and made a quiet scoffing noise. "Little worth telling, I'm certain. My youth is not something I've ever had any desire to talk about—at all."

"Perhaps that's the best reason of all to talk about it; perhaps you *should* talk about it."

He turned his head on the pillow; his eyes became deeply reflective. "Perhaps," he said, and she realized that was his intention. "Reginald died the month before I was born; he was barely two, I believe. As a child I hated just hearing his name. It took me years to even figure out exactly who he was, but my mother talked of him constantly. He'd died at the age of two, but one might think he'd lived an entire lifetime of perfect achievements by the way she spoke of him to anyone who would listen for more than a minute. She was certain that had he lived he would have surely done this, or done that, and he would have done it better than anyone else." His voice saddened, and his eyes grew distant. "To my mother, Reginald was a saint, an angel, the beginning and end of all that was meaningful to her. I was invisible."

"And what of your father?"

"He was indifferent . . . about her, me, everything. I was invisible to him too."

"That's horrible," Eleanore whispered, maintaining the quiet level of their conversation so as not to wake David.

"Yes, I believe it was," James said. "But clearly I survived it."

"I never imagined . . ."

"Imagined what?"

"That your childhood was so difficult."

"My needs were met."

"Except the most important one. Above all else, surely a child must know love from its parents."

"Yes, I agree with that."

"Did you?"

"I believe that I was somehow blessed to come to this world with some . . . extra sense of . . . logic perhaps. It's difficult to explain. Even as a child I remember watching my parents and thinking, 'I know they love me because they're my parents, even if they don't know how to show it.'"

Eleanore laughed softly and reached over the top of David to touch her husband's face. "So you were *always* astutely mature and deeply methodical."

"Is that funny?" he asked, mildly defensive.

"No, of course not. It's just . . . you. It's who you are. It's how you've always been. It's one of the things I love about you."

"Well . . . yes, I suppose I was, in a way. Maybe I needed to be to survive emotionally."

"Maybe you did." She softened her touch to a compassionate caress. "And what of your sister?"

"*She* wasn't invisible. She died unexpectedly of an illness, but long before that . . . right from the start . . . the very fact that she was female put her immediately into the same position as Reginald. She didn't have to compete with him the way I did. She could do no wrong, and was horribly spoiled. I remember when she was born, vaguely at least. I was four, I think. I loved to hold her, be around her. But the nannies were ridiculously protective, and my mother behaved as if I might carry the plague. Once she became old enough to play with, she was so utterly spoiled that I didn't *want* to play with her. If I were anywhere near her and something went wrong it was always my fault, and I was punished for it."

"That's *horrible,*" Eleanore repeated, more emphatically. "It's difficult to believe that you were so . . . so . . ."

"What?" he pressed.

"That you were treated so wretchedly. I've just always believed that people were mostly a product of their upbringing."

"So, given what you just learned about me, you think I should have grown up to be some kind of monster?"

Eleanore felt taken aback, both by the statement and by what she'd just learned about him. She admitted with humility,

"Clearly I was wrong. It's evident you came into this world with an inner strength."

"I believe that, Eleanore, I do. I remember the day I realized it. I was nearly eighteen, and I came upon my parents in the midst of an argument—which was typical. I often attempted to break it up, tried to help them see reason—usually to no avail. They were paying no attention to me whatsoever, and I remember as clearly as if it were this morning, standing there looking at them behaving as they always had, and I thought, 'Heaven help me. These people are crazy. I can't let myself turn out like this. I can't.' And they were so *unhappy.* That's when I became obsessed with figuring out what constituted a *good* marriage, which of course is at the core of a good family. I traveled the world, observing marriages in different cultures. I asked questions, talked to people, read everything there was to read. I truly became obsessed. I was determined to counteract what I'd been raised with."

Eleanore smiled at him again. "So that's why you're such a good husband."

"Am I?" he asked as if he truly didn't know. Eleanore considered this revelation in light of all she knew about him. She recalled his attitude about their marriage at the beginning. It *had* been very methodical and logical. He'd done everything right, in spite of being resistant to giving her his heart. Still, he'd been tender and sensitive, and very conscious of giving his children a loving environment and a positive example. Her admiration for him deepened, and so did her compassion. She'd never once stopped to wonder why he'd never discussed his upbringing. She'd never discussed hers either. They were both the only children in their families, and their parents were all deceased. It had never seemed important. They'd come together to make a new family, and the past had been conveniently left in the past. Now she'd been given a glimpse into aspects of her husband's character that she'd never comprehended. She felt deeply grateful for the strength and insight he'd been blessed with that had allowed him to rise so nobly above such horrific examples. If that were not the case, she either wouldn't have married him, or she would be married to a difficult man. She far preferred the present situation to any other option.

"Oh, yes," she said and left it at that. For now she preferred to let him keep talking rather than slowing his momentum by expressing her own thoughts.

His gaze intensified. "I've tried to be, Eleanore; I truly have."

"And you are," she assured him firmly.

James leaned onto one elbow. "Do you mean that, Eleanore? And don't lie to me to spare my feelings."

"I wouldn't. You should know that. Is this some roundabout way of trying to tell me that I'm lacking as a wife or—"

"No, of course not." His genuine surprise eased her concerns.

"Then, what? You're practically a perfect husband, James. You always have been."

"Not *always.*"

"Even when you so boldly declared you would not love me, you still treated me like a queen. I never had cause for complaint."

"Now, *that's* not true."

"Neither of us is perfect. That's not what this is about. But I love you, and you love me. We *do* have a good marriage and a good family."

"Yes, we do."

"I couldn't ask for anything more," she added.

"Now you *are* lying, Mrs. Barrington. And I know exactly what you would ask for." For a moment she looked away, feeling almost guilty. "Don't tell me you wouldn't prefer a husband who actually *lives* your religious beliefs."

She looked at him sharply. "I *prefer* the husband that I've got, exactly as he is. Our differing views on religion have *never* constituted enough discord between us to even minutely cause what I would define as a challenge in our marriage, or to make me wish for anything more or less than what I have being married to *you.*"

He gazed at her while his eyes flickered, and she sensed him struggling to believe her. She felt compelled to point out, "This is not the first time you've hinted at such feelings, James. Why don't you just . . ."

David stirred in his sleep, drawing their attention to him. Eleanore was amazed at how deeply he was sleeping, but surely that was good for him. He rolled over and settled further into the bed. James tucked the blankets tightly over him, then stood and stoked the fire before he went to the window and looked out. Eleanore took up the shawl she'd left over the foot of the bed and wrapped it around her as she stood beside him.

"Talk to me," she said softly. "Tell me what you're feeling . . . thinking. It doesn't have to make sense. Just . . . share your thoughts with me."

He took a deep breath while he studied her face, as if he might find there the courage to heed her request. He folded his arms over his chest and looked out into the darkness. He cleared his throat, and the muscles in his face tightened. "When I married Caroline . . ." he said, then paused. And with those four words a level of understanding settled into her. He only had to mention his first wife's name for Eleanore to be reminded of what a horrid, difficult woman she had been. Eleanore had always known that he'd only shared very minimal information with her regarding their relationship, but what she'd been told led her to believe that what he was still holding inside had to be ugly. She'd simply never considered before that it might be affecting his attitude about *this* marriage. When he'd told her that he'd forgiven Caroline, and he'd forgiven himself for being such a fool, she had assumed it was over and done. Apparently not.

After several seconds passed without him finishing the sentence, she attempted to urge him along. "When you married

Caroline, you expected her to have integrity and put the same effort into the marriage that you were willing to put in."

"That's right," he said, surprised.

"But she didn't."

"Not even for a month," he said. He sighed loudly. "I felt confused and frustrated, but I believed that by loving her with my whole heart, her heart would soften, and with time all would be well. It only got worse. After the truth came out—a few years into the marriage—everything suddenly made perfect sense. It had all been a lie. The plain and simple truth was that she'd married me for my money, and she did an excellent job of saying and doing all the right things to make me believe that I was marrying her for the right reasons. I poured my heart out to her about my quest for the perfect marriage, how I wanted our family to be strong and happy. I gave my love to her with no restraint, believing that love could surely cure all ills, and the more eagerly I gave it, the more she would feel loved and blossom into her greatest potential." His voice became gruff. "She took everything I gave her, and gave everything she had to someone else. And I was oblivious, too naive to have any comprehension that *my* wife would do something so hideous. The day I found out I was . . ." He stopped, startled. "There is no reason for you to hear any of this."

He tried to move away but she put a hand on his arm to stop him. "Maybe it doesn't matter whether or not I hear it, except that I'm your wife, and it may give me a better understanding of who you are now because of what you've been through. How can there be *complete* trust between us when you've been holding secrets in your heart?"

He became mildly defensive. "I don't know any more about your past than you've known about mine."

"I don't *have* a past, James. Beyond the deaths of my parents, I was happy and secure in my upbringing."

"Yes," he said with noticeable irritation, "a child scrubbing pots and shoveling ashes."

For the first time, she realized that her once doing so actually bothered him. She calmly pointed out, *"Our* children scrub pots and shovel ashes."

"Not in servitude. They do it as a contribution to a family. It's different."

"It bothers you . . . that I was a servant."

"Don't twist this, Eleanore. The differences that once existed in our social stations—which immediately ceased the moment I put that ring on your finger—have *never* bothered me. The fact that you were a servant in *my* household bothers me very much. What was going on in my life while you were on your hands and knees mopping my floors? You should have been out climbing trees and riding ponies."

"That's not the life I was born to, but I was *happy.* Something that you obviously were *not.* Now why don't you stop trying to divert my attention with a silly argument and finish telling me what happened with Caroline. Maybe it's not so important that I hear it, as it is that you speak it, that you let it out of wherever you've been hiding it." She wondered if he would argue or change the subject or simply tell her that he didn't want to talk about it. He looked frustrated, then resigned, as if he could come up with no reasonable protest. He looked down and sighed. She added gently, "What *was* going on in your life while I was mopping floors and shoveling ashes?"

He let out a bitter laugh. "There we were, right under the same roof, completely oblivious to each other."

"I was a child when you married Caroline. What might you have done differently?"

"Well, I wish I'd never married her, for certain. I was a fool."

"No, James, you were deceived. As human beings we all make mistakes, but she put great effort into deceiving you. How can you blame yourself for that? And how could you not want David and Iris?"

"Of course I want David and Iris, but I would have preferred for them to have a mother who was kind and decent and—"

"And if Caroline were not their mother they would be different people. They are who they are because she *is* their mother. You can't wish that away."

He sighed. "Yes, you're right. And I know that; I do. There are just moments when . . . the choices I made haunt me. I've forgiven her, and I've tried to forgive myself. But maybe I haven't."

He sat down and pressed his head into his hands. Eleanore checked on David to find him snoring softly, then she quietly moved a chair right next to her husband's, partly facing him. She took his hand and said gently, "Talk to me, my darling."

He played with her fingers for a long moment before he murmured, "I don't know what else to say, Eleanore. I suppose I just . . . feel sorry for them."

"Who?"

"Caroline. My parents. Did they even know *how* to be happy? And I wonder why I would be so blessed, when I often feel . . ."

Eleanore saw his chin quiver and heard his voice crack. Whatever he'd intended to say came from somewhere deep. She waited, but he didn't finish.

"Tell me what you often feel," she urged, almost holding her breath. He looked into her eyes as if he were measuring some level of trust. After all they'd been through, did he still struggle with trusting her with his deepest feelings? She saw his lips press together and his cheeks tighten, as if they would prevent him from saying any more. Trying to make it easier for him, she added gently, "Just one word, James. Tell me one word to describe how you often feel."

She waited while he thought about it, then his eyes became decisive, and his countenance revealed the mustering of courage. Eleanore had known he found it difficult to expose his emotions.

And from what she'd known of his first marriage, that was certainly understandable. But now her understanding deepened as she considered Caroline's betrayal, in combination with the poor parenting in his home. In that moment, she grasped more than she ever had how fragile his heart still was. The effort it took for him to heed her request was startling, but it made past conversations suddenly make sense. For all his confidence and self-assurance, there was part of him that was hurt and scared. It was surely the same part of him that had resisted giving her his heart for so long, and perhaps it was the part that resisted embracing the gospel. The channel of her thoughts, and the validity behind them, fell neatly into place when he finally said, "I feel . . . undeserving."

"Of what?" she asked softly, feeling the need for clarification for him as much as for her. He was talking, and she wanted him to keep doing so.

"Of . . . everything—everything good in my life."

"But you're a good man, James. Your life is a result of choices you've made. Trials come in spite of anything people may or may not do; the story of Job is evidence of that. But we have a happy home because you've worked hard to make it that way. Clearly your parents were *not* happy because they made different choices."

"Maybe they didn't know any better."

"Maybe they didn't. We do. We've been very blessed."

"Yes, we have." He looked down, and she sensed there was something more he wanted to say. She waited, and wondered why his thoughts would be wandering into such territory now. Had the trauma of searching for David in the storm prompted something to the surface in him? He glanced toward the sleeping child and added, "Maybe they were so miserable because they'd lost a child, and then they lost another. Maybe they never got over it."

Eleanore took a sharp breath. At this point they had no reason to believe that David wouldn't be fine, but she wondered if James had some kind of feelings to the contrary. "Do you think we're going to lose him?"

"I don't know. Maybe I'm paranoid."

"And maybe the Spirit is preparing you for something." He looked at her sharply. "Will you not share such feelings with me?"

He did so, but with an edge to his voice. "I've felt for a long time that something was going to happen. I've been fearing it would be with you or the baby. Now I wonder."

"Just because he got so ill last time doesn't mean it will happen again."

"And it doesn't mean that it won't."

"We must accept God's will, whatever it may be."

He stood up so abruptly that his chair nearly tipped, startling Eleanore. David slept on while she attempted to quell her pounding heart, then she rose and stood beside her husband. She put a hand on his arm. "Do you think we couldn't survive losing a child?"

That edge was still in his voice as he muttered, "I could not survive losing anything I love, Eleanore—not you, not David. Nothing. No one. I couldn't survive it."

"Of course you could. You don't know your own strength, James."

"And you don't know my greatest weakness."

Again she felt startled but kept her voice even. "I'll know if you tell me."

He looked at her hard, and she could feel him once again measuring whether or not he could utter words from the darkest crevices of his heart. Apparently he decided against it when he said, "We must pray that David stays healthy, and that all goes well with you and the baby."

"Of course," she said, and he left the room. Eleanore sank back onto her chair, attempting to feel her instincts on behalf of David—and her husband. After many minutes of thought and prayer and careful measuring, she felt more afraid than she ever had in her life.

* * *

David's peaceful rest ended somewhere in the night with a sudden bout of sneezing and coughing that kept him awake into daylight. The spring snow melted quickly, and the weather was sunny but cool. For three days the temperatures outside rose to the point where the family needed to open windows, and David's cold symptoms persisted but didn't worsen. Still, Eleanore found her husband rarely leaving David's side. He gladly assigned many of his own chores to Frederick or Ralph, which was too out of character for Eleanore to ignore. She too stayed near David, keeping a close eye on her husband as well as their son. Her concerns were difficult to define and too illogical to talk about, but impossible to ignore.

On the fourth day, David seemed better. The doctor had checked back twice and now assured them he was on the mend. On the fifth day, his cough became dramatically worse without warning, and then the fever set in. When James discovered that David's face was hot, he gave Eleanore a frightened glare, then hurried into the hall. She found him there with his head and hands pressed to the wall, struggling to breathe. When she touched his arm he retracted it and cursed, then he shrugged off her attempts to tell him all would be well before he returned to David's side and showed a hopeful smile to his son. He'd once declared that he could be a very good actor, but she'd never seen the evidence so apparent as now. He was terrified, and she knew it.

The doctor declared it to be pneumonia, and three days later when David's condition had only steadily worsened, Eleanore couldn't deny the validity of her husband's fears, or the fact that she concurred completely, even though they'd hardly uttered a word to each other throughout the course of their shared bedside vigil. He'd expressed concern about her catching the illness, but she assured him she'd learned in her youth how to be careful about such matters and she was not going to leave him alone with David. They were grateful, however, to have Iris in the care of the other adults in the home. They brought food and all else that was needed, but they stayed out of the room. The doctor came twice more, but his reports were not good. Apparently there was little to be done except wait it out and see if the fever and the cough would relent and leave the child to recover and regain his health.

Five days into David's fever, a storm set in. Or was it six? Eleanore had lost track. The child was utterly miserable when he was coherent at all, and the fear in James's eyes left Eleanore doubly afraid. Each day David's ability to breathe became more strained, and his father became more agitated and upset. His capacity to put on a brave face had completely disintegrated. David seemed calm in spite of his growing inability to draw breath, but he knew his father was terrified.

Darkness settled in while the wind pounded the rain into the windows and the fire cast eery shadows about the room. The dim glow of two lamps on either side of the bed barely illuminated how pale and ashen David had become. And Eleanore knew in her heart what the outcome would be. Three days earlier she had asked Frederick to give David a priesthood blessing. He'd been glad to comply, but the blessing had not given the promises that Eleanore had hoped for. There was no mention of healing or recovery, only a promise of peace and understanding, and an indisputable declaration that David's life was in his Savior's hands. Frederick's expression when he finished the blessing had left a somber impression that had caused Eleanore to question the outcome. But she could not question the source of the blessing or the power behind it. James, however, *did* question it. He'd followed Frederick into the hallway, and Eleanore had followed too, sensing her husband's frustration.

"Wait," James said, putting a hand on Frederick's arm. "I thought this priesthood gave you the power to heal."

"This is God's power, and subject to God's will."

"Are you saying it's God's will for my son to die?"

Frederick was slow to answer. Eleanore felt heavy from the implication of Frederick's hesitation and noted her husband's expression turning sour. Frederick finally admitted with solemnity, "I'm saying I had the impression that it was his time to go, but I'm only one man, James; and I'm human. I just don't know."

"Well, it's not true," James hissed quietly.

"Apparently you believe it is, or you wouldn't be so upset."

James only scowled at him and went back into David's room. Eleanore shared a concerned gaze with Frederick, then followed after her husband. In the days following the blessing, Eleanore had prayed and wrestled and fought internally over the matter, begging God to spare herself, and especially James, from having to face such a horror as losing their sweet son. But the answer was always the same, and only in accepting it had she been able to find any degree of peace. With the peace came her knowledge that David's mission, or at least that portion of it that he could accomplish while in this world, was complete. His suffering would soon be over. But then her husband's suffering would only begin. While the thought of letting David go threatened to crack her heart wide open, facing her husband's grief threatened to make it crumble. How could he bear it? How would she ever console him? He'd said he could never survive such a loss. If he truly believed that, could she ever talk him out of emotionally crumbling beyond recovery? As David's life became measured with each strained breath, Eleanore feared that the joy of her marriage and the tranquility of their home would die with him.

The wind howled while David's struggle to breathe only worsened. It became so difficult to watch him that Eleanore began praying that if he was truly meant to go, God might take him quickly and free him from this horror. She wept silently but without ceasing while she sat on one side of David's bed and James sat on the other, holding his son in his arms, rocking him, pleading with him to breathe, to live, to hold on.

"Breathe, David!" he almost shouted, not for the first time.

The frustration in both their eyes became too much for Eleanore to bear. She felt compelled to intervene, even though she knew James wasn't going to like what she knew needed to be said. She moved off of the bed and around it to sit facing her husband. While he held David against his shoulder, his eyes met hers over the top of the child's head.

"You need to let him go," she mouthed more than spoke, not wanting David to hear, even though his coughing and raspy breathing likely made it impossible.

James's eyes widened, then turned brittle. "No!" he whispered back. "I can't. I *can't!*"

Eleanore touched his face and kept her voice gentle. "You can't make him live, James. Do you want your final moments with him to be filled with your demanding something of him he can't do? He wants to please you, but he *can't* breathe any more. You have to let him go." She felt tears slide down her cheeks as his eyes showed comprehension, then unfathomable sorrow. "Tell him what you want him to know. Tell him what he needs to hear."

She saw him tighten his hold on the child as if that might prevent the inevitable from taking place. David's attempt to breathe became more strained, frantic. James held the boy's head in one of his hands and drew back to look into his eyes while new tears filled his own eyes, then spilled.

"I love you, David," he said, his voice breaking. Eleanore moved behind David and wrapped her arms around both of them. "I'll love you forever," James continued with growing emotion. "You're such a good boy; the finest son a man could ever ask for." He sobbed as something warm and peaceful replaced the fear and frustration in David's eyes. "I don't want to let you go." He sobbed again. "I'll miss you so much." He sobbed harder. "But if you need to go . . . I understand. All right?" David gave a perceptible nod, then went into a horrible fit of coughing that prompted James to sob audibly while he held him close. For more than an hour David coughed and struggled to breathe, with the span of seconds between each breath growing longer. James and Eleanore both spoke to him gently and held tightly to each other's hands while they each kept an arm around the child. A fit of strained coughing stopped abruptly, then the child went limp against his father's arm.

"No!" James cried and took David's face into one of his hands. "Don't leave us!" He wrapped David in his arms and wept without restraint while Eleanore sat beside him and did the same. Their weeping evolved into mutual shock while they sat in silence in David's room, attempting to accept that his lifeless form had been left behind, and was quickly turning cold.

Eleanore finally stood and put a hand on her husband's shoulder and whispered as if David was only sleeping and she didn't want to wake him. "We need to tell the others, and . . . make arrangements."

James felt terrified to leave the room, as if remaining there might somehow prevent this from being real. But he knew she was right. He touched David's cold face once more and took Eleanore's hand as she opened the door. In the hall they found a lamp burning and the door to Iris's room left open a crack, as it always was when she'd gone to bed. They crept quietly into their daughter's room where she was sleeping soundly, and they each carefully touched her face, as if to be assured that she was warm and breathing, unlike her brother in the next room. James was glad she'd been spared the horror of David's illness and death, but he wondered how they would tell her, and how they might help her through this loss. As if Eleanore had read his mind she wrapped her arms around him and pressed her face to his chest, clinging to him desperately, whimpering softly against his shirt. He just held her and cried silent tears while the shock wore off only slightly for just a moment before it settled back in place to protect his emotions. Once Eleanore was composed, he walked with her down the stairs where they found Frederick and Lizzie in the parlor, with Mary Jane asleep on one of the couches.

"We were just about to come and check on you," Frederick said, then both he and Lizzie showed alarm as the truth dawned on them. Either James or Eleanore had been with David for days; they'd not left him alone for a minute. But now they were together. And surely their faces showed evidence of their grief.

"What's happened?" Lizzie demanded in a hot whisper.

James cleared his throat, and Eleanore squeezed his hand. He forced his voice enough to just say it. "He's gone. It's over."

Lizzie immediately started to cry. Frederick put his head down and blew out a harsh breath. But neither of them seemed at all surprised. James had nearly forgotten about the blessing Frederick had given David a few days ago, but now he felt freshly angry over it. If the power of the priesthood existed, why could it not have saved his son? He forced back the temptation to voice his opinion, fearing his grief would explode in a fit of anger. It was surely best to keep such thoughts to himself.

James held Eleanore close throughout the night while they both cried more than slept. He finally got up before dawn and returned to David's room. Unable to bear the lifelessness there, he went to Iris's room instead and sat close to her bed, taking in the evidence of life radiating from her even as she slept. He was still sitting there when she came awake. She accepted the news of her brother's death with tears and simple faith, declaring firmly, "He's with Jesus now."

"Yes, I'm certain he is," James said. He felt no sorrow or fear on David's behalf. It was being left behind that caused him grief. He just didn't know how he could go on living without his son.

Chapter Thirteen
THE HUMAN HEART

Throughout the hours and days leading up to the funeral, James was occasionally stricken with unfathomable sorrow that racked his body with heaving sobs unlike anything he'd ever experienced. Between bouts of tears, the shock would settle in and allow him to make rational decisions and share practical conversations regarding the death of his son. Eleanore's grief was similar to his own. At times she cried so hard he feared she would put herself into labor. He stayed close to her, determined to see that she didn't do anything to risk her health. Neither of them could handle any more loss or trauma, and he prayed hourly that the outcome of this pregnancy would be favorable in every respect.

James and Eleanore agreed without question that David should be buried in the woods near the house, a place where he'd loved to play and had always been happy, as opposed to the city cemetery, which was too far away. The perfect spot was found, and a lovely iron fence was put up to protect an area large enough to allow James to imagine himself and the rest of his family all being buried there one day. Neighbors and members of the church congregation they met with all gathered for David's burial. The minister they listened to every Sunday spoke over the open grave, but James didn't at all like what the man said. While it was difficult to pinpoint exactly what bothered him, he was left with an uneasiness over the concepts of life and death that this man was preaching, especially in regard to relationships. It just felt wrong. But in the days following the funeral, James couldn't bring himself to talk about it with Eleanore or anyone else. He felt sure she would have answers according to her own religious beliefs, but that didn't necessarily feel any more right to him. In fact, *nothing* felt right. Nothing. He felt like a ghost, hovering on the planet with no purpose or meaning, lost in some endless abyss that had swallowed his son. He'd never fathomed that grief could be so consuming and mind-altering.

James was startled from a deep stupor when Eleanore sat beside him on the couch in the library and touched his arm. "Did you hear anything I said?" she asked.

"No," he had to admit. He hadn't even realized she'd been in the room.

"I'm worried about you, James. We must talk about this and—"

"You who have stared at walls and stayed in bed for weeks after losing a baby have no right to tell me that I need to talk." He realized how sharp he'd sounded when he saw her eyes widen, but he couldn't bring himself to take it back.

"You don't need to snap at me, James. I lost David, too. I thought we were in this together."

"I need to be alone," he said and hurried out of the room, fearing he'd say something else to hurt her.

Eleanore watched James leave and immediately became assaulted with a fresh wave of tears. She didn't know how it was possible to cry so much. She had believed that losing her babies had taught her grief. But it had never been like this. Having David taken from them was the hardest thing she'd ever faced, and yet she knew it was harder for James. For all of Eleanore's grief, she knew in her heart that David's death had not been happenstance. His life had been—and was still—in God's hands. While she missed him beyond comprehension and her sorrow could not be denied, it was buffered by her knowledge that it was meant to be. She felt peace. But she knew her husband didn't. It was for him that she feared.

A while later, Eleanore found Iris crying, which was not uncommon since the death of her brother. But this time her grief was more centered in feeling neglected by her father. She expressed a mature concern for him, and a childlike need that wasn't being fulfilled. She was accustomed to having her father actively involved in every aspect of her life, and he'd hardly spoken a word to her since he'd told her of David's passing. Eleanore did her best to console the child and assure her that all would be well with time, then she sought out her husband in his office, knowing he needed to hear what she had to say, whether he wanted to or not. She found him sitting in the chair, staring at the wall.

"What?" he growled quietly when she'd been in the room for a minute and hadn't spoken.

"As your wife it's my responsibility to point out anything I'm aware of in the household that might be a problem."

"Yes?" he said, at least looking at her.

"Iris needs you, James. She needs her father."

He turned back to the wall. "I have nothing to give her that won't make her more upset."

"Then you're going to have to *find* something to give her. Let her know that you love her. She's lost her brother. Will you allow history to repeat itself and make your other children feel invisible while you refuse to come to terms with losing this one?"

He glared at her sharply, but a while later she found him sitting on Iris's bed with her while they read together one of David's favorite stories. After Iris had been tucked into bed, Eleanore found James sitting on the edge of his own bed, sobbing into his hands. Eleanore sat beside him and put a hand on his shoulder. He clutched onto her and muttered through his tears, "Don't let me become like my father, Eleanore. Our children deserve better than that."

"You're a good father, James. You always have been. Believe it or not, Iris understands your pain. The two of you can find strength in sharing your grief."

He cried harder and then became silent with his head in her lap. "You are a wise woman, Eleanore Barrington," he said, his voice hoarse. "I can't imagine what I ever did without you."

Eleanore gratefully regarded the evidence that the man she loved still existed inside the shell he'd been hiding behind. But the following day, that shell was neatly back in place. She crawled under the covers that night beside her husband who had once again gone to bed much earlier than normal, leaving her to put Iris down for the night, and to answer the child's questions about life and death and why her father wouldn't talk to her. One bedtime story had clearly not appeased her needs.

"I know you're awake," Eleanore said, "so you can stop trying to pretend you're asleep when I come to bed. You can't imitate how you breathe when you're asleep because you've never been awake to hear it."

She'd hoped for the tiniest indication that he might find some small bit of humor in her comment, but he only said, "Good night, Eleanore." She turned over and cried, well aware that he had to know she was crying, but he made no effort to hold her close or discuss their common grief. He felt more distant to her than when she'd been scrubbing floors in his household and he'd not known of her existence.

Eleanore came abruptly out of a sound sleep, as if a noise had startled her. But she heard nothing beyond the pounding of her own heart. It only took a moment to surmise that James was not in the bed and not in the room. A heartbeat later, words came to her mind with no degree of subtlety. *Find your husband. He needs you.* Eleanore didn't hesitate even a moment to get out of bed and grab the robe she'd left on the chair. She felt her way down the stairs, not wanting to even take the time to light a lamp. But at the bottom of the stairs, she could see nothing. She groped around on a table in the hall to find a lamp and matches, then hurried toward the back of the house, which was completely dark. Her instincts drew her out the back door, which she left open as she turned and saw him. He was oblivious to the sudden glow of the lamp she was holding, and she was so astonished she could hardly breathe. There he stood, some kind of angry determination etched into his face, holding a pistol that was aimed directly at the dog. Jack sat obediently where he'd been tied to the porch rail. His ears were down as if he sensed that something horrible was about to happen, but he didn't move. Eleanore heard the gun cock and screamed, "No!" James turned to glance at her. There was no shame or guilt in his expression, only some kind of hard vengeance in his eyes. She set the lamp on the porch and rushed toward him as he corrected his aim. She grabbed his wrist and shouted softly, "Don't you dare do it!" She hadn't even known he owned a gun.

"Let go, Eleanore," he muttered hotly; she'd never heard him so angry.

"I'm not going to let you do it," she insisted, then realized that her holding his wrist could not prevent him from pulling the trigger. "Put the gun down and talk to me."

"Just go back to bed and—"

"No!" she shouted, but again he adjusted his aim in spite of her effort to push his hand down. "You'll regret it, James. Iris loves the dog. Would you take him away from her too? *You* love the dog, James; you know you do. You'll hate yourself if you do it." He said nothing, but he didn't pull the trigger. "It won't bring David back, James. It won't." Still he kept his aim steady; she could feel his determination. "Then you'll have to kill me too." Abruptly she let go and rushed toward the dog, putting herself between Jack and the pistol, wrapping the animal in her arms.

"Eleanore!" James shouted. "Don't be ridiculous!" Eleanore hoped that Iris wouldn't wake up and become privy to her father's intentions.

"How dare you call *me* ridiculous while you stand there with a gun in your hand? You're hurting. That's understandable. But this is *ludicrous!* It will solve *nothing!* Now, put the gun down!" Eleanore prayed even as she shouted at him. "He's my dog, too! And David is my son, too! Don't try to tell me that you love him any more than I do." She sobbed. "Now, stop this madness and talk to me." He moved his finger from the trigger but still he didn't lower the gun. "If you think that—"

"What on earth do you think you're doing?" Frederick said in a calm voice, coming out of the darkness. He took advantage of the distraction caused by his appearance to grab the pistol and twist it out of James's hand. Eleanore gasped with relief but kept her hold on the dog. She watched her husband stare at Frederick, looking as if he'd just been snapped out of a stupor, having no idea of where he was. He staggered slightly and hung his head as if holding the gun had somehow been holding him together, and now its absence had left him disoriented and weak. Frederick uncocked the pistol and tossed it to the ground before he put an arm around James to steady him. Eleanore heard her husband sob as he dropped his head further. Frederick moved with him toward his own home, saying over his shoulder, "Hide that gun, Eleanore. I'm going to keep him with me for a while. I won't let him out of my sight. I promise. Try to get some sleep."

She watched them disappear into the darkness, James leaning heavily against Frederick as they walked. Eleanore held the dog more tightly and wept without control until she realized how cold she'd become from sitting on the ground. She untied the dog and took him up to her room, where she curled up in bed and wept again with Jack resting near her feet. She prayed as she cried, and cried until she slept. She woke up to daylight and Jack scratching at the door to go out. She put on her robe and followed him outside. He went one direction, and she went the other to Frederick's kitchen door. She knocked lightly, and Frederick answered. Before she could utter a word, he said, "He's asleep. He spent most of the night crying and screaming, but maybe he just had to explode and get it over with. I said some things he needed to hear. I pray they sank in."

"As do I," she said and hugged him. "Thank you for being there."

"Well, it was hard to ignore all that shouting."

He stepped back and squeezed her hand. "He'll be fine. But you should be resting. You need to be careful."

"I know," she said, then told him where she'd hidden the gun. "Will you please get it and put it where he can never find it? I didn't even know he had one."

"It was his father's," Frederick said. He forced a smile. "You look after that pathetic dog, and I'll look after James."

Eleanore nodded and went back to the house, telling Amanda, who had just arrived that she was going back to bed, that they'd had a bad night. Amanda offered to care for Iris, who wasn't awake yet, and Eleanore was grateful, as always, to have Amanda in their household. She was so much like family. Ralph was already busy doing James's chores. Again Eleanore crawled into her bed and cried until the exhaustion of mourning combined with pregnancy lured her into an oblivion marred by strange dreams. She woke up feeling briefly disoriented, then fresh grief surged through her, both for David and for how the loss so deeply consumed her husband. While Eleanore stared at the wall, her tears came like a recently familiar companion, and she turned her face into her pillow and wept without restraint.

Eleanore was startled to feel a hand on her arm. She gasped and glanced over her shoulder to find her husband lying on his side behind her. He pressed a hand over her belly and held it there tightly, as if he might connect to this child they had created. "Forgive me," he murmured, and she knew he was crying. "I went crazy, Ellie. I don't know what I was thinking."

"You're holding too much inside, James," she said, "until it has no choice but to explode." She turned over and touched his face. "You must talk to me."

James blew out a long breath, knowing she was right but hating it. He just forced himself to say what he was feeling, as foolish as it might sound. "I don't understand . . . why God would allow this, Eleanore." He lay back on the pillow and let out a weighted sigh while his eyes drifted to the ceiling. "Why?"

"What are you saying?" Eleanore leaned up on one elbow. "That God is punishing us or something by taking our son?"

He looked at her intensely. "That's how it feels."

"Many families have lost a child, James. I don't think this trial is exclusive to us. David is the lucky one. He's free from the sorrow and pain of this world."

"I believe that, Eleanore, I do. But still . . . being without him hurts too deeply to comprehend ever being able to accept it." He looked at her harshly, as if she'd done something wrong. *"You* feel peace over his death," he said as if such a feeling were criminal.

"Yes, I do," she said. "And don't try to tell me that I love him less than you do. He has been my son for years now. You loved him no less than you do now when you believed he was *not* your son."

"Then *how*, Eleanore? How can you feel peace over this?" He stood up and began to pace; she leaned against the headboard and wrapped her arms around a pillow as if that might protect her from his heated emotions.

"How can you *not*, James?" she asked with quiet firmness. "That is the question. And since you asked, I'm going to give you the answer, but I have a feeling you're not going to like it. Still, I would hope that given your history of being a relatively teachable man, and humble in most regards, you will eventually come to realize that what I have to say is true."

She hesitated, and he said curtly, "Just say it and get it over with."

Eleanore looked at him sharply. "This has brought out a bitter, ugly side to you, James Barrington, a side that I don't understand, and I want no part of. Were you this belligerent when you lost Caroline?" His eyes snapped toward her; they both knew she was talking about her betrayal, not her death. Before he could answer she said, "Ah, yes. I recall now . . . the way you spoke to her in the library when I overheard you. I thought then that you were a harsh, cruel man, and I had no desire to know you. Now I see that facing certain difficulties brings out the worst in you. How could you ever hope to find peace while you harbor such anger and resentment, James?"

"Well, I *am* angry," he said. "My son is dead and—"

"*Our* son," she corrected. "Now, to answer your question. I can feel peace over this because the Savior's Atonement makes it possible to feel peace over *any* hardship this life might bring. I felt His love comfort my heart, James. And I know that everything will be all right. We will get through this, and we will yet have much joy in our lives, and we will have the opportunity to see David again." He looked dubious, even angry again, and she added the point that she knew needed to be made. "When it comes to matters of your heart, God and I have much in common, don't we?"

"I have no idea what you're talking about."

"Do you not see how you pledge your undying devotion to God? You will do whatever He asks of you, so long as it doesn't cross one firm boundary. You will not give Him your heart. Is love not part of the deal?"

James was assaulted with a pounding heart before her words even penetrated his clouded brain. His mouth went dry, and his palms became sweaty while she went on. "You're a good man,

James. I know it and God knows it. But I wonder what kind of fear is wrapped around your heart, with pride there to protect it. And don't tell me I don't know what I'm talking about. *I*, of all people, know your heart. What are you afraid of, James? That if you wholly give your heart to God, He will hurt it? The way your parents did? The way Caroline did? You have learned to trust me. Can you not trust Him?"

James felt his own defensiveness jump to defer the question. "Like the Mormons have trusted Him?" he asked, and she looked as if he'd slapped her. "What kind of God allows such persecution to be the measure of devotion? How can a *loving* God stand by while *His* people are driven, raped, murdered, while they die of disease and exposure on all sides? How can He . . . let innocent children die and . . ." The last came out on the wave of a sob.

Eleanore was surprised at how well she knew the answer. "The same kind of God who gave every human being the gift of free agency and the opportunity to have it tested through the course of this life. The same kind of God who stood by and watched His Only Begotten Son suffer more than any human being could possibly imagine." James stopped pacing and looked at her. "Because *His* suffering was the *only* way we could ever hope to find peace in the midst of the difficulties that would inevitably come to us here as Satan fights to oppose all that is good." She sighed slowly, relieved to find his eyes riveted to hers, and receptive. "The Saints have suffered immeasurably, James. No one can dispute that. Some have fallen away, but most remain steadfast and true no matter the horrors they've had to endure, the children they've had to bury. They have the peace of knowing that while God cannot take away the free agency of others, nor stop the natural course of life and death, He loves them. They are in His hands. They feel the peace He offers. They understand the perspective of eternity."

James felt quieted and stunned by the firmness in her eyes as well as the tranquility in her voice. Then she pushed aside the pillow she was holding and leaned forward as she added, "Don't you see, James? That's why they're willing to suffer, to sacrifice so much. It's not about this life. It's about eternity. It doesn't have to end with death, James. We can be together forever, all of us . . . but not if you allow your pride and fear to keep you from taking hold of what you know in your heart is true. You *know* it's true. The same way you knew you loved me long before you would ever admit it—even to yourself. If you want to be with David in the next life—with me, all of us—you must have faith enough to reach out and take what God has offered you."

A sudden weakness prompted James to stagger to a chair while he kept his eyes carefully connected to hers. He started to tremble as the truth of her words took hold of his frightened heart, reminding him of how he'd once willfully kept his heart from her when she had deserved it so fully. Was it true? Had he really done the same with God? Had fear kept him from accepting and embracing what God was offering him? Was that the reason he'd stubbornly resisted what everyone around him had embraced? Had his own fear of mortal suffering and heartache prevented him from accepting what had given Eleanore such undeniable peace and conviction? Could it be possible that his attempt to avoid grief and suffering, for himself as well as for his family, was the very key to not being able to let go of the heartache he felt now? Could it be that simple? If he gave his whole heart to God, would God in turn grant him peace over the loss of his son?

Eleanore watched her husband's eyes grow distant, his expression troubled. She sensed him weighing and measuring all she'd just said and prayed that his heart would receive it. She'd expected some degree of protest, not because he was antagonistic by nature, but because his present pain went so deep. He met her eyes again, and she saw moisture gathering there. While she was hoping for the conversation to continue, he shot to his feet and muttered, "I need to be alone." She heard his booted feet hurrying over the wood floor of the hall and down the stairs, then the back door slammed in the distance.

James ran once he was out of the house. Far into the woods he dropped to his knees and wrapped his arms around his middle, curling around them while fresh pain poured out of him with a volatile barrage of tears. And while he cried he prayed, pleading for understanding—and forgiveness. Was Eleanore right? Had he been withholding his heart from God out of some kind of deep-seated fear? Was that the reason he couldn't find any degree of peace over David's death?

James lost track of time as minutes faded into hours while he remained on his knees, lost in prayer and internal torment. He recounted the painful episodes of his life, all culminating with the death of a child. *His* child. When his knees burned and his back ached, he rolled onto the ground and lay on his back, looking up through the trees toward a star-scattered sky. Again time slipped by while a calming sensation slowly trickled into his spirit. While he assimilated it into himself and affirmed its validity, a different kind of tears burned his eyes. He knew he had a long way to go to get the answers he needed, but for the first time since David had become ill, he felt a glimmer of hope. He felt some tiny measure of understanding, even if he couldn't possibly put it into words. And he felt forgiveness. He knew that God understood the weakness of his human heart and was there to carry him in spite of it. And perhaps with time, he would come to fully understand all that God might be willing to teach him. He left the woods with a prayer that he could overcome his fears and fully give his heart to God. It seemed a small price to pay for all that God had blessed him with. And if God could grant him peace over David's death, and also the will and means to press forward and find happiness, as Eleanore seemed convinced was possible, then surely James should be willing to do whatever God asked of him. While it was likely easier said than done, James felt the tiniest spark of hope that such a thing might be possible. He just needed time . . . to think, to pray, to understand.

Eleanore held her breath when she heard James come in the back door. She had paced and stewed and worried for hours on end, but had felt it was important not to go searching for him. It was dark, and he'd missed two meals. Iris had already gone to bed, and the others had all gone home. Eleanore stepped out of the kitchen and met her husband in the hall, relieved to see something tranquil in his eyes, but it was coupled with a great weariness.

"Forgive me," was all he said before he put his arms around her and held her tightly for a long moment. "It's late; we should get some sleep."

"But you haven't eaten."

"I can't," he said and started up the stairs.

Eleanore followed him as he slipped into Iris's room and pressed a kiss to her forehead while she slept. Silence hovered between them as they went to their own room to prepare for bed. She sat down to brush out her hair, and he knelt in front of her, pressing his hands, then the side of his face, to her well-rounded belly, as if he might hear the baby whisper.

"I love you, Eleanore," he murmured and lifted his head to kiss her. "I do."

"And I love you," she said, touching his face. He kissed her again, then moved away to get undressed for bed. A few minutes later when she came out of the bathing room, he was beneath the covers and already asleep. Eleanore lay beside him and prayed for him until she too drifted off to sleep. She woke sometime in the night to find a lamp burning in the bedroom. She turned over to see her husband sitting near the lamp, scratching Jack's head, which was planted in his lap, while he read from the Book of Mormon. She pretended to be asleep, not wanting to interrupt or make him self-conscious. She wept silently and prayed some more, certain they were on the verge of a miracle.

She slept again, and when she woke up the following morning, he and Jack were still there. This time the book was closed on his lap, with his finger between pages, while he gazed toward the window. His eyes looked strained with lack of sleep, but bright with wonder.

Eleanore felt it best not to bring too much attention to his reading the book after all this time. Instead she simply asked, "Are you all right?"

He looked up at her. "Better, thank you. And you?"

"Just . . . very pregnant."

He smiled. "It's what you've always wanted."

"Yes, it is. So I won't expect you to feel sorry for my aches and pains."

"Oh, but I do!" he said. "Just because you asked for it doesn't mean anyone ever expected it to be easy."

With this confirmation that he was more like himself, Eleanore silently thanked God for such progress and got dressed for the day. James went back to bed after breakfast and slept through lunch. He was up and dressed for supper, not saying much but behaving pleasantly. His subdued attitude indicated his ongoing grief, but he had apparently discarded the gruff, closed attitude he'd been holding onto.

That evening he spent time with Iris and tucked her into bed, and the child clearly felt more at ease and secure. Eleanore heard her say to her father as he doused the lamp, "It will be all right, Papa. We'll be with David again someday."

Again Eleanore caught her husband reading in the night, but she said nothing about it. He was up early and kept busy throughout the day, more engaged in doing the usual chores and work in the garden than he'd been since David's illness. Over the next few days, he kept busy as he always had. He'd let the household books get way behind as he grieved over David's death, and he spent long hours in his office putting them in order. And he took a trip into town to see that they had everything they needed.

After James had tucked Iris in for the night once again, Eleanore found him sitting on David's bed, lost in deep thought. She entered the room quietly and opened a drawer to retrieve something she'd been waiting to show her husband. She sat down beside him and put a leather-bound book into his hands.

"What is this?" he asked.

"David's most recent journal," she said, and his eyes widened. "The others are here," she added, referring to the other four books she was holding. "I haven't read them yet. I thought you should be the first." She set the books on the bed and stood to leave the room.

"Ellie?" he said, and she turned back.

"Do you think that God would take my son from me in order to teach me what I needed to learn?"

Eleanore was grateful to have an answer. "I believe it was David's time to go. How God works His purposes into such events is surely beyond our comprehension. Whatever David came to this earth to do, it was done. We need to let him go."

Eleanore left James to read, wanting to give him time alone as much as she wanted to avoid having him exposed to her own emotion. In spite of her convictions and peace over David's death, she missed him so much it hurt. She found herself in the library where she pulled out the family Bible and sat down to read in a way that had been her habit for many years. While she randomly flipped through pages, hoping it might fall open to something that would offer some peace and understanding, she felt guided to the very front where the family records were kept. She'd not looked here since she'd seen her own name put there along with the date of her marriage to James Barrington. She actually felt startled to see David's name next to his death date, and she wondered when James had made the effort to put it there. And above that were three separate death notations that simply stated *Unnamed Baby* and the corresponding dates.

Eleanore wept freshly over the grief associated with what was written there, then she forced herself to follow her original goal and find a message in the Bible that might give her strength. She was led to the story of Job, marveling that all of his children had been killed in one horrifying accident, and yet he had responded firmly, *The Lord gave, and the Lord hath taken away; blessed be the name of the Lord.*

* * *

James felt almost hesitant to read David's journals, but once he got started he became immersed in the childlike perception of events that James knew well. David had written of Eleanore becoming the governess, how he loved and trusted her, and how he'd struggled with his mother's death. He wrote of his joy in having his father marry the governess, and his pleasure in going to America. And he wrote of daily events and life-altering decisions with amazing insight. James read far into the night, unable to stop until he'd read them all. The penmanship and flow of words had gradually improved as David had matured; memories and feelings oozed off the pages. James laughed and cried and thanked God for this tangible remnant of his son's life, and for the opportunity to know David's most personal convictions on matters of life and religion. When he slept, it was in David's bed, and he woke to daylight with Eleanore lying beside him, her hand on his face.

"Are you all right?"

He kissed her and said, "He was an amazing child."

"So much like his father." She kissed him again. James drew her into his arms and couldn't deny his growing belief that everything would be all right.

* * *

Eleanore was pleased as always to receive a letter from Sally. It spoke of the everyday matters of her family and the community, and the rising walls of the temple. While the Saints still grieved over the loss of their beloved Joseph, Sally felt confident that the Church was in good hands and that God was still in charge. She barely mentioned that there was ongoing trouble from outsiders, as if it were minimal and nothing to be concerned about, but Eleanore suspected that Sally was simply trying to be optimistic. As always, Eleanore kept Sally and her family in her prayers, as well as all people everywhere who shared her beliefs. And she prayed for her husband, that his quiet search would lead him to peace and understanding. He seemed more calm and tranquil than he'd been since David had become ill, and occasionally she caught him reading. But he said nothing, and Eleanore was certain he would talk when he was ready.

Eleanore finally sat down to write to her friends of David's death. The letters were difficult to write, and she cried many tears during the process, but once they were mailed she felt one step closer to being able to put the loss behind and move on. They would never stop missing David, but she knew from the deaths of her parents that time did aid in healing.

A month after the most horrible night of their lives, Eleanore sat next to her husband in bed while they read from separate books prior to settling down for the night. Since James had been dominating the Book of Mormon, she read from it when he was busy elsewhere and was now reading from the Bible he'd given her during their engagement. She knew that David's copy of the book was in his room, and there was an unread copy tucked away that she'd purchased in Nauvoo just to have it on hand, but this arrangement felt right for now.

"Listen to this," he said eagerly, and she wondered if he would finally share his feelings on what he'd been reading.

"I'm listening," she said, and he read aloud. *"Now, concerning the state of the soul between death and the resurrection—Behold, it has been made known unto me by an angel, that the spirits of all men, as soon as they are departed from this mortal body, yea, the spirits of all men, whether they be good or evil, are taken home to that God who gave them life. And then shall it come to pass, that the spirits of those who are righteous are received into a state of happiness, which is called paradise, a state of rest, a state of peace, where they shall rest from all their troubles and from all care, and sorrow."*

James lightly slapped the page with the back of his hand. "It's incredible," he said. "That minister who buried our son had *no* answers, no comfort to give us, no understanding whatsoever. But here it is. David truly is in a better place, Eleanore."

"Yes, he is," she said and squeezed his hand. She resisted the urge to add, *provided you believe that book is true.* She wondered if he *did* believe it. Well, obviously to some degree he did, or he wouldn't be so thrilled over what he'd just read. But she knew from her own experience, and the experience of others, that he needed to *know* it was true for himself, beyond any doubt. He kept reading to himself, and she left him to it, certain that with time he would find the full depth of his answers. In the meantime, she prayed for him and continually expressed her gratitude to God for all they'd been given, and for how far they had come.

* * *

James was beginning to think he might actually be able to find peace over losing his son when Iris became unexplainably reluctant to get out of bed. She simply said she didn't feel well, but overall she seemed fine, wanting to sit up and draw, or read, or play with her dolls. Her being under the weather with no apparent cause for concern suddenly turned, in the middle of

the night, to a raging fever and a great deal of moaning and
writhing from the child, as if she were in great pain. And James
wondered if his fragile heart could take any more. The panic
that seized him was like unto the news of David's pneumonia,
only more so. The prospect of losing a child had been devas-
tating—the reality of it beyond comprehension. The very idea of
repeating the nightmare threatened to rip his human heart to
shreds.

Frederick went for the doctor when it was barely daylight.
He came back to report that the doctor would come as soon as
he delivered a baby that was getting close. Frederick saw to the
animals' needs, and while they waited for the doctor, Eleanore
suggested they pray. James knelt to face her and took both her
hands into his. He prayed verbally with all the strength of his
heart and soul that they might be guided to know what to do
for Iris, that she might be spared from whatever illness had
taken hold of her young body. James felt reluctant to get off his
knees, afraid he might not have the answer that he would have
to face a horrific possibility. Iris's moaning prompted him to end
the prayer. Once the amen was spoken, Eleanore moved to the
child's side while James paced beside her bed, almost crippled by
the smoldering anxiety in his stomach.

He heard Eleanore ask, "Does it hurt anywhere, sweetheart?"

James listened for an answer but didn't hear one. He turned
to investigate Iris's silence and found her looking at Eleanore
with guilty eyes.

"What is it, Iris?" James asked tenderly. "You can tell us
anything, my darling. Anything."

"And you won't be angry?" she asked, and tears rose in her
big eyes.

"Of course not, sweetheart," Eleanore said while she shot a
confused, mildly panicked glance toward James.

After some serious hesitation and more tears, Iris finally
admitted, "I hurt my foot." The words flooded out of her, barely

comprehensible through her tears. "You told me not to walk in the woods in bare feet and I did it anyway and I stepped on a sharp twig and I didn't tell you because I was afraid you'd be angry because I didn't do what . . ."

She stopped and gasped when James threw back the bedcovers while Eleanore demanded, "Is that why you've stayed in bed?" Her voice was kind in spite of its urgency. "Your foot hurt, and you didn't want us to know?"

Iris nodded, and her tears turned to audible sobs just before James found the guilty foot and words of hushed terror escaped his lips. "Heaven help us."

He found Eleanore right beside him, felt her attempting to accept, as he was, that this was the ugly culprit for Iris's fever. The injury was blistered and full of pus, with redness and swelling radiating all around it.

"Please, no," Eleanore muttered and took hold of James's arm with trembling hands. He felt his heart turn cold and threaten to stop. He'd never seen anything like this, but he'd heard of it. And he found it difficult to believe that his little daughter would survive this; at best, she would lose her foot. Even the thought of that made him ill.

James was grateful for Eleanore's calm fortitude as she soothed the child and assured her they weren't angry; they were just worried. Eleanore was honest as she told Iris that the sore on her foot, now that it had gone unheeded, was the reason she'd become so ill, but they loved her no matter what, and they were going to do whatever they needed to make it better.

"The doctor will be here soon," Eleanore said. "I want you to be a brave girl and do what he asks. Your father and I will be right here with you. Do you understand?"

Iris nodded. "Is it going to hurt?"

"Yes, I believe it will," Eleanore said, and Iris clutched onto her and cried. "We must pray," she added and immediately began a verbal prayer, asking that the child would be calm and comforted, that the doctor would be guided, that this horrible infection would not be irreversible. But James felt little hope. The reality was plain, the logic too profound to ignore.

Chapter Fourteen
DAVID'S DREAM

The doctor's report was not a surprise. Eleanore held the child close while James paced the room and listened to the doctor explaining how the redness moving up the veins in her leg meant that the infection had passed a crucial stage. He asked James and Eleanore to step into the hall. Eleanore assured Iris they would be right back, and she nodded bravely. In the hall, the doctor said, "I'm so sorry, truly." James took hold of Eleanore's hand and found her shaking as much as he was. "At this point, attempting to amputate the leg would only give her undue suffering that would not likely alter the outcome. We can lance the ulcer and do some things to help draw the infection out, but I fear it's gone way too far to do much good."

James felt his mind drawn immediately elsewhere, clinging to a source of hope that the doctor couldn't give them. "Do everything you can," James said to the doctor, feeling distracted.

The doctor nodded and said to Eleanore, "I'll need to use your kitchen for some preparations."

"Of course," Eleanore said.

"I'll take you down," James said and nodded toward Eleanore. "You stay with Iris."

James left the doctor in the kitchen with Amanda, instructing her to help him, then he rushed outside and found Frederick in the barn.

"I need you," he said without preamble. "I need you to give Iris a blessing—now. I need it done now."

Frederick looked alarmed, then concerned, then hesitant. "The last time I did this, you disagreed with the results." James couldn't blame him for his curt tone. "Why would you ask again?"

James heard his own voice crack. "Because it's the only chance she's got."

Frederick's concern overrode his hesitance as he asked, "Why? What's wrong with her?"

James barely kept from bawling like a baby as he gave Frederick a brief explanation. He concluded with a firm plea, "She needs a blessing; I beg you."

"You don't have to beg me," Frederick said gently. "I'm more than willing, but . . ."

"But what?" James wished it hadn't sounded so sharp.

"I didn't think you believed in that kind of thing. Clearly your desire for me to do this is more than respecting the beliefs of your wife and daughter."

"Clearly I would not be asking if I didn't believe it could help."

Frederick offered the subtlest of smiles and put a hand on James's shoulder as they left the barn. On their way up the stairs, Frederick said, "It would be more ideal for two men to do this, you know."

"I'm certain God understands that we only have one available."

"Yes, I'm certain He does," Frederick said. "But do you?"

James stopped walking, and Frederick did the same. The sharp glance he aimed at his friend quickly came back to him, and he looked away in an attempt to hide how the question pierced his heart. But he couldn't think about that right now. His daughter might die. And the power that Frederick held seemed the only possible way to save her. In Iris's room he found Eleanore leaning against the headboard, holding Iris close to her. The child was crying and writhing with pain and fever. Silent tears trickled over Eleanore's face. James choked back his own tears and discreetly lifted the sheet to show Frederick the ailing foot. He heard his friend gasp and was grateful to note that Iris was oblivious.

Eleanore remained where she was while Frederick put his hands on Iris's head. As the blessing began, new fear pounded into James's heart. What if the answer was the same as it had been for David, that nothing could be done? What if it was God's will for this child to die? While James prayed silently that such might not be the case, he was surprised to realize that he had no choice but to accept God's will. As difficult as that would be, he found himself silently telling God that he *would* accept His will. Still, he begged for the miracle, pledging to do whatever God required of him for the remainder of his life. The words of Frederick's blessing became distant while James spoke to God in his own mind, begging forgiveness for his prideful heart, for the fear that he'd allowed to rule him, for his stubbornness. And he pledged his heart, his whole heart, to the God who had given him life. He was startled from his prayer when he heard Frederick hesitate; a noticeable silence filled the room. Even Iris's moaning and crying had ceased. James opened his eyes to see if something might be wrong. He almost wondered if the child had died, but he could actually see her breathing. Frederick's eyes were squeezed tightly shut in concentration, his hands remained firm on Iris's head. James closed his eyes and waited, holding his breath, wondering if he would hear a pronouncement of imminent death, steeling himself to accept it without the anger and bitterness he'd indulged in when he'd lost David. And then Frederick said it. In a voice that was firm and forceful, he commanded her to heal and be strong, to live and to grow, to have children of her own, and to help build God's kingdom on the earth. Iris was told that she would share peace with the Saints in Zion and raise a family there without persecution or suffering.

James felt tears slide down his cheeks even before the blessing was completed. He reluctantly opened his eyes, hesitant to let go of the powerful Spirit present in the room. He saw Frederick slowly remove his hands from Iris's head. Both he and Eleanore were weeping as well. Iris was apparently sleeping soundly for the first time in many hours. Eleanore looked on in awe; Frederick looked terrified. While James could almost guess the reasons, Frederick readily admitted, "What if I'm wrong? I can't explain by what force those words came out of my mouth. But . . . what if I'm wrong?"

"It's *not* wrong," Eleanore said with hushed reverence. "I felt the truth of it as you spoke." She sobbed quietly and held the child closer. "She's going to be all right."

They were all startled when the doctor opened the door without knocking, entering the room with Amanda, who was carrying a tray of medical instruments that had apparently just been cleaned. They both stopped. The doctor said, "Did we interrupt something?"

"Uh . . . no," James said. "We were just . . . praying. We were finished."

"Can never have too much of that," the doctor said. James and Frederick moved aside to let him do what he needed to do.

"I think her fever's gone down," Eleanore said, putting a hand on Iris's cheek.

The doctor touched the child's brow and looked puzzled. "I believe you're right. It's gone down significantly." Then he threw back the sheet covering Iris's feet and gasped. He froze, staring. He opened his mouth as if to speak, but no sound came out. James didn't dare move, or look, until the doctor finally said, still staring, "That must have been quite some prayer."

"What do you mean?" James demanded, stepping forward.

The doctor motioned toward Iris's feet. "There is nothing wrong with this child that a few days won't take care of." He looked directly at James. "If I hadn't seen it myself, I wouldn't believe it."

James sank weakly onto the edge of the bed, taking hold of the foot that had, not so many minutes ago, been threatening to take his daughter's life. He saw only a scabbing wound with no redness or sign of infection. He heard Eleanore start to sob before she put a hand over her mouth. He met her eyes, he met Frederick's, he turned to the doctor and barely managed to ask, "Do you have any explanation for this?"

"I think they call it a miracle," he said with a smile. "I've seen a few in my day, but nothing like this. Apparently God wants this child to live." He started gathering his things. "I dare say this little one is destined for great things."

"Indeed," James said and wiped fresh tears.

Amanda wiped her own tears on her apron and showed the doctor out once he'd declared that there was no further need for him to be there. On his way out the door, he said he would see them when the baby came, and hopefully not before.

Iris slept until late afternoon, with either James or Eleanore staying with her. They were both in the room, quietly talking of the miracle, when Iris opened her eyes and asked for pancakes, three of them, with hot maple syrup. They both laughed and hugged her, but tears came with their laughter.

"Why are you crying?" Iris asked. "Are you angry with me because I didn't wear my shoes and—"

"No, my darling," James said. "Although you *should* wear your shoes in the woods. We only ask that because we don't want you to get hurt. You can go barefoot around the yard where the ground's not so rough. But whenever you get hurt, for any reason, whether it's something you've done wrong or not, we want you to tell us straightaway. We probably could have prevented your getting so ill if we'd known about the injury on your foot right when it happened. Do you understand?"

Iris nodded penitently. James took her hand and moved closer. "Now," he said, and Eleanore saw a sparkle in his eyes, "we must tell you of the miracle that saved your life, my dear. You must write about it in your journal, and one day you will tell it to your children and grandchildren. This was a great day in your life, Iris." He became emotional again. "God saved you this day, and you must always praise Him for that, as we will. And you must always remember that He let you live when He could have let you die. For that reason and many others, you must always live as He would have you live."

Iris shed tears herself as her father repeated what the doctor had said, which now horrified the child. But then he quickly recounted the miracle. Iris investigated the recently ailing foot and gasped. She kept touching the healing sore there as if she couldn't believe it. Then she hugged both her parents tightly, apologized again and repeated her request for pancakes.

Amanda gladly complied, and while she mixed the batter and poured it onto a griddle, Eleanore heated up the syrup. Once Iris was full, she wanted to get out of bed, but her father insisted she stay there for the remainder of the day, just to be on the safe side. She'd been very ill. She asked for her journal and used the time to write down the story her father had told her of the miracle, then she let her parents read it. She slept well that night and was up and running before breakfast the next morning, as if nothing in the world had ever been wrong.

The day was busy with catching up all that had been neglected during Iris's memorable illness. Although Eleanore felt far too slow and achy from her pregnancy to believe her meager efforts contributed much to the household, she was grateful for Lizzie and Amanda, who not only kept everything in order, but fussed over her like a couple of mother hens. Eleanore decided that every woman in her condition could use a little mothering.

James went into town, spent hours in his office, and helped Frederick and Ralph in the garden. That night after supper, Eleanore sat in bed with a book while her husband bathed in the next room. He entered the room while haphazardly combing his wet hair back off his face with his hands, then he bent to kiss her.

"Oh, you smell good," she said.

"A stark contrast," he said with light sarcasm, "from all that sweat."

"Ah, but sweating becomes you. I don't think you did much of it before you came to America."

"No, I didn't," he said and settled against the headboard beside her, apparently intent on reading himself. "But I confess, I love the life we've found here." He kissed her again. "The opportunity for a man to work up a good sweat every day isn't a bad thing."

"No, it certainly isn't," she said, touched by her ongoing admiration for her husband, and comforted by the evidence that he'd gotten past the crippling grief of losing their son. She caught him shedding tears now and then, but he was healing— so gradually that she wondered if he had fully noticed his own progress. He picked up the Book of Mormon and began to read. He'd still said nothing about his feelings on the book, beyond occasionally reading a verse or two aloud and discussing its concept with her. She'd felt compelled to keep her thoughts to herself and allow him all the time he needed to come to his own conclusions. But tonight, with Iris's miracle still fresh, she felt the need to say, "Apparently you're rather taken with that book. It *is* compelling."

"To say the least."

"So, talk to me. It's been my favorite book for years, but we've rarely talked about it at all. We *always* talk about the books we read."

James sighed, and his eyes showed suspicion over her motives, but it was suspicion laced with humor. He closed the book but left one of her hair ribbons there as a marker. "It's magnificent, Eleanore. It's everything you ever said it was." Eleanore wanted to hear more but didn't know how to press the topic without making the situation awkward. She was relieved when he added, "I'm certain you're wondering where I stand when it comes to this book and all else that's tied into it. So I'll tell you. You certainly have a right to know." He set the book aside and leaned forward. "I want to be baptized, Eleanore," he said, and she took a sharp breath, "but not until I absolutely know for myself, beyond any doubt, that it's true and right. I'm grateful for the miracle we were just given with Iris, and I don't dispute its source. But I don't want God to think that I'm some kind of sign seeker; I don't want to do this impulsively in the wake of a miracle."

Eleanore smiled and touched his face. "I wouldn't expect you to do anything of importance in your life without careful thought and consideration."

James saw tears in her eyes and felt compelled to admit his deepest thoughts. "Why, Ellie? Why would God give me such . . . profound, undeniable . . . proof of His existence in my life?"

"Perhaps because He knows that in spite of your weaknesses, you're a good man with a good heart, and your faith in Him was not nearly so absent as you might have believed. He's known your heart all along, James." She smiled. "Perhaps He just wanted you to admit it."

He laughed softly, then closed his eyes as new tears unexpectedly tingled there. How could he not see—and feel—the parallels? He'd loved Eleanore from the start and had been too proud and stubborn to admit it until he'd been forced to recognize his absolute dependence on her in every respect. Had he known in his heart all along that the gospel was true? Had it taken evidence of his utter reliance on God to show him what he'd known from the start? Whatever the case may be, he was done playing games with his life *and* his salvation. His heart had been spread wide open, and he meant what he'd told God during the moment of crisis. He *would* devote the remainder of his life to living the way God wanted him to. He simply needed to know, beyond any question, exactly what that entailed, so that he would never have to question it again, never have to look back and wonder.

Eleanore fell asleep while James was still reading. She woke up in the dark, not certain of the time. She crept quietly into the other room to relieve herself, longing for the day when this baby was no longer consuming her entire body. She lit a lamp only long enough to check the time and found that it was nearly five. She eased silently back into bed, and her husband immediately moved close to her, wrapping her in his arms.

"I tried not to wake you," she said, but she couldn't say she was sorry when he pressed a kiss to her lips.

"You didn't wake me," he said. "I haven't been able to sleep."

"Why?" She touched his face. "What's wrong?"

"Just a lot on my mind, I suppose," he said, but offered no further explanation. "How are you feeling?" he asked.

"The same," was all she said and set her head against his shoulder. She quickly relaxed until she was startled out of fresh sleep by a strange sensation. It only took her a moment to figure out what had happened. It had happened to her once before, but then it had been way too early for the baby to survive. Now, it was less than a week before the estimated due date.

"James, are you awake?" she asked and slid up into a sitting position.

"Yes," he said, but she could tell from his voice that he had drifted off and she'd roused him. Just when he was finally able to sleep she was going to deny him that privilege. She wasn't about to go through even a minute of this alone. "What's wrong?"

"Would you light a lamp, please?" she asked, and he did so. As soon as a glow came over the room, Eleanore threw back the covers, relieved to find only a wet spot where she'd been laying, and no apparent cause for concern.

"What is it?" James asked, turning back toward her.

"My water just broke," she said.

He gasped and sat up straight. "We should send for the doctor and—"

"No," she took his arm, "I've not had so much as a single contraction. We'll know when it's time to send for the doctor. This isn't it. Just . . . hold me."

He sighed and put his arms around her, asking softly, "Are you afraid, Eleanore?"

"Yes," she said, "but not nearly so afraid as I was the last time. Now I have every reason to believe the results will be good. I would endure almost anything just to have a strong, healthy baby."

"I would agree with that on all counts," he said, holding her close. "I only wish I could do more of the enduring. I hate to watch you suffer."

"Just . . . don't leave me. As long as you're with me, I can do anything."

"I'll be here," he said. "I promise."

She let out a long, slow breath. "We still don't have a girl's name picked out. What if it's a girl and you have no idea what to call her?"

"I'm certain we'll come up with something," he said and rubbed her belly. "But I still think we should consider a different name for a boy."

"No, I'm firm on it. He shall have his father's name. We will call him Jamie to differentiate. I've always loved the name Jamie. Before my father died, there was a boy in our neighborhood, a playmate. His name was Jamie. He was very handsome."

"Your first love?" James asked lightly.

"I was five."

"He didn't try to kiss you?"

"No," she laughed. "We played marbles and hide-and-seek, and his mother made the most heavenly plum tarts."

"Jamie it will be then, in memory of your first love."

She laughed again. "No." She touched his face. "In honor of my only love." He smiled and kissed her. "And if it's a girl?"

"Perhaps she will whisper her name to us when she arrives."

"Perhaps," Eleanore said, then felt a tightening across her lower back. "Oh, I think it's starting."

James fought to cover his concern and alarm, and instead distracted her with conversation while he carefully watched the clock. It was late morning before the pains were close enough that he felt justified in sending Frederick for the doctor. Already the evidence of her pain was difficult to bear; he prayed the rest would go quickly and without complications. But the hours of labor dragged incessantly and with great misery for Eleanore, while James could only try to encourage and distract her from the pain. Early in the evening, she finally gave birth to a perfectly healthy boy. And James had never known such happiness as the moment that baby was placed in Eleanore's arms and she looked up to meet his eyes. It was the fulfillment of so many years of wishing and hoping and surviving disappointment. It was a miracle.

Later, after the ordeal was over and everything had been cleaned up, Eleanore lay resting while James sat on the bed beside her, holding his infant son. He knew he should be tired, but he didn't feel it. He wanted only to try to accept yet another miraculous moment in his life. He'd become a father before, and while he could not compare the love for one child to another, the sharing of this experience with a woman who loved him with her whole heart and soul was immensely different than what he'd known with his first wife. He had only to look into Eleanore's eyes to know that this was not only about bringing a child into the world; it was a manifestation of the love they shared. And his heart swelled with perfect joy.

Iris was so completely thrilled with her baby brother that James could hardly stop laughing while she held him with extra care and expressed wonder over every part of his new little life. Everyone else in the household was equally excited, and happiness filled the house as little Jamie was passed around and admired with firm declarations that he looked like his father.

Eleanore drifted in and out of sleep while James made himself comfortable beside her with little Jamie sleeping in the crook of his arm. He thought she was asleep when he heard her say, "I think David and Jamie had a few moments together before he was due to arrive."

"I'm certain you're right," he said and touched the baby's thick, black hair.

Eleanore was struck with a thought and gasped at exactly the same moment that James looked at her with wide eyes, as if it had occurred to him as well.

"That dream," he murmured with hushed reverence. "David's dream. Do you think it's possible that . . ." He didn't finish but Eleanore didn't need him to. She knew exactly what he meant.

"Yes, I think it's possible," she said and felt tears trickle down her face at the same time they showed in James's eyes. She knew, as she knew he did, that David had been given a glimpse of heaven when he'd been shown the moment he would be with his baby brother. Whether such a thing had actually occurred or not didn't matter; the message was evident. There were no words needed to express the peace present in the room as they internalized one more piece of evidence that their lives, in this world and the next, were in God's hands.

James looked again at the baby and said with a cracking voice, "He seems to still have a glow of heaven about him."

"So do you," she said, and he found her hand on his face.

James met her eyes and admitted, "You've made me happier than I ever could have imagined." He wrapped an arm around her while the baby remained asleep in the other one, and together they cried with a joy that was equal to all they had suffered together.

A short while later Jamie woke up and demanded to be fed. While Eleanore nursed him and James sat beside her, gently examining the baby's feet, she ventured to share her thoughts. "I have a confession to make."

"I'm listening."

"Do you know the story of Leah . . . in the Bible?"

"Vaguely," he said. "Isn't she one of Jacob's wives?"

"That's right. But Jacob always loved Rachel, her sister. His marriage to Leah was purely convenience."

James bristled a litte at that last word. They both knew their marriage had initially been exactly that.

"On the evening of the day I accepted your proposal," she went on, "we were in the library, and I was thumbing through the Bible. It fell open to a particular page, and a phrase jumped out at me." She started to cry, and he reached across the baby to wipe her tears, wondering over her emotion related to the topic. "I was never able to forget it, even though I tried. And I think . . . I believe . . . there was a time . . . although I probably didn't even admit it wholly to myself . . . that I felt the same way . . . the way Leah felt. But it didn't turn out for me the way it did for her." She smiled. "You gave me your love a long time ago. And maybe God wanted me to be sure that your reasons for loving me had nothing to do with my giving you a son. And now that I have, everything between us is simply all the more wonderful."

"Yes, it is," he said, feeling confused. "What did it say?" he asked. "What did that line in the Bible say?"

She closed her eyes and spoke it from firm memorization. *"And Leah conceived, and bare a son . . . for she said, Surely the Lord hath looked upon my affliction; now therefore my husband will love me."*

James took a sharp breath and sorted silently through all she'd just said. For a moment the heartache he'd surely caused for her in the past pierced him. But it was in the past. He understood the meaning in what she'd just told him. And there was nothing more to say, except to declare once again, with all the conviction that he felt, "I *do* love you, Eleanore."

"I know," she said with a gratified smile. "That's why my life is perfect."

He watched her focus turn to the baby as he finished eating, and together they laughed when James got a loud burp out of him. While Jamie went back to sleep in his father's arms, Eleanore slipped into much-needed sleep herself. James rose and laid the baby in his bassinet before he got back into bed. His life was perfect too. Almost, anyway. But he knew exactly what to do to make it that way.

* * *

"Eleanore, there's something I need to ask you." He sat beside her on the bed and took her hand while she fed the baby. The afternoon sun was pouring into the room. "If circumstances had been different, do you think you would have married me?"

Eleanore looked into his eyes and realized that for whatever reason this had come up before, it hadn't been resolved. "That's difficult to answer when I can't go back in time and change the circumstances. Why don't you just get to the point about what is specifically troubling you regarding the reasons we were married." He looked surprised, and she added, "You should know you can trust me, James. Just tell me what's troubling you, and let's talk about it."

Eleanore saw his eyes soften, and he pressed her fingers to his lips. "Yes, you're right. Truthfully, I've felt . . . uneasy over the matter for some time . . . without really knowing why. I've had to give it some thought . . . and prayer . . . to fully understand. But now I think I know." He looked down, but not before she saw marked vulnerability in his eyes. "I told you when I proposed that I could never love you; I could never give you my heart. And you know that I stuck by that very firmly for a long time. Even after you declared your love for *me*, I held my heart back. When I realized that I *did* love you, I couldn't deny that I'd loved you for a long time; I'd simply been too afraid of having my heart broken again to admit it." He lifted his eyes and took her in with an encompassing gaze. "Don't you see, Eleanore? Although I didn't consciously realize it, I wasn't so much afraid of giving my heart as I was . . . afraid that you would never give me yours. Perhaps I believed that if I never allowed myself to love you, I would never be disappointed when you didn't love me. But I loved you from the start, Eleanore. I asked you to marry me because I loved you." Tears glimmered in his eyes before he closed them and lowered his head. "Of course I had weighed everything very practically, and the arrangement *was* logical and convenient. And I knew then as I know now that tender feelings alone will never make a good marriage." Again he met her eyes. "This doesn't change my beliefs about what makes a good marriage, Eleanore. But you need to know . . . I need to tell you . . . that I've loved you from the start."

"James," she said and touched his face, "when you first told me you loved me, you told me you'd loved me all along. And I knew that you had, so why—"

"No, Eleanore. Let me explain. When I proposed marriage to you, I *wanted* to tell you that I loved you. The words hovered in my mind, but I convinced myself that it was only a desire to tell a woman what I believed she wanted to hear, that it had nothing to do with my real feelings. I believe I was lying to myself more than I was lying to you. But I believe those discrepancies in my feelings and behavior have been catching up with me, leaving me confused and unsteady. And what I really want to say . . . need to say . . . is that you were right. You were right when you said that I was withholding my heart from God the same way I had once withheld it from you. I want to thank you for having the insight to see what I couldn't, and the patience to see me through while I struggled to understand myself." He leaned forward to kiss her and found tears in her eyes as he drew back. "I love you, Eleanore."

"And I love you," she murmured.

"There's one more thing I need to say."

"I'm listening," she said and wiped her tears while the baby kept nursing, oblivious to the miracle taking place around him.

"One of the things I've always loved best about you, my dear, is the way that you love and honor God above all else. I've told you before, and I meant it, that I wouldn't want it any other way. But I've realized that I've fallen short myself in that way. And now I intend to follow your example in every way, Eleanore Barrington. From this day forth I will honor God above all else, and I will commit my life—and my heart—to Him wholly. I promised Him that I would, and I must keep my promise. I must do whatever He asks of me."

Eleanore examined the sparkle in her husband's eyes and didn't know whether to laugh or cry. Too stunned to do either, she just took him in with absolute amazement. With his baby in her arms and his heart fully open, Eleanore felt as if the glory of heaven had just cascaded directly into the room.

While she was still too astonished to speak, he smiled broadly and said, "Aren't you going to ask me what it is that God wants me to do? Or do you already know, the same way you knew I loved you long before I admitted it?"

She smiled and touched his face. "I already know because you told me; you said you wanted to be baptized. You just had to know for certain that the Book of Mormon was true."

He let out a joyful laugh. "Oh, it *is* true, Eleanore. It *is!*"

"I know," she said and sobbed through a burst of laughter.

"When I set out to learn the truth for myself, I never expected that my answer would be so firm, so undeniable. But it was. I've never had such an experience, Eleanore. Seemingly out of nowhere, pure, clear thoughts flowed smoothly and gently into my mind with such perfect clarity. In an instant everything changed. I knew that this church is true, and I felt God's love for me as I had never felt it before. And I knew . . ." His voice broke and his eyes moistened. "I knew . . . that David's mission on this earth was done, but his life is eternal—and we will be with him again. We will! And everything will be perfect."

Eleanore wrapped her free arm around him and wept without control. In all her longing for the desires of her heart to be answered, she never would have dreamed that the reality could be so blissful. Everything was *already* perfect.

* * *

Eleanore would always remember the spring of 1845 as a season of great miracles. They lost a son, but they were also given one. Jamie could never replace David, but he helped fill the void left in his brother's absence. With the time and heartache that had preceded the arrival of this child, how could his birth not be considered a miracle? And of course, Iris's healing was something that only those who had seen the evidence could truly comprehend. Still, for Eleanore, the greatest miracle of all was seeing her husband lowered into the river and brought back up again. He stepped out of the water and immediately wrapped her in his arms, allowing the moisture to soak into her clothes as surely as his joy and conviction soaked into her spirit. He took her face into his wet hands and firmly repeated his conviction with words she had never dared hope to hear him say. "As soon as the temple is finished, my dear, we will go there, and we will see that everything is in order. Forever isn't long enough to be with you, my dear sweet wife." And then he kissed her.

"This is a baptism, not a wedding," Frederick said as he stepped out of the water.

James just laughed and kissed Eleanore again until Iris interrupted by throwing her arms around her father's waist with a burst of laughter.

Late that evening Eleanore was sitting in bed, nursing the baby, when James slipped between the covers and settled his head close to her side, putting his arm around her. "What a glorious day, Mrs. Barrington," he said and eased a little closer.

"Indeed it is," she said and pressed the fingers of her free hand into his hair, thinking that it was barely dry from the marvelous step he'd taken today.

"Eleanore," he said in a cautious tone that indicated she might not like what he had to say.

"Yes?" she drawled, and he leaned up on one elbow to look at her.

His eyes became intense. "Maybe we should move to Nauvoo." Eleanore held her breath while she examined the conviction in his eyes. "Wouldn't it be marvelous to attend Sunday meetings with people who know the truth and discuss it freely? Wouldn't it be tremendous to just . . . live among such people, interact with them each and every day?"

"Yes," she said, unable to hold back her tears, "it would." She found it ironic that she felt the need to point out, "But persecution continues, James. We could be exposing ourselves to potential hardship."

His expression tightened, but he said, "I know. But . . . if God wants us to be with the Saints, then that's where we need to be. Pray about it, my dear, and I will too—as we've done before. We'll know what's right, and we'll take it on the best we can."

"Of course," she said and smiled. He returned her smile as he sat beside her. Then he kissed her. "Oh, Eleanore." He looked into her eyes and touched her face. "You have brought such joy into my life, right from the moment I had the good sense to ask you to marry me."

She touched his face in return. "I assure you that I have given no more joy than I have received, my dear. I love you more than life, James."

He kissed her again. "Then it's only fitting that our marriage last forever." He turned his attention to the baby and touched Jamie's dark hair. "We will all be together forever, Eleanore. All of us."

"Yes, we will," she said and took his hand.

A moment later Jamie was finished eating and James took the baby to get a burp out of him, laughing frequently at his son's funny noises and expressions. His resemblance to James was strikingly obvious. Just seeing them together filled Eleanore with a peace and contentment unlike any she'd ever imagined, coupled with her husband's newfound convictions that had finally made them completely and irrevocably of one heart.

Iris came in a few minutes later and sprawled herself on the bed, wanting to hold the baby. James placed the infant in her arms. The child beamed and talked in a funny voice to Jamie, who only answered with silent eyes that seemed to be taking in this world where he'd so recently arrived. Eleanore put her head on James's shoulder and watched them, certain David was as close by as Iris in that moment. After all, it had been a glorious day for their family.

A few days later, Eleanore was disappointed to realize that God meant for them to stay exactly where they were for now. But she was touched by the evidence that her husband's disappointment was far deeper than her own. Still, mingled with their disappointment was some measure of relief when news came through letters that the unrest in Nauvoo was growing, and some believed it was likely to get worse. Eleanore wondered, as she often had, why her family would be guided to remain aloof from the body of the Saints. While they were safer, and didn't have to fear ongoing persecution, they were also denied the privilege of living among the Saints and the blessings that surely came as a result. Still, Eleanore believed, as James did, that eventually they *would* be given that privilege, even if it meant taking on the accompanying hardships. And wherever they might live, they knew that God was with them.

Sitting on the side porch with little Jamie in her arms, watching Iris and James while they worked and laughed together in the garden, Eleanore pondered the serenity of her life and couldn't help wondering how long the peace might last. Thoughts of her friends in Nauvoo prompted a prayer on their behalf. It seemed that praying was all she could do beyond holding to her faith. If more trials were on the horizon for the Saints, or for James and Eleanore and those who constituted their family, she prayed that they would all be able to endure them well.

Eleanore saw James stop working long enough to glance her way, and she could see her own tranquility mirrored in his contented smile. Whatever the future *did* hold, they were in it together. They were truly of one heart in every respect, and she could ask for nothing more than that.

AUTHOR'S SUGGESTIONS FOR READERS GROUP DISCUSSION

1. How does this story illustrate the purpose of trials in this life?

2. While James and Eleanore are made aware of the circumstances of the Saints in Nauvoo from a distance, how does their viewpoint coincide with our own as we study Church history with the distance of time?

3. How do the characters' decisions demonstrate the importance of allowing God to guide the decisions we make in our lives?

4. As we learn more about James's childhood and first marriage, how do we gain a deeper understanding and compassion for his fears? Do we sometimes judge weaknesses in others without comprehending what might have motivated them?

5. As enduring hardship brings James's weaknesses boldly to the surface, he is confronted with an emotional turning point in his life. How might he and his family have suffered if he'd become bitter over the loss in his life?

6. How does a role reversal take place with James and Eleanore as they experience the grief associated with losing a son?

7. How is the importance of friendship and finding unity with others in living the gospel illustrated in this story?

8. How does your prior knowledge of Church history, especially regarding the fate of Nauvoo, influence your perspective of the characters' decisions?

9. If you could put yourself into the place of James or Eleanore, knowing the inevitable course the Saints will be forced to take, what emotional and spiritual dilemmas might you be faced with?

10. When Eleanore tells James that the Saints are willing to sacrifice so much for the sake of eternity, what message does that give us regarding the way we live the gospel today?

ABOUT THE AUTHOR

Anita Stansfield, the LDS market's number-one best-selling romance novelist, is a prolific and imaginative writer. Her novels have captivated and moved hundreds of thousands of readers, and she is a popular speaker for women's groups and in literary circles. She and her husband Vince are the parents of five children and reside in Alpine, Utah.